Worcester Nights

The Box Set

Books One to Four

Ophelia Sikes

D1616888

You are unique out of seven billion people.
Let your individual gifts and talents shine!

Book 1: Dwell in Possibility

DWELL IN POSSIBILITY

OPHELIA SIKES

A WORCESTER NIGHTS NOVELLA

Chapter 1

Dwell in Possibility.
-- Emily Dickinson

Crash!

My shoulders instinctively hunched as I spun to look through the large row of plate-glass windows which fronted the bar. Kelley Square sprawled in full, glorious view under the sharp moonlight, eight roads converging into a chaotic mess which is routinely nominated as the worst intersection in Massachusetts.

If Boston had been designed based on Colonial-era cow-paths, Kelley Square had been constructed by wild, lust-crazed gerbils drunk on Jack Daniel's.

The source of the ear-shattering crunch was easy to spot. A fire-engine-red Ford F-150 had T-boned a bumblebee-yellow hummer. I was surprised tangerine-colored shards weren't spewed across the pavement. A muscular black man leapt out of the first, a beefy Hispanic out of the second, and they launched into a shouting match worthy of the WWE.

A bystander in a leather jacket stepped forward like he might try to intervene. Worcester was no place for heroes. They wound up maimed – or dead.

Trouble was a heartbeat away.

Don't do it. Please, just –

He turned and stared right at me. I could only see his shadow in the dark night, but something sizzled, and my breath caught.

Then he was stepping into Death Match Round One.

I jolted back into reality. My hand reached automatically for the phone hanging above the cash register of the bar, but I needn't have bothered. A Worcester patrol car was already screaming its way into the mix. A pair of lanky patrolmen leapt from the vehicle and hauled the combatants apart.

The stranger melded into the mist and vanished, as if he'd never been there at all.

There was the sharp crack of pool balls as the game swung back into motion at the far end of the room. The remaining patrons – all four of them – turned with disinterest to the large-screen TV on the wall opposite the windows. Just a few days prior the Sox had won the World Championship – in Fenway Park no less. Somehow all other sports seemed to have lost their luster. The middle-aged men watched apathetically as the Celtics strove to hold their own against Milwaukee.

I sighed, grabbed a clean rag from beneath the sink, and ran it across the main counter's mahogany surface. Jimmy, the owner, did a decent job of trying to make a go with this place. The chairs and stools were clean, forest-green vinyl. The walls were mostly dark wood, decorated with Cork road signs, Guinness promotions, and a few posters depicting rolling green hills dotted with sheep. If the scenery out the window could morph into a line of pastel-colored row houses, rather than the chaotic swirl of cabs and cars trying to dent each other into origami shapes, we might almost be in County Kerry rather than an hour west of Boston.

The phone rang, and I brought it to my ear. "O'Malley's Bar. How can I help you?"

The voice on the other end was male, no-nonsense, and thickly brogued. "It's Seamus. Get Jimmy for me."

"Of course, Seamus. Just a minute."

I put the phone down by the cash register and waved a hand to the thin, lanky guy sitting on a stool by the door. Joey was practically a bar fixture, arriving when we opened, hanging around until the lights went out. His mouse-brown hair was uncombed and his eyes had a slightly unfocused look.

"Joey, watch the bar for me for a second?"

He nodded, his eyes not leaving the TV. "Sure thing, Kate."

I turned left and walked through the open doorway to the narrow hallway which ran the length of the bar. There were the restrooms, the store room, Jimmy's office, and then a door leading to the back parking lot. Not that cars could fit in there, of course. Between the dumpster, the shed, and the rusted, burnt-out hulk of a 1982 Camaro, you'd be hard pressed to fit even a motorcycle through the mess.

I came up to Jimmy's office door and rapped my knuckles on it. "Jimmy?"

No answer.

I sighed, then pushed the door open. I had a good guess what I'd find.

Sure enough, Jimmy was sprawled, naked, across the ancient oak desk which stretched across the back half of the small room. I'd take bets that the reason he bought such a massive piece of furniture was for this very purpose. A nude young woman with short, dark crimson hair and breasts the size of watermelons straddled him, rhythmically bouncing up and down.

His wispy brown hair sprawled even further askew as he turned his head to growl at me. His voice came in time with her bounces. "Jesus – Mary – and Joseph – What – the Hell – Dy'a Want?"

The woman – perhaps twenty – looked as if she had a pair of angry water balloons strapped to her chest and they were fighting for supremacy. Jimmy had to be at least twenty years her senior. His paunch jiggled in time with her movements, which had not let up at my entrance.

I'd grown up with four older brothers. You'd think I'd have gotten used to this by now. But my father had passed away when I was thirteen. Those brothers had turned into my knight protectors, and as a result I'd barely dated in high school. I'd also been carefully shielded from all of my brothers' testosterone-laden adventures.

My cheeks flamed with heat and I kept my gaze on the wall behind the desk. My voice was tight with embarrassment. "Seamus is on the phone."

Jimmy seemed half-willing to grab the woman's waist and finish off the process, but then he cursed and rolled, plunking her into the faux-leather chair behind the desk. He barely glanced at her as he grabbed up his jeans from alongside the desk.

"You stay put – I'll be right back."

I turned and went back out to my position at the bar. Jimmy joined me in just a few seconds. He grabbed up the phone. "Yeah, Jimmy here."

Seamus's blast came so strongly through the earpiece that I could clearly hear the words. "Do you have another whore at the bar?"

Jimmy's jaw went tight. "No, no, Seamus, of course not."

The hard edge of Seamus's voice drew tension along my shoulder blades. "If my sister finds out, I'll never hear the end of it."

Jimmy was shaking his head before Seamus finished. "She don't know nothing," he swore. "I've got it under control."

Seamus's voice dropped into a lower register and I couldn't hear his response. Jimmy nodded a few times, mumbling "sure" and "yes," and then he hung up the phone.

The woman came out of the hallway, dressed in tight jeans and a black, spaghetti-strap tank with Elmo smiling across its front. She attentively chewed at a wad of gum in her mouth as if she were a cow who had found the most delicious clover patch in the field.

She spoke in a bored tone to the room in general. "My sittah leaves in five minutes."

Jimmy's brow furrowed, but he waved to me, and I nodded. I picked up the phone and hit the first button on it.

An elderly male voice answered. "Ethan's Taxi Service."

"Ethan, it's Kate."

A smile brightened his response. "Oh, sure, Kate. Need a pickup?"

I gave a wry smile. "That we do."

"Be there in five." He hung up.

Jimmy went around the bar to give the girl a hug. She glanced around the bar before carefully agreeing to the most distant of embraces. Then she turned with a swoosh of her crimson hair. The bell above the door gave a high tinkling noise as she stepped out to the sidewalk.

A minute later Ethan's yellow taxi pulled up smoothly through the maelstrom of traffic. The girl vanished within, and he was gone.

Jimmy slumped onto one of the six stools fronting the bar, running a hand through his thinning hair. "Pour me some Redbreast, Katie."

I turned and pulled the green bottle of whiskey from the shelf, pouring him his double, neat. I put the glass in front of him, placing the bottle alongside it.

He waved a hand at the glass. "Have a sip."

I had only been filling in at the bar for about a month. The usual bartender, my good friend Eileen, had gone to County Kildare to be with her ailing grandmother. But I already knew well enough not to argue with Jimmy. He liked for me to take a sip before he began drinking, and truth be told, I'd come not to mind. The whiskey was one of his local favorites from County Cork and had rich flavors of toffee, honey, and raisin.

I took my drink, rolling the flavors around in my mouth, coating my tongue. Then I handed the rest back to him. He took down a swallow, staring at the amber liquid for a moment. Then he shook himself and looked over at the far wall with its TV and memorabilia.

"I'm going to make this into a proper place, Katie," he vowed. "We'll put on a second floor for the offices and be able to expand this level to hold a trio of dart boards. We'll host a team. We'll have local bands in here on the weekend. We'll make it into a real bar."

"Sure, we will, Jimmy," I soothed him. I'd heard this every night for a month. But every day, rather than working on his dreams, he was sliding his hand into another co-ed's shirt and dragging her back into that rat-infested room that passed for an office.

I was counting the days before Eileen returned, before I could get back to my job search. I had graduated in May, but with my degree in journalism, work was hard to come by. Then again, in this economy, it seemed that everybody was having it rough.

Jimmy went on with his rambling, the few patrons trickled out to their homes, and finally it was time to close up. Ethan picked me up as usual, his wiry, grandfatherly warmth pleasant in the two a.m. moonlight. He drove me the short half-mile to the sturdy three-decker I boarded at. My landlady would be sound asleep by now, so I was careful with the front door, then turned right into my room.

I sighed as I stepped into my small sanctuary. My acoustic guitar rested against the left wall, my futon mattress filled the right corner, and the one small window looked out over a quiet street lined with three-deckers nearly identical to mine. A set of sagging laminate shelves held my textbooks and journals.

I peeled off my sneakers and slumped down onto the bed. My life seemed stuck, bogged down, as if somewhere along the way I'd stepped into deep mud and hadn't even realized it.

There had to be some way for me to escape.

Chapter 2

The overhead bell tinkled as I pushed my way into the bar, the orange flow of sunset already tracing across the scattered tables. Good God, it was only 4:30 p.m. and already darkness was coming. As much as I looked forward to a white Christmas, there were some aspects of a New England winter which I could do without.

A sturdy, middle-aged woman, built like a Mack truck and outfitted in a nicely tailored sapphire blue dress, was working efficiently behind the bar, slicing up limes. She looked up and nodded in approval.

"You're always right on time. I value that."

I smiled and moved around to join her, hanging my Holy Cross hoodie on the hook at the far end. Aside from my textbooks, it was my one memento from the four years of time I'd invested in that place.

I picked up the rag and wiped down the bar. "It's good to see you, Mrs. O'Malley."

"Ah, lass, call me Bridgit," she insisted, as she always did. I found it hard to comply. Her presence was such a force, her movements so full of bull-like strength, that I thought of her as apart from the rest of us mere mortals.

"You should stay around for the night," I suggested. "I'd like the company." I brought my eyes down to the bar before me, pretending to focus on scrubbing out a spot. It was much more than the company; I felt intensely guilty about being a silent partner to her husband's continual cheating. It was as if I was now complicit in his activities, expected to lie to his wife for him, when all I wanted to do was turn the cheating bastard over to her fury.

But when Eileen had taken her sabbatical from this job and asked me to cover for her while she was gone, she made me vow not to disturb the balance of the bar. She wanted to come back to a quiet work environment. So, as much as it tore into my heart every day, I went along with it.

Mrs. O'Malley shook her head with gusto. "Sorry, lass, far too much to do. Tonight's the baby shower for my niece. As soon as Jimmy pries himself out of that office of his, we'll get going. Just what does he do in there all day long?"

I bit my lip and focused tenaciously on the swirl of wood before me.

There was a movement from the back room, and Jimmy strode out, wiping his hands. He nodded to his wife. "Ready to go?"

"Of course," she responded, finishing up with the limes. "The present's in the car."

Jimmy turned to me. "You know how to lock up, Katie. Make sure you call for the taxi when you are ready to head home. I know you don't live far, but don't walk there. You know this neighborhood. Those Cubans are fockin' bastards who can't be trusted around a woman."

I internally noted the disconnect of him making a statement like that, but wisely held my tongue.

Mrs. O'Malley came out from around the bar and nodded in agreement with her husband. "And that halfway house across the street – the Jefferson Hotel – you can't trust any man who's staying there."

I'd already heard this lecture numerous times. "I'll be fine," I assured them. "Besides, Joey's here to protect me."

The lanky man's eyes semi-focused for a moment as he heard his name. He turned from the TV, giving a thumb's up.

Jimmy rolled his eyes, but his wife hooked his arm and gave him a tug. "The lass'll be fine. We need to get going." A tinkle of the door's overhead bell and they were walking around the corner to wherever they'd found street parking.

I sighed, looking over the quiet crowd. It was Saturday night, supposedly the most happening night of the week. But we had only our six regulars – two lethargically battling it out over pool, four at the tables. The TV was running coverage of the celebrations for the Red Sox.

First I made sure we had plenty of limes, lemons, cherries, and other detritus that made a bar run smoothly. Next, I ensured every wood surface in the place gleamed. I handled the occasional drink order. The clock next to the TV ticked slowly, methodically, and it seemed to get louder as the evening dragged along. This was my life. This was my youth, my energy, all vanishing, never to be retrieved again. If Eileen didn't return soon, I would become trapped here, lost forever, and the ticking clock would mark the passage as my hair turned grey and my bones brittle.

At one in the morning I allowed myself the pleasure of a task that involved at least a little mental activity. I turned and did an inventory of the liquor. This could keep me busy for at least a half hour, if I examined each bottle carefully and gave thought to where it had come from.

I smiled as I reached the top shelf. Jimmy must've had a rough day – the Redbreast was nearly empty. We were also running low on Glenmorangie and Jack Daniel's. The men in here tended to go for the harder stuff. Maybe the run-down atmosphere of Worcester did it to them. Once a mill town, it had struggled to re-invent itself with twelve colleges and a few large medical centers. That might have been great for the dance clubs, but for the middle-aged men seeking basic jobs, there just wasn't that much out there.

I felt for them. My own future seemed fairly bleak.

I caught Joey's attention. "I'm just going in back for a sec."

His nod seemed almost a sleepwalker's motion. "Sure thing, Kate."

I wasn't quite sure if he was fond of an apathy-inducing drug or if he had mental issues. He was friendly enough, and well meaning, but there was a gap between his brain and the rest of the world.

The TV blared a rich rendition of "Sweet Caroline" as I moved into the storeroom. It was haphazardly piled with boxes and bags, with no rhyme or reason to the layout. It was always something of a treasure hunt to dig through here, and I felt a rich sense of triumph when I was able to locate all three bottles I was seeking. I tucked the Redbreast under my arm, took the other two bottles one in each hand, and returned back to the main room.

I had only taken my second step across the wood floor before a strange sensation tickled between my shoulder blades. I drew to a stop by the corner of the bar, depositing my three bottles on it, before sweeping my eyes across the room.

The pool players were finishing up their game, looking as if they might call it a night. The four staring at the TV could, for all purposes, have fallen asleep. And there –

Time crystallized, and the world around us faded.

There was a stranger in the back corner. His chair balanced, tilted, against the far wall. His moss-green eyes held mine with a look far beyond any intensity I had ever experienced.

I lived between breaths as I soaked him in. He appeared in his late twenties, well built, with loose, dark brown hair which just skimmed his shoulders. A shadow of a beard caressed his face. His black t-shirt hugged his body, emphasizing his six-pack stomach and firm biceps. His jeans did the same for his muscular legs. A soccer player, maybe, with a build that was both lean and strong.

Emotion swirled in his eyes as he drew his gaze down me. A distant part of me wondered that I was not nervous, not filled with all the usual butterflies and lustings that came during this stage of the mating dance. But this was different than anything I had ever felt before. I was mesmerized, captivated, and wholly connected with the man before me. Rather than feeling hesitant, I arched my shoulders, meeting his gaze, feeling viscerally the movement of his eyes down my dark blue long-sleeve, lingering on my slender waist. He traced the gentle curve of the jeans on my hips, slid down my lean legs, and drew to a stop at my mid-heel leather boots.

I wanted his eyes back on my own. I craved that connection, that stunning blast of electricity, that had awakened something dormant within me. I raised my fingers and ran my hand through my long, dark hair, pushing it back from my face.

The barest hint of a smile danced at the edge of his sensual lips. And then he drew easily to his feet.

A bolt of lightning zagged through me, and my skin crackled with energy. My heart pounded against my ribs.

I wanted him with every cell in my body.

Yes. Yes.

The two pool players put their cues in the rack and moved in front of him, waving at me as they headed out the door. "See ya tomorrow."

That seemed to shake the other four out of their TV stupor and they stumbled to their feet, leaving their glasses where they lay. Joey gave a distracted nod. "Guess it's about time for us, too."

I barely heard them. My sole focus was on this one man, on how I had been waiting my entire life for this one moment.

He was here.

The thought sent a fresh flare of longing through me.

Thank God there were no other men in my life right now. It had been eight long months since I'd broken up with Derek, that bastard, and I'd come to accept my nun-like status as I dealt with the pressures of finals. It was as if the universe had held me open, waiting, prepared for this one moment.

Joey shook himself, as if he were just coming awake, and he looked over at the stranger. "Hey, you, the bar's closing up now. Time to head out."

The man paused as if he'd barely heard the order. He held my gaze, a hint of a question in his eyes.

I could feel every pulse of my blood through my body. The tsunami of desire threatened to drown me, capsize me, wash away all reason. The sane spark of me, deep within the roiling waters, pleaded with me to take it slow, to at least take a breath before losing myself totally within whatever whirlwind was around us.

His smile spread in knowing understanding. He nodded at me and turned to the door. The four regulars made way for him, waiting until he was down the street before waving at me and heading out. The room echoed with the silence.

It took me a moment before I stepped over to the door, turned the bolt, and flipped the sign from "Open" to "Closed."

I found myself going over to the corner he had been sitting in. I eased myself down into the seat. It was still warm from his presence. I breathed in the aroma of musk and pine. A powerful ache soaked through me, roiling in my chest, sinking to much, much lower.

My thoughts went to *The Godfather* by Mario Puzo. In the novel, Michael Corleone had been hit by *Colpo di Fulmine* - The Thunderbolt. *"This was an overwhelming desire for possession, this was an inerasable printing of the girl's face on his brain and he knew she would haunt his memory every day of his life if he did not possess her. His life had become simplified, focused on one point, everything else was unworthy of even a moment's attention."*

I had laughed when reading that, thinking the description outrageous. Nobody felt a connection like that any more. That was a fantasy from fairy tales, from Snow White glimpsing her Prince by the edge of a wishing well.

Now I knew better. Now I realized that – for the rarest of individuals, perhaps just once in a lifetime – that bolt of electricity could sear your soul in a way which would change you forever.

I closed my eyes and let out my breath, drowning in a need I'd barely known I had submerged within me.

Chapter 3

I glanced at the door for the fiftieth time, desire honing me like a glowing metal rod ready for the anvil. He had to come back. Whoever he was, he had to return to me.

My mother's cautionary voice tickled in my ear. Was he one of those recently-released felons that appeared at the Jefferson Hotel, struggled to keep their head above water for a few weeks, and then sank into the mire of their own history?

I fervently hoped not. Because, the way I felt right now, I wasn't sure I would care.

The door's bell chimed and I spun with a pounding heart. My shoulders sagged. It was a waif-like teen, perhaps five-seven, with blonde pigtails and a peach skin-hugging dress which barely reached below her thong.

A dark cloud grew within me. Thunder rumbled as Jimmy sauntered out from the back hall, took her by the arm, and vanished again with her.

I knew I'd promised Eileen, but this was getting to be too much. I vowed to text her again tomorrow to find out when she'd be coming home.

Joey turned from his perch by the door to wave his empty glass at me. "Another Bushmills, Kate."

I snagged the bottle, noting it was closing in on empty. The amount the crew could drink in a day was just mind-boggling. It was probably the only reason Jimmy could keep the bar going – although it baffled me that the place broke even. I moved to Joey's side and poured out his glass. The last drips shook out.

I nudged my head. "I'm going back for another one. Watch the bar for me, would ya?"

"Sure, sure," he agreed absently, his eyes glued to the set. His hand took the whiskey to his mouth as if set on auto pilot.

I dropped the bottle into the recycling bin – a concession Jimmy had made to me when I complained about the waste of throwing all this glass away. I shouldered my way into the stock room, then began digging around for the Bushmills. If yesterday's trip here had been a treasure hunt, this time it was more like trying to locate Atlantis. I was sure I had opened up every single box in the room before finally locating a bottle stuffed behind the back radiator.

I wrapped my fingers around its neck, walked back along the dimly-lit corridor, turned the corner –

He was sitting at the bar.

The shock of it staggered me to a stop. He was staring right at me, those moss-green eyes holding a glint of amusement as they drew down me. I glowed under his gaze, seeing myself through his eyes. My grey cashmere sweater hugged my body, soft, inviting the touch. The low cut allowed my silver Saint Michael's medallion to glitter between the curves of my breast. The jeans and boots accentuated my slender figure.

A swirl of desire built in his eyes; the corners of his mouth eased up in a knowing smile.

Heat washed through me, and my throat went dry. I moved behind the bar, focusing on putting the Bushmills where it belonged, striving desperately to regain my center.

I'd never had a man affect me like this – never. The thunderbolt. It was real. And it was dangerous. I knew nothing about this man sitting in front of me. He could be a dangerous felon for all I knew.

I didn't care.

The thought flashed in my brain, hot, powerful, and I squelched it before it could take root.

I had to get this under control. I had to figure out who he was.

I took in a deep, steadying breath and turned to face him. He was wearing a dark brown leather jacket over a black shirt. His hair had that same tousle, his chin that same stubble that made me long to run my thumb along it. The glass before him was nearly empty, with only a slight glisten of amber liquid in it.

I nudged my head at the glass. "You want some more?"

His gaze traced down to my neckline, then back up to my eyes again. His voice was rich, resonant, and shimmered throughout my body. "That depends."

My throat went dry, and it was a moment before I could reply. "Depends on what?"

His smile grew, and he dropped his voice down lower. "Are you a betting woman?"

I couldn't help it. I stepped closer to the bar, leaning against it. I told myself it was so I could hear him better. But as I breathed in that scent of his – musk and pine – waves of heat washed through me. It took me a moment to remember what his question had been.

Something about betting.

"Depends on the stakes."

He nodded at that. He held up his glass before me, turning it so it caught the light. "You tell me what I was drinking, and I'll tip you twenty for your bartending skills."

A thrill of excitement darted through me. I could use twenty. I might be able to forego ramen for the week and get several nights of Ziti's pizza.

"And if I can't guess it?"

His finger slid along the glass. "Well, then, I guess you'll just have to …"

My heart thundered in my chest. "… have to?"

His eyes held mine. "Have to tell me your name."

My breath whooshed out of me, and I burst out laughing. He seemed caught by me, and for a moment he didn't speak, just watched as I soaked in my joy. Then he held up the glass, his eyes holding a new emotion, something deeper. "So you'll drink?"

I grinned. "Absolutely."

As I reached out to take the glass our fingers brushed each other's. An electrical charge shimmered through us; every corner of my body resonated with the power of it.

I was thankful that I was still leaning against the bar. Drawing my fingers away from his was like pulling away from a powerful magnet. When the contact broke, I curled my fingers tightly on the glass.

Take your time, I warned myself. *You need to learn more about him.*

I brought the drink to my nose, closed my eyes, and took in a few gentle sniffs. I didn't hold out much hope of figuring this out – we must have had forty whiskeys on our shelf – but I would give it my best try. A trio of nice sausage pizzas was on the line here, after all.

I drew in the aroma of …

I stopped in surprise. Raisin. Honey. Toffee.

Nobody in the bar besides Jimmy drank this stuff. Could I really be that lucky?

I raised the edge of the glass to my mouth, taking in the remaining swallow. The liquid coated my tongue, slid along my throat, and sent a warm shaft of desire into my core.

I opened my eyes.

He was staring at me, transfixed, as if I were Venus rising naked from the ocean on a clam shell. His jawline was tight, and when he spoke there was a hoarseness to his voice.

"Well?"

I gave the side of the glass a thankful kiss for bringing me such luck, then placed it down before him. I turned to the back wall, selected out the bottle of Redbreast, then faced him again. Without a word I poured him a fresh glass.

He turned the glass in place, his eyes still on me, now brightening with respect. "Apparently you have some experience."

"Oh, more than enough," I agreed with a smile.

He ran his thumb over the section of the glass that I had kissed, and the flames within me cranked higher. I could imagine him running that thumb down the side of my neck … under the curve of my breast …

His eyes twinkled, and he reached with his other hand to his back pocket, pulling out a worn black leather wallet. He flipped it open; his driver's license and some sort of a business card showed in the sleeves. He drew out a worn twenty and held it out to me.

"I always follow through on what I say," he murmured, his eyes holding mine.

I couldn't help it. When I reached out to take the bill, I let my fingers run along his, and the burning desire within me billowed to new heights. I pressed my thighs together, trying to rein in the out-of-control hormones which were raging within me.

I barely knew him!

I folded the twenty in half and slipped it into the front pocket of my jeans.

Jimmy's furious shout echoed from the side of the room. "Jesus, Mary, and Joseph! What the fock, Katie?"

Sharp, violent heat flared in the man's eyes, replaced so quickly with stillness that if I hadn't been staring right at him I'd never had seen it. He turned on the stool, looking calmly at Jimmy. "That was a tip for good service," he coolly stated. "I'm running a tab for my drinks."

Jimmy took an angry step into the room, his paunch jiggling with his emotion. "The hell you are."

Joey spoke up from his stool, drawn from his stupor by Jimmy's loud voice. "Uh, I started the tab, Jimmy," he explained. "It's there on the cork-board by the phone. Kate was out back getting me some more whiskey when he came in."

Jimmy stalked over to the corkboard, stared for a moment at the white note, and all of a sudden he was the friendly, pedophile-uncle again and not a raving ball of fury. "Ah, right, of course, lass. You're one of the best bartenders we've had. Only a month and I've got you well trained." He patted me on the shoulder.

The blonde girl came out of the back room, her hair now in one long ponytail behind her. "I gotta get home or my parents will kill me."

Jimmy looked at me, and I punched the taxi button on the phone. A few minutes later she was safely on her way. I wondered if she'd make it in before her curfew or if she'd be grounded.

I wondered if her parents had any idea what she was up to.

Jimmy looked over the man before him as if Jimmy were the stallion of a herd and a rogue horse had just come up on the horizon. He glanced down at the wallet which still lay open on the bar. His voice held more than a hint of challenge in it. "So, staying at the Jefferson?"

I looked down in surprise. The business card did have their logo in the top corner, as well as the name and title of the manager of the place.

My chest constricted. I should have known …

The man calmly nodded, unfazed in the least. "Name's Sean Miller."

Jimmy's eyes drilled in on him. "What were you in for?"

Sean could have been talking about the weather. "Armed robbery, in New York City. Sentenced to fifteen, let out in seven."

"What did you rob?"

"Italian restaurant. They were causing trouble for my friend's bar. Trying to run them out of business; thought we were the wrong sort for the neighborhood. Me and a few of my friends went to teach them a lesson."

Jimmy's gaze became considering. "And did you?"

Sean's lips twitched into a smile. "They never reopened."

Jimmy reached back and tore the note from the corkboard, dropping it the trash. His grin was expansive. "First two drinks are on the house, as a welcome to your new life. But we run a clean establishment here. No trouble, you understand me?"

Sean gave him a toast. "Loud and clear."

Jimmy glanced around the room, then turned to me. "I'll be in my office."

I nodded. "Sure thing, Jimmy."

My heart was thumping against my ribs as he turned the corner, effectively leaving me alone again with Sean. The remaining patrons could have been window mannequins for all they figured. Questions tumbled one after another in my mind, and I fought them all down with furious energy.

Sean watched me, a glint of curiosity in his eyes. "So? What d'ya want to know?"

I steeled myself. He seemed open to talking, and this might be my only chance for some answers. "Why did you do it?"

The corner of his mouth quirked up. "I told you. The Italians were muscling in on us. Thought we Irish trash should clear out of their territory."

"Wasn't there another way?"

He paused for a moment, looking at me with consideration. His voice was more measured when he spoke again. "I would have preferred it," he admitted. "However, the rest of the crew was beyond talking at that point. I went along to make sure nobody got hurt."

A tremor of nervousness ran through me. "And did they?"

He shook his head, holding my gaze. "I made sure I was the only one with a gun, and I focused their energy on smashing the place. We locked the patrons in a back store room. Nobody was hurt."

I thought of him in that tense situation, a rowdy mob set out for revenge on one side, and only Sean stood between them and their victims.

"I guess sometimes you do the best you can," I murmured.

"That you do," he agreed. He nudged his head toward the back hallway. "I see you know something of that yourself."

I found myself smiling. "Certainly not the job I thought I'd land when I graduated," I agreed.

"Holy Cross?"

My throat went dry. Had he been stalking me?

He chuckled, his eyes flicking to the back wall. "You wear their hoodie," he pointed out. His gaze shadowed. "Or is that your boyfriend's college?"

I shook my head vehemently. "He went to Worcester Tech," I snapped.

I flushed, realizing that even after all these months I thought of Derek as having power over me, as still being a presence in my life. "Ex-boyfriend," I clarified. "And good riddance."

He grinned. "Sounds like a story." He took a sip his drink. "Let me buy you a drink, and you tell it to me."

I knew I should resist, but I found my hands reaching for the Redbreast and pouring the glass. He clinked his against mine, and I felt the vibration of it deep within me.

I took in a mouthful of the whiskey, and it was all I could hope for. Somehow it loosened the gears of my long-silent machinery, and once they began turning, the words flowed out.

"Bastard seemed charming at first. Attentive, that sort of thing. But in a short while it crossed over into full blown jealousy. He said one of my friends was too needy and drove her away. Then another was too flashy. God forbid I talk to a male. By two months in he was watching my every move, screaming at me every night, and I was almost afraid to leave him. I thought that might just make it worse."

He nodded, his eyes holding mine. "But you did."

I took another drink. "Yeah, my friend Eileen went with me to tell him and to get my stuff from his apartment. Good thing, too. He was furious. I stayed with her for the next two weeks, just in case he got some wild idea in his head." I gave a wry smile. "Luckily when he graduated, his company sent him out to the Berkshires." I shrugged. "So I'm all right now."

His gaze sparkled. "I'd say you were more than all right."

I looked down in my drink, flushing. I had gotten so used to Derek's snide commentary and harsh language, to his continual put-downs, that handling the compliment seemed a completely foreign task, like trying to juggle flaming torches. I rolled Sean's words around in my mind, soaking in the feeling of it, and Sean sat quietly before me, sipping his whiskey, acting as if we had all the time in the world.

It struck me that I'd never been this comfortable with anybody. Derek would have been launching into a monologue right now to fill the silence, ranting about my choice of friends or the clothes I wore. Nothing was ever quite right to please him. But with Sean we simply were. It was as if he were the exhale and I was the inhale. I could breathe him in, breathe deeply, and his strength would fill me.

Sean laid his fingers along mine, and I could feel the texture of them in every corner of my soul. The warmth filled me, lifted me, and brought exotic flavors to the liquor in my mouth.

His words were a soft caress. "I want to know."

And I told him.

For long hours I described what it was like to grow up in Waterbury, Connecticut, a run-down brassware-industry town which had fallen in on itself and decayed. My father was a cop, my mother, a teacher, and my four brothers and I lived a wild but happy life in our pothole-riddled street with houses jammed cheek-by-jowl against each other. We knew nothing else. We had a sense that we could hold out against anything.

And then there was that day that we came home from school to find our mother weeping on the couch. My father had been shot and killed in the line of duty.

Everything changed. My brothers took their mission to look after me with serious intent. They watched my every movement, examined every boy who showed interest, and ruled that none met their stringent standards. When I finally escaped to college, I thought this was my time to be free and find myself.

And then I had met Derek …

There was a noise from the hallway, and I looked up in surprise. Jimmy came out, shrugging on his coat. "Time, boys," he called out to the room.

I blinked. Could it be closing time already? It seemed only the blink of an eye, but the clock was right there on the wall. I had never had a conversation like that with a guy before. Sean had been attentive, concerned, and he hadn't interrupted to find ways to "fix" things. He'd simply listened, offered support, and been there for me.

My heart whirled into even deeper emotions, and I didn't want him to leave.

Sean peeled another twenty out of his wallet, placing it on the counter.

I shook my head. "That's too much. My drink was only —"

He folded his wallet and tucked it back into his pocket. "Get some mozzarella sticks to go with that pizza," he suggested.

My eyes widened. "How did you know?"

He chuckled. "When I mentioned the twenty the first time, your eyes flickered over in the direction of Ziti's. If this bar is your source of income, I figure you're living on chicken soup and pretzels."

I took up the twenty. "I appreciate it. Thanks."

He held my gaze for a long moment. "My pleasure."

The way he said it sent waves of longing down my body. And then he was turning, walking through the door, and only the echo of the bell was left.

Chapter 4

I stepped through the bar door wearing the best clothes from my closet. A rose-colored top with a plunging neckline; its silver embroidery made my Saint Michael's pendant sparkle. The jeans had a hint of silver on their back pockets as well. I looked around …

He was sitting at the bar, his eyes on me, his mouth turning up in a knowing smile.

I flushed, forced my feet to stay in motion, and Mrs. O'Malley's voice rose above the thundering of my heart.

"Ah, you're such a good lass, Katie. Come around back here with me."

I hung my hoodie on the hook and joined her. She passed over the small, white cutting board of limes she was working on. I took up the knife, carefully making even wedges of them.

She leaned against the side of the bar, looking at me. "You know to be careful of those guys from the Jefferson," she stated in a matter-of-fact tone. "Half of them go right back in the joint a month after release. It's the life they know. It's just their nature."

My cheeks flushed with the heat of a blacksmith's forge. She was clearly doing this in front of him on purpose. It was all I could do to nod.

"Unreliable guys," she continued, her gaze steadily on mine. "Trained to lie. They'll say anything. You can't trust 'em."

I focused on the lime before me, carefully cutting my way through its skin. I knew Mrs. O'Malley meant well, but Sean wasn't like that. When we'd talked last night, he hadn't tried to manipulate me. He'd simply listened and been there for me. I wished fervently that she'd finish with her little sermon and move on her way.

My savior came in the shape of her philandering husband, stepping in from the hallway. "Bridgit, my dear, won't you be late for that mah jongg game?"

She glanced at the clock and nodded. "You're quite right. I just wanted to make sure I had a chat with Katie here before I left." She stepped forward to lay a hand gently on my shoulder. I could smell the jasmine and orange of her perfume – it was all she ever wore. Then she moved around the bar.

Jimmy went with her to the door. "I'll be home late again."

She rolled her eyes. "Of course you will. When is it any different?"

Jimmy turned to me. "Oh, Katie, come here a sec."

I went around to join them. He handed me a key on a ring with a large, Crayola-green shamrock on it. "Thought you should have this. So you can lock up with your own key for now on."

I thought of refusing it. Surely Eileen would be back home any time now and I'd be free of the place. But I bit my lip, remembering my promise to her to not cause any trouble. There was no harm in taking the key, after all. I'd just give it back when I could quit. I nodded to Jimmy and tucked it in my back pocket.

Mrs. O'Malley gave a wave of a ringed hand, then turned and walked out the door. She headed right around the corner to the side street.

I had barely gotten halfway back to Sean when the doorbell tinkled again. I turned and sighed. This girl was

Japanese, if I had to guess, with straight black hair to her waist and a delicately pale, oval face. She wore a simple white shell and black leggings, with black, satiny, slipper-like shoes.

It was all I could do not to shake my head. Had she been lurking in the street, waiting for the very second she could enter the room?

She stepped toward Jimmy, digging her hand in the massive Coach bag at her side. It was decorated with dark pink hollow circles on a paler pink base. A delicate frown creased her forehead as she stuck her hand further into its depths.

"I can't find my cigarettes."

Jimmy waved a hand at her. "We'll get you some later. We should –"

She pulled away from his outstretched arm, stepping back to the door. "I need my cigarettes," she insisted. "I'll pop across the street to the liquor store. I'll be back in a sec."

He looked as if he would protest, but she turned and slipped through the door, the chime announcing her departure.

Jimmy sighed in exasperation and moved over next to Sean. His voice was a growl. "Women."

Sean's eyes held twinkling amusement, but he did not answer. I found myself lost in that gaze, in the rich greens, in the subtle flecks of gold …

There was the tinkle of a chime behind me, and confusion flitted through me. Surely she couldn't have made it across the madness of Kelley Square and back again that quickly. Maybe she had found the cigarettes –

Sean's gaze was hardening, steeling, and a shaft of fear drilled through me. I'd seen that kind of look in my father's eyes, a few times in the depths of Waterbury's grittier blocks. I knew what it meant.

My heart thundering, I turned in place.

A pair of massive men, nearly contenders for sumo wrestling, stepped through the doorway. They had skin the color of café au lait, and if I had any question about their background it was dispelled by the large Cuban flags each had tattooed on his right bicep. They wore red muscle shirts and faded jeans.

The one on the left was larger, thicker, with a bald head which shone under the bar's lights. The one on the right had tight curls against his head and a scar under his right eye. He seemed to be the leader. His gaze honed in on Jimmy. "You in charge here?"

Jimmy's paunch swung as he turned to face the intruders. "Yeah, I'm Jimmy. Jimmy O'Malley. Whatd'ya want?"

Curly-head looked at Jimmy dismissively. "We got a message for you. We don't want you here."

Jimmy's hands clenched into fists. "Yeah, well look around, *rafter*. There's still signs up on Millbury Street for kielbasa and kiszka. You jerks are just the latest wave to come in and try to stake your ground. This spot here is mine, and I ain't moving."

Curly-head glanced at his friend, and the bald man stepped forward.

Jimmy strode up to stand right in front of him. "You get out of my place, or I'll –"

The bald man grabbed him beneath each arm, arced him up in the air, and slammed him down on his back into the nearest table. It smashed, its legs giving way, sending Jimmy to the ground in a cascade of splinters and planks.

The bald man turned to look at me, a leer growing on his face.

Sean seemed to move between time. One moment he was on his stool, the next he had interjected himself between bald-guy and me, driving a left uppercut hard into the Cuban's jaw. The Cuban's head rocked back, and Sean drove a right roundhouse into the side of his head. The man flew back against the wall by the door and leaned against it, staggered.

Curly-head snarled and drove in like a bull. Sean stepped aside, evading the charge, and slammed his elbow down into the guy's kidney. The Cuban howled in pain and rage, spinning in place. He raced again at Sean, and this time Sean threw a jab at his temple, the momentum of the man's body giving it extra force. The man's legs buckled, folded, and he drove head-first into the door.

Sean balanced on the balls of his feet, looking at the two men, his eyes alert for any sign of movement.

The bald man blinked himself back into awareness. He looked at Sean for a long moment, his fingers flexing, considering another round. His eyes moved up to Sean's – and he stopped. Something he saw there made him let out his breath and drop his eyes. He bent down to drag his friend up, draping one of the curly man's arms over his shoulder. Then he drew open the door with his other hand and together they lurched around to the right.

Sean moved to the door and shut it behind them, turning the bolt. Then he went over to Jimmy and gently hauled him up, his shoulder muscles flexing with the weight. He looped Jimmy's arm over his shoulder and eased him over to the stool.

Sean's voice was low. "You all right?"

Jimmy groaned, rubbing at his lower back. "I think so." His gaze filled with anger. "But if those bastards –"

There was a hammering at the door. Jimmy flinched, curling in on himself. Sean turned in place, his hands solidifying into fists, his shoulders braced for action.

The Japanese girl stood there at the other side, her lips closed in a red pout. Her high voice scraped through the glass. "What the hell, Jimmy?"

Sean stepped forward to open the door. As she stepped into the room her mouth went into a round O. She looked from the smashed table to the numerous cuts on Jimmy's arms. "What in the world happened?"

"It's the fockin' Cubans," snapped Jimmy. "We'll teach them. They should go back to that fockin' island where they belong!"

The girl wrapped her arms around herself. "I wanna go home."

Jimmy growled, but he nodded at me. I went around behind the bar and grabbed the phone, punching the button. Ethan didn't even bother to greet me when he picked up. Caller ID in action.

"I'm around the corner," he said, hanging up.

The girl took one last look around the place, then went back out to the street, rubbing her hands on her arms to keep warm. Ethan pulled up and they were gone.

Jimmy looked at me. "Pour me a double. Some for you, too. And get him whatever he drinks."

I put out three glasses, grabbed the bottle of Redbreast, and poured out the drinks.

Jimmy looked at Sean in surprise. "You drink Redbreast? Are you a Cork man?"

Sean nodded. "Born and raised there, at least until I was nine. Then my ma sent me to live with her sister in Hell's Kitchen, in the heart of New York City."

Jimmy raised a toast to him. "To standing your ground."

We all clinked glasses and drank down the rich liquid, honey coating our throats. Jimmy rubbed at his neck for a moment before looking back to Sean. "You learn to fight in the city?"

Sean gave a slight shrug. "My old man was a boxer, small time stuff. He could be a foul mouth when he drank, but when he was sober he spent time boxing with me. It was what we did. I thought this was how all boys grew up, learning footwork and making the speed bag dance."

Jimmy raised an eyebrow. "Whyd'ya move to the states?"

Sean's lips pressed. "Sometimes my old man would use my ma as a punching bag. When I was nine, I tried to defend her one time, and he turned on me. My mother moved us out the very next day. She sent me to the states, and she moved back in with her parents in County Kildare."

"And your dad?"

He shrugged. "He got drunker, got run out of town, and we haven't heard from him since. For all I know, his liver failed on him."

Jimmy patted him on the shoulder. "Well, whatever that man did wrong, he did one thing right. He taught you how to defend yourself. And that, my friend, is a valuable talent."

The phone rang, and I turned to pick it up. Seamus's voice was terse. "Put Jimmy on."

I handed the phone over to Jimmy. "It's Seamus."

Jimmy paled, but he took the phone, placing it to his ear. "Yeah?"

The stream of swears and fury was so thickly brogued that I could hardly make out individual words. Jimmy listened through it without saying a word. When the verbal assault ended he clicked off the phone, handing it back to me.

"We're closing up, boys," he said to the rest of the room.

I'd completely forgotten the others were even there. They seemed frozen in states of shock, sitting in their seats or standing by the pool table. One by one they creaked into life, putting down their items and heading to the door. They skirted the broken table as if it were contagious with the plague.

I went toward the broom, but Jimmy shook his head. "Trai Hok and his wife will come by and take care of all of that. You're going home. Call Ethan back. Make sure he watches you until you get into the house. You understand me?"

I nodded and pushed the button. Ethan picked up on the first ring. "Thought so," he said without preamble. "Be there for you in a jiff."

Sean started to get up out of his seat, but Jimmy put a hand on his arm. "I'd like you to stay. Seamus wants to meet you. Give thanks for your help here."

Sean eased back into his seat. "Sure, if you want."

He looked across the bar at me, his eyes creased with concern. "You all right?"

I nodded, forcing a smile to my lips. "I'm fine," I assured him. I drained down the last of my whiskey and put the glass back on the bar.

He reached his fingers to rest on top of mine for a moment. They were tender, warm, and I thought how only minutes ago those same fingers were curled with tight precision, were keeping me safe from a world of hurt. My body blazed with heat, and for a wild moment I wanted him to come home with me. I wanted him to be the one to escort me to my door, to my bedroom, to …

His gaze swirled with passion, and I could see the ripple in his shoulders, feel the press of his fingers against mine.

His voice was hoarse. "You stay safe."

There was a honk by the door, and I forced myself to draw my fingers away. I pulled on my hoodie and went around the bar. As I passed Sean, I couldn't help myself. I ran my hand along the back of his brown leather jacket, drinking in the texture of it, that smell of leather that is equaled nowhere else in nature. His head turned to meet mine, and I could see the strength there, the power.

Then I turned, and the whirling dervish of Kelley Square ran on before me as if nothing had happened. On the opposite side of Kelley Square I could see Seamus's black Escalade entering the intersection.

I stepped into the cab and settled back into the stale-cigarette-smelling interior.

Ethan rattled away the whole ride home, about the Cubans and who knew what else, but I barely heard it. I could only see Sean in motion, a panther, a control of muscle and power that I had never experienced before. Ethan drew to a stop before my house, and I was in a daydream as I unlocked the door, closed it behind me, and stepped into my room.

I slumped into my bed, fully dressed, my head delving deep into the pillow. All I could see was Sean, heart-stopping Sean, and I wanted him with every ounce of my body.

Chapter 5

The hem of my purple-swirled shirt barely skimmed the top of my jeans; the cool November wind sent an edge of chill against the exposed skin as I crossed from the taxi to the bar's door. I stepped inside, swept my gaze around – and I stopped in confusion.

He wasn't there. Not only that, but half the chairs were gone, too. The two pool players were silent in their game. The other four patrons had huddled together around a single table near the corner pocket, as if their solidarity would protect them.

I automatically hung my hoodie on its hook and began mechanically chopping limes, but my brain was racing like a freight train.

He had left.

He had gotten into a fight, his parole officer had found out, and he'd been moved. He could be who knows where.

I might never see him again.

My heart thundered in panic. Sean was the one man I'd ever wanted, the one man I'd connected with. And he was gone.

Jimmy poked his head around the edge of the hallway and nodded when he saw me. "Good. You're here. Seamus and I are having a meeting back in my office. Bring us the Redbreast and the Bushmills."

Of course!

My shoulders relaxed in overwhelming relief. A smile spread broadly across my face. I'd been foolish. That explained all the missing chairs. Surely Sean was part of the gathering. After all, he'd saved the day.

I grabbed the two bottles. My feet were light as I went down the hall to the office. I could hear muttered voices and scraping chairs as I approached.

The room was jammed with probably a dozen men, all serious and in low discussion. Seamus, his body lean and hard even though he must've been nearly fifty, was at the desk with Jimmy. I pushed through to deposit the two bottles on its gleaming wood surface. I grabbed up the two empties that were waiting for me. Then I turned and swept the men, looking –

He wasn't there.

I blinked in disbelief, looking again. There were a collection of ages, from twenty to sixty. The builds ranged from slim to chunky. Some even looked in fairly good shape. But none of them were the one man I wanted, I craved with all my being.

My shoulders sagged as I slowly took the path back to the main room. I swung down the two bottles – and sighed. The recycle bin was overflowing.

I wanted to find the rewind button on this day. I desperately needed to restart and try again.

Somehow I carefully balanced the two new bottles on top of the others. Then I gingerly lifted the whole tub in my arms. I turned to glance at Joey.

"Joey, I'm going out back for a sec."

He absently waved a hand at me, intent on the basketball game.

I hefted the container more snugly in my arms before setting into motion. The office door was closed as I passed it. It took some juggling before I was able to draw open the outside door and move out into the back lot.

The nearby street lamp shone a cold glow into the small area of blacktop. The dumpster was large, black, and the lid kept in most of the stench. A smaller receptacle next to it was half-filled with bottles and lids. I upended my own container into it, making a loud clatter in the night air.

There was an echoing clatter from within the shed.

My heart pounded in my chest, and I turned slowly, staring at it. The shed was corrugated aluminum, perhaps ten by fifteen, and held snow shovels and other sundry equipment. I hadn't noticed before, but the door was half-way open.

Had a raccoon gotten in there, or was it something worse?

I carefully put down the empty container and reached for the tire iron leaning behind the dumpster. My brothers had drilled into me the idea of keeping a weapon in locations you might be vulnerable, and this dumpster certainly applied. I wrapped my fingers along its grip, keeping it low along my leg, then crept carefully toward the opening.

There was no light coming from the shed, and when I got to the door I carefully peered around the edge of it. All I could see within were shadowy shapes. I stepped into the opening –

A man moved before me, large, muscular.

I reacted on instinct, fire pounding in my veins. I swung the tire iron in an arc, up, around, aiming to drive the end of it solidly into his head.

His hand flew up with lightning speed. He caught the top part of the iron inches from his skull.

He stepped forward into the light.

It was Sean.

My breath came out in an explosive gasp. "Jesus Christ, Sean, I could have killed you!"

He gave a wry smile, taking the tire iron out of my hand and putting it down against the shed wall.

I shook my head, my breath still coming in heaves. "What the hell are you doing in here?"

He pushed the door open fully, letting in the light. "With everything that happened yesterday, Jimmy said I could keep her in here. Just in case the Cubans get ideas of retaliation."

I stepped forward into the shed. "Keep what?"

And then I saw it.

The room had been swept, cleaned, and organized. Years of chaotic debris and flotsam now sat stacked and neat along the edges of the wall. In the center of the room sat a black Triumph motorcycle, its silver handlebars gleaming in the streetlight. It could have been a mirror image of the one James Dean had ridden.

My eyes rounded as I approached it, running a hand along its black leather seat. "It's *gorgeous*," I sighed. "What year is it?"

"1955. All original," he stated with a hint of pride. "I had it in storage while I was in prison. Just got it back out again."

"No wonder you want to keep this safe," I breathed. The large front headlight was like a beacon, calling me. The words were out before I thought. "I want to ride it."

He came over to stand before me, looking down at me. In the darkness his face was in shadows, his leather jacket blending into the night.

His voice was hoarse when he spoke. "God, Kay, you are amazing."

I leant back against the wall, looking up at him, my heart thundering in my chest. Kay had been my father's endearment for me. When Sean said it, it sounded soft, sultry, and just right.

I reached out for his hand. My fingers slid along the back of his, and he groaned.

His throat tightened, and he gave his head a short shake. His voice rasped. "You should stay away from me, Kay. Far away. I will be trouble for you."

I found myself sinking into those moss-green eyes, losing myself in their depths, and everything else fell away.

"I can handle the trouble."

His shoulder muscles rippled as he held in place and looked down at me with smoky eyes. Then in a heartbeat he was pressed up against me, his broad chest pushing hard into my breasts, his lips finding mine, claiming them. I gasped as his tongue slid into my mouth. Liquid gold coursed through me, sending my nipples tingling, and heat lower down. I opened my mouth fully to him, losing myself into the sensations of his kiss, utterly lost. Nothing in my life had ever prepared me for the feelings that shook me.

His hands came to my hips, pulling me in harder, then they slid up along the bare skin of my back. Shivers raced down me as he deftly undid the snaps of my bra. My breasts burned with heat as they were freed, as the delicate nipples raked against the moving fabric. He slid his hands around to my breasts, taking one in each hand, sliding his fingers up so they straddled each of my nipples. He squeezed, and the sensation that flooded through me staggered me.

He trailed kisses down my neck, down my chest, and with a slide of his hands he'd pushed my top and bra up over my breasts to expose them to the night air. The nipples hardened further in the cold, and I groaned in pleasure. He squeezed again, and the sensations layered into something indescribable. Then he brought his mouth down to my right breast, and I reeled at the feeling. He slid his hands down to cup my rear, supporting me, and I arched into him, craving more, craving that swirling tongue on my other breast.

"Please," I groaned.

He chuckled, moving his head to the other side, and I wrapped my hands in his thick hair, holding his head in place. I wanted that mouth on every part of me. I wanted his body against mine, I wanted us naked, I wanted –

Jimmy's voice called, loud, sharp, from the entry to the bar. "Katie, you out here?"

I squeaked in shock, grabbing to pull my shirt down over my breasts. I hastily reconnected my bra and brushed back at my hair.

Sean's eyes were still dark with passion, but he gave me a wry smile as he stepped back.

I moved out of the shed and looked over at Jimmy. "Just admiring Sean's bike," I stated, hoping the darkness covered my burning cheeks.

Jimmy nodded, already turning. "Get him in here, too. We're about to get started."

Sean came up behind me, closing the door and snapping the lock shut. His hand slid along my hip, and the heat of desire flooded through me again, swelling my breasts, moistening my sex.

His voice sounded low against my ear. "We'll finish that up later."

He picked up the empty container for me and guided me through the door before closing it behind us. He gave me one last look, fragrant with promise, before moving into Jimmy's office and closing the door behind him.

The hours ticked past with maddening slowness. If normally the night moved by at a glacial pace, tonight it was as if I were watching sand dunes creep slowly, lethargically, under the steady efforts of the wind. My body was aflame, and every move or twist of my body sent it into new surges of desire.

Finally there was the sound of feet and a stream of men emerged, heading across the bar to the door. Jimmy came with them. "Seamus will be staying around with me for a while. You can head on home. Sean's out back – he said he'd take you."

I grabbed my hoodie and had my arms through it before I got halfway down the hall. I stepped out through the back door.

The motorcycle was out on the pavement, pointed at the street. Sean was astride it, a full head helmet on, the visor up. A second, matching black helmet hung in his hand.

He handed me the helmet, and I put it on without a word. I climbed on back. The vibration of the bike beneath me, and his firm, leather-clad body before me, nearly sent me over the edge. I wrapped my arms around him, pulling myself as close as possible.

He groaned, revved the engine, and then we were pulling out into the street. The bike was like butter beneath his guidance, smooth, easy, almost floating along its path. I felt as if I were in another world. I blinked in surprise when my olive-green three-decker appeared out of nowhere.

I didn't want to go in.

He looked back at me, his eyes swirling with a mix of emotions. Desire seemed intertwined with the tightest reins of restraint.

"Kay, I am warning you. If we start down this path –"

Every cell in my body craved him. My throat nearly closed up.

"You are right for me. You are the one man, the only man in the world, who has ever been this right for me."

He groaned with desire, then looked at the three-decker. "Do you have a leather jacket?"

I nodded, climbed off the bike, and ran inside, not even taking off my helmet. I grabbed the jacket from the closet, then ran back outside. I didn't want to give him the chance of changing his mind, of riding away and leaving me alone on this dusty street.

I zipped it up as I climbed back on behind him, wrapping myself around him again. I tapped him on his thigh, putting my head near his ear.

A playful urge tugged at me, and I called out, "I feel the need – the need for speed!"

A rev of the engine, and we were off.

He took us away from the bar, north, and I didn't care where we were going, just that we were together. The bike's vibration sent waves of pleasure coursing through me; his body before me was sturdy, strong, and all I could ever want. The night was glorious, the sky full of twinkling stars against a black velvet backdrop. He took us up onto 290, the elevated highway swirling amongst the buildings of Worcester, then over Lake Quinsigamond.

We moved beyond the city limits, into suburbs, then forests, and then we turned north onto 495. We passed a scattering of cars and trucks – but to me it was as if we were alone, two travelers in a large, empty world. Nothing else existed besides us two.

The bike's rumble eased, and we curled off an exit ramp down into Bolton. The town was one of apple orchards and dairy farms. My heart began beating more quickly. Just what did he have in mind?

He guided the bike off the main street, up narrow, winding roads until he reached the opening to an apple orchard. There were no buildings in sight. He steered the bike onto a dirt path, and we climbed up through rows of trees for perhaps two miles. At last we reached the crest, and he drew to a stop, leaving the engine idling.

The vista was stunning. The autumn hillside sprawled out beneath the moonlight, and in the distance I thought I could see the twinkling lights of Worcester. It was magical.

He turned in place, put his hands under my arms, and lifted me, his shoulders rippling with the effort. I curled my leg as he brought me around, settling me down to face him on the gas tank, my legs astride his. He reached forward to undo my helmet clasp, then hung it on one of the handlebars. He undid his own, placing it on the other side.

The bike rumbled beneath us, his thighs were warm beneath mine, and I wanted him with every beat of my heart.

Our lips slammed together with mutual need, our mouths open, his tongue tantalizing me, driving my already hot flames into searing heat. His hands were at my chest, pulling the zipper of my jacket and stripping it off me with ruthless efficiency. Then he was pulling my top over my head, tossing it on the ground next to my jacket, and pressing kisses all down my neck, my chest, to the curve of my breasts where they were exposed from the bra.

His voice was hoarse. "These last hours have been torture."

I laced my fingers in his hair, pressing his lips against my breast, and his hands undid the bra. I momentarily released my hold to shrug it off, then gasped as his lips seared my nipple. My hands came up around his back, pulling him in, as his teeth teased at first one nipple, then the second. The night air was brisk, and my entire body shone with desire.

He groaned, reaching forward to switch the engine off, then he wrapped his hands beneath my rear and stepped over the bike, carrying me with him. He strode the few steps to a nearby apple tree, pressing me up against its bark. His mouth found mine again, and my breasts flattened against his chest as he drove in against me, his need for me evident against my stomach.

He dropped to one knee in front of me, undoing my jeans, sliding them down my legs to my feet. He pulled off one boot, then the second, then my socks. My toes relished the feel of the soft ground beneath my bare feet. Then he was pulling my jeans fully off.

He looked up at me and groaned in desire. He moved his head forward to start kissing along my thigh, running his tongue along the edges of my panties. I leant back against the trunk, nearly fainting with desire, the rough bark tantalizing my skin.

He hooked a finger around each side of my panties, then slowly, languorously, he pulled them down until my sex was revealed. He let them drop to the ground. I stepped out of them, and he looked up at me, his breath going out of him. The moonlight shone, silver, on my naked body, and my nipples stood hard, ready, eager for him. The only thing I wore was my Saint Michael's medallion glistening at my breast.

I reached for him, my throat all but closed up with passion. "Oh, Sean."

His eyes swirled with emotion, and then his lips moved to my sex. The impact of his tongue rolled my head back against the trunk, and my hands came down to twine in his hair. His fingers kneaded my ass, squeezing, pinching, as his tongue danced against my hard clit. I could feel my juices easing down my leg as his tongue picked up speed, as his hands squeezed and urged me on.

I held in my moans with every ounce of energy I had, but one finally escaped me, shuddering my body.

He looked up at that, his lips glistening. His eyes shone in the moonlight. "I want to hear you."

I flushed. In all the years I'd been with Derek, I had trained myself to be silent. Not that there were many times that I reached orgasm, with his self-centered approach to sex. But both of our apartments had thin walls, and he hadn't wanted anybody else to hear any noise I made.

I'd never had sex without muffling my reactions.

He pinched my ass, and I groaned at the sensation, craving more. His eyes held mine.

"The nearest house is miles away. There's nobody to hear you. I want you set free."

He brought one hand around, maintaining his gaze, then slid two fingers up inside me.

The pleasure of it nearly sent me over the edge. I leant back and a low, guttural groan coursed from me.

"That's my Kay," he murmured. "Sing for me."

He pressed his fingers in deeper, and my groan was lower, richer. He withdrew his fingers and brought them to my lips. "Taste yourself. Taste how beautiful you are."

I sucked in his fingers, swirling my tongue around them, and he groaned in response, pushing his head back into my sex. His tongue moved into action, and my body danced with his motions, arcing, pulsing, with his fingers in my mouth, his hand on my ass, his tongue delving and swirling, sucking and pulsing.

Suddenly I could feel the crest build and I dug my fingers into the hair at the base of his neck. He brought both hands back to support me from my ass, pulling me in hard, driving his tongue deep inside me. The waves rose, rose, carrying me with them, and then they were crashing, exploding like fireworks, and my groans shook through my body, filling my soul, tremoring every corner of my being.

My knees wobbled, and Sean's hands moved under my arms, lowering me down to kneel before him.

I put my hands on either side of his face, my breathing slowing from its breathless heights. I drew his mouth into mine for a long, heartfelt kiss. Time drifted away.

When I finally drew back, I stared at him in amazement.

"I had no idea," I breathed. "No idea at all."

He ran a hand through my hair, his gaze caught on mine. "You are so beautiful," he murmured. "You deserve so much."

I put my hands on his hips and pulled left. He drew to his feet at my urging, and in a moment I had him placed against the same apple tree that had recently supported me. I stayed kneeling before him, and began undoing his belt buckle.

His cock throbbed hard against his jeans, and he groaned. "Oh, Kay."

The buckle came free, and I undid the button, then the zipper. I gave a hard tug, and the jeans slid down to his ankles. His black underwear was pressed out by the pressure of his cock. I slid a hand against the fabric, against the hard member beneath it, and the breath left him.

Slowly, gently, I slid the underwear down his body, admiring his form. The man was in incredible shape – and his cock matched him in every way. I moved my mouth to the top of it, carefully, gently sliding my mouth just over the head, letting my tongue swirl the pre-cum around its top.

Sean shuddered, bringing his hands down into my hair, holding my head in place.

I brought my hands around to grip his firm ass, using only my mouth to slide down deeper, ever deeper, along his shaft. His hips rocked with my motions, and I ran my nails along his skin, smiling as he arched in response, as his breathing grew hoarser, more guttural. He was already close, so close.

I slowed down and he groaned with desire, his fist in my hair tightening, but I resisted his motions. I tantalized him, licking him, pressing my lips in a ring, letting the thick head of the knob pop in and out of that pressure.

His voice was ragged. "Jesus Christ, Please, Kay –"

I dug in my fingers, slammed my mouth against him, and took him fully into my throat. He gasped with pleasure, let out a long groan, and then he was coming, hot and salty, deep into my throat. The pulses went on for long moments, his breath coming in shuddering gasps.

And then, at long last, the pulses slowed, eased, and I sucked gently on him, taking down the lingering remnants of his desire.

He pulled me up to my feet, drew me against his chest, and I wrapped my arms within the leather jacket he was still wearing. He brought his arms around me, pressed his head down against mine, and we were one.

Chapter 6

I hesitated for a moment before climbing out of the cab. I felt so different, so alive, and I wondered if every person in the bar would see it in me. I didn't care. Let them laugh, let them tease me as much as they wanted. Nothing could spoil my mood. Not as long as Sean was there waiting for me.

I stepped to the door, pressed it open – and frowned.

It was hard to take in. For the month I'd worked here the room had always been near-empty. But now it was packed with men, standing room only, talking in tones that seemed oddly out of place. It was not the lively banter of a Friday night out. It was rich with a tense energy, of anticipation and shadowed darkness.

It came to me. It was the way my father and his friends had talked when a dangerous assignment was looming on the horizon. Like they knew the risks – and they were looking forward to it.

I pushed my way through the crowd to the bar, joining Mrs. O'Malley there. She nodded at me. "Need three more pints of Guinness and two Harps," she stated without preamble. I grabbed up the glasses as she continued pouring out whiskies.

I tried to glance around for Sean as I filled and set out the drinks, but in the throngs it was hard to see individual faces. My heart pounded against my chest. Clearly they were gearing up for action against the Cubans, and they would want Sean in the thick of it.

Sean could get hurt – or worse.

There was a hand on my shoulder, I turned, and Sean was there. A wealth of emotions swirled in his eyes, and I folded in against him, wrapping myself into his chest. His arms came up around me, holding me tight.

All of a sudden it was that momentous morning again, the last time I had seen my father alive. I had hugged him this very way, sensing something in his tension, something hovering in the air. I had begged him not to go. He had kissed me on the forehead, said he loved me, and then he had gone.

He had gone.

My throat closed up on me, and the urge to beg Sean to stay nearly overwhelmed me. I clung to him as if I were on a life raft in the middle of a raging storm.

At last he gently pushed me back, looking down at me. His gaze held steady promise. "I'll be all right."

"You can't know that," I moaned.

He gave a wry smile, brushing one hand along my cheek. "You're my lucky charm."

My hand went to my medallion.

I brought both hands behind my neck, undoing the latch. The latch that had not been released since that day of my father's funeral.

I held it in my hands for a long moment, then looked up to Sean. "This was my father's. I want you to wear it."

His eyes stilled, and he looked at me in stunned silence. At last he found his voice.

"Kay, are you sure?"

I nodded, holding out my hands.

He dropped to one knee before me, and I brought the chain around his neck, bringing my head next to his to do the clasp. I lay my hands against his neck for a long moment, feeling the strength in his shoulders. Then I slid my hand up to twine in his hair, and he bowed his head.

I kissed the top of his head. My voice was a mere whisper. "Be safe. Come home to me."

He reached up to gently take my hand, then he turned it as he brought it around to his lips. He pressed the softest of kisses against the inner part of my wrist. I could feel it course through me, down to my very toes.

When he rose again, his eyes were steady and firm.

Pride shone within me. If anybody could get through what was to come, he would.

Seamus climbed up onto a chair by the TV, hitting the wall with his fist a few times to get the room to settle down. He drew his eyes around the crowd.

"You know what to do. Now let's go do it. Nobody disrespects us in our own place. Nobody."

The men growled in agreement, and the stream began moving out the door. Jimmy came by the front of the bar, glanced at his wife, and kept walking, with Seamus close behind.

Sean held my gaze for a long moment, and I stepped back. I wrapped my arms around each other and gave him a small smile. I would be right here until he returned to me.

He nodded, turned, and then he was lost in the crowd.

When the room cleared there were the six regulars along with two stout men in their forties. The newcomers took seats right by the door.

Mrs. O'Malley nudged a head at them as she went around to gather up glasses. "They'll keep an eye on us here, just in case," she commented to me. "But we won't need them. Seamus will teach those bastards a lesson. Nobody messes with our family and gets away with it."

It seemed I couldn't go sixty seconds without glancing over at the door, but Kelley square swirled on in its maddeningly complex dance of slammed-on brakes and screeching tires. An ambulance screamed through, delving across the center of the chaos like a surgeon's blade through a cancerous tumor.

And still the door remained motionless.

I went out to wipe down the tables, to refill Joey's Bushmills, and it was maddening, maddening. How could I be cutting up limes, as if nothing at all were happening, when somewhere out there Sean was diving into Hell? Where were they? What were they doing? What kind of a place were they going to assault – and who was there to fight back?

Mrs. O'Malley shook her head. "Lass, you're going to have a nervous breakdown at the rate you're going," she warned me. "Take deep breaths. Here, have some Redbreast. It settles the nerves." She poured me a shot.

I took the glass without hesitation and downed it in one smooth swallow. It hit me hard; I leant against the bar for a moment, but I welcomed the distraction. And she was right. The chaotic thoughts eased up, if only for a bit.

"They'll be fine," she calmly assured me. "Seamus knows what he's doing. Done this many times, back home."

I looked over at her, at her deep brown eyes heavily lined with mascara. "How about Jimmy?"

She snorted, glancing at the gold wedding ring on her finger. "It should've been Liam, his brother," she murmured. "Now *there* was a man. He was Seamus's partner, you know. You had the two of them side by side, and nothing could stand in their way. We were engaged, once."

I could hear the ache of longing in her voice.

"What happened to him?"

Her eyes grew cold. "The British bastards," she snapped. "Shot him six times. In the back." Her eyes swung to the door. "My brother would have gone up to take them all on, but I managed to convince him to come with me to the states instead, to get Jimmy out of harm's way. Things were tense back then."

She shrugged. "Jimmy was a miserable failure as a soldier, but he was a sweet talker, and somehow I gave in to him. I thought that he might grow into his brother's shoes." She snorted. "He never did."

"Still, you two seem to love each other," I offered.

She snorted again. "That bastard would stick his cock into a tub of ice cream, if it had a hole in it," she snapped. "But a vow's a vow, and he's not a mean drunk. We have our separate worlds, and he makes sure the bills are paid. So that's life."

I pressed my lips together. That didn't sound like much of a life at all. I wondered how people got themselves into these situations, got so used to misery that they began to think of it as normal and even something to hold onto.

Sean's face came into my mind, and with it a longing which nearly toppled me. There was a man worth loving, worth risking all for. At every turn he'd defended those he cared for. His mother, his friends, me.

He had to come back to me unharmed.

The bell tinkled, and my heart stopped. I gripped the edge of the bar and looked up.

Sean had Jimmy's arm draped over his shoulder and was half-carrying him in through the door. Jimmy's right leg had a spreading bloodstain on the front of the calf and he wasn't putting any weight on it. Sean had a dusky-purple bruise on his temple and his black shirt was torn in several places.

Mrs. O'Malley grabbed up the Redbreast and was around the bar in a heartbeat. For all her talk, her face was filled with concern as she helped her husband into his seat and handed over the bottle. He swigged down a mouthful, returning it to her.

"Tripped over a case of beer," he growled. "Missed half the fight."

There was a honk outside, and he looked up. "That's Seamus. He'll take me to the hospital." His eyes turned to Sean. "You lock the place up, and you and Katie get over to our house. The guest room is up the stairs and on the left." He dug in his back pocket, bringing out a key on a ring. "Lock up after you get in there. Don't open for nobody until me or Bridgit get home. Understand?"

Mrs. O'Malley put her arm under Jimmy, gently hauling him to his feet. "I got ya."

Sean opened the door for them, and they walked the few steps to the waiting Escalade. In a moment they were inside and it pulled away from the curb.

The remaining men in the bar didn't need a word. They filed out into the darkness. Sean set the bolt, flipped the sign to "closed", and then turned to me.

My breath returned to me. I raced to him, my arms threading within his leather jacket, needing to feel his body against me, his skin, to know he was all right. He groaned in pain as my fingers pressed against his back, but he didn't pull away – just held me tighter against him. He pushed me back against the bar, and I went willingly, my mouth turning up toward his, my body aching with need for him.

He looked at me, hot with passion, and then he growled with desire. "God, Kay, what you do to me. I have to get you somewhere safe." He turned with me, moving me in front of him down the back hall. We got out into the parking area, and his Triumph was waiting. We climbed on, put on our helmets, and then we were roaring down the street, deep into the heart of Worcester.

I barely took in the twists and turns before we pulled up in front of a dark blue Colonial house with a two-car garage on the side. The houses on the street were close but not oppressive. He took the bike around the side of the garage, through a gate, and brought it to a stop in the neatly mown back yard. High fence surrounded us on all three sides.

We climbed off the bike and went to the back door. He used the key, pushed it open, and we stepped into the kitchen.

I reached for the light, but he caught my hand in his, shaking his head in the dark. He closed the door behind us, locking it, then led us through the shadows, somehow navigating his way across what must have been a living room. We reached the front door and he guided us up the stairs. The door to the left was open, we went through, and he pushed it closed behind us.

The moonlight streamed in through the open windows, gilding the world with silvery edges. His eyes shone with hot desire and need. His voice was guttural and strained. "Kay – I'll warn you –"

I threw myself at him, pressing my mouth into his, holding nothing back.

He groaned, his shoulders rippled, and then he was lifting me and carrying me over to the bed. He dropped me on it so my hips were at the lower edge, my legs hanging off the end. His hands popped my jeans button, raked down the zipper, and the fabric ripped off of me, taking my underwear down to my knees at the same time. He yanked them the rest of the way, then his hand drove into his back pocket, coming out with a foil pouch. He had his jeans loose and sliding down to the ground as he latched his fingers on his underwear and sent it in the same direction. His cock throbbed hard, huge, and I gasped at the size of it.

He slid the condom on, my knees came up on either side of me of their own accord, and then he delved into me.

My cry of pleasure echoed throughout the empty house as he filled me, stretched me, plundered me in a way I'd never even imagined possible. The cry became a long, drawn out moan, a song, and he groaned in response, twining his hand into my hair. He pounded into me, harder, harder, and my body arced in response, desperately needing him. My ankles crossed at his waist, pulling him in more deeply, and his breath came in short, urgent gasps.

"Kay – I – My God – Kay –" and then he was shuddering, exploding, throbbing deep within me. That was all I needed. I shattered, a million crystals rising high into the night sky, reflecting silver light, turning, spiraling.

Then, at last, at long last, I was drifting, falling, settling down into a quiet river.

He lay down on top of me. I relished the weight, the sense of security, the feeling of his cock within me and his strength all around me. I drew both hands around to his back, pulling his shoulder blades in against me.

He turned his head to look at me, and the emotion which shone in his eyes took my breath away. It was all I could do to get his name out.

"Oh, Sean."

He stilled for a long moment. Then he leant forward to tenderly, gently press his lips against mine.

Within me, I could feel his shaft give a soft but noticeable throb.

I nuzzled against him with my nose. "You sure you aren't too sore from tonight's adventures?" I gave a soft tilt with my hips.

His cock twitched again, and a gleam came into his eyes. His mouth came down to mine, gentle at first, then more insistent, and the world fell away.

Chapter 7

The mattress beneath me was soft and comfortable, the comforter on top billowy and jasmine-smelling, and I blinked my eyes open in confusion. Golden sunlight streamed across an unfamiliar room, dancing on the royal blue covers and thick cream carpet. The walls held small watercolors of forget-me-nots.

I rolled to my side, but the bed was empty. A single rose lay on the pillow, its crimson petals glistening.

I smiled, taking up the stem and admiring the blossom. Sean was astounding. His body brought me to heights of pleasure I'd never thought possible. And he truly cared about me as well.

For some reason nervousness whirled in the pit of my stomach. It all seemed too good to be true. Something would happen. Surely something awful would happen, to take this all away from me.

I pushed the thought away, climbed out of bed, and gathered up my clothes from where they were scattered around the room. I took a few minutes in the bathroom to freshen myself up, then picked up the rose. There were quiet sounds of movement coming from downstairs, so I headed down the stairs and across the neat living room with its dark green couch and flat-screen TV.

Mrs. O'Malley was in the kitchen amongst her pine cabinets and white marble island. She nodded in welcome as she sliced tomatoes. Sausage and eggs were already frying on the stove, and the aromas sent my stomach grumbling.

"Morning," she said with a smile. "The boys will be back soon. They're just off with Seamus to check on things." She tossed the tomato slices into the pan and shook it around. She nudged her head at one of the stools by the counter. "Take a seat. Coffee? Tea?"

"Tea would be fine," I responded. In a minute a steaming off-white mug was sitting before me. Next came the plate with the fragrant breakfast. She put hers alongside mine and came around to sit.

I took a bite, soaking in the delicious flavors. "How is Jimmy?"

She drank some of her tea. "He's an ox – he's fine. Just twisted something and scraped off a layer of skin; the doc said to take it easy for a few days. There weren't any serious injuries, thank God."

She looked over at me. "I might'a been wrong about Sean. I'm woman enough to admit it. Seamus says Sean was a key part of what went down last night. When Jimmy got hurt. Sean was right by his side, holding off three of the Cubes until he got on his feet again. Then Seamus came in with the cavalry. A few of our boys wanted to escalate, but Sean talked them 'round. He was a good soldier."

My cheeks warmed. That was my Sean she was talking about. He was a man to be proud of.

And yet that twisting came back into me. He'd just been in a turf war – and this was only going to get worse. A voice in my head said we should run, run, run …

The back door pushed open, and Jimmy came through, then Sean. He wore the same dark brown leather jacket, a dark grey shirt nearly identical to the black one from yesterday, but somehow he seemed even more handsome than the first day I'd seen him. His eyes had richer depths, his shoulders had a stronger set.

He was mine.

The corner of his mouth quirked up into a smile, and he came around to my side, sliding his hand along my waist and giving me a squeeze. His lips met mine for a long kiss. When he drew back, he traced his fingers along my face. "Good morning, beautiful."

Mrs. O'Malley looked over at Jimmy. "So?"

He plunked down on the stool on the other side of her. "Looks like it worked. The Cubans weren't expecting that kind of a show of force. They thought me and my bar were all they had to deal with." He grinned. "Now they know better."

He nudged his wife. "We did good, huh? Just like the old days."

She gave a snort. "You fell on your ass while Seamus and Sean took care of business," she returned. She ate the last bit of egg off her plate and stood, taking the plate over to the sink to rinse it off.

Jimmy's shoulders fell, and he looked down at the counter for a moment. At last he turned to Sean. "Joey's going to run the bar today, to give Katie a day off. Just in case, you know. So you take her out, have some fun." He reached into his pocket, pulled out his wallet, and drew out some bills. "Get her some real food. Not that ramen crap she's been eating."

Sean took the bills and tucked them into his own wallet. He looked over at me. "Ready to go?"

My plate was empty, and I stood, putting my hand into his. "Absolutely."

We walked out to the Triumph. As I picked up my helmet I noticed an odd, thick wire sticking out of the lower part of the visor. "What's this?"

He smiled as he put his on. "In-helmet communication. Figured it might be nice to be able to talk while we're riding." He climbed onto the bike, and in a moment I was at his back, hugging myself close to him.

I chuckled. "Testing, testing."

He turned the key, and the bike purred into life. "Got you loud and clear," he responded. He turned his wrist, and the bike glided out of the back yard and onto the street. "Swing by your house so you can take a quick shower?"

"Sure, my landlady gets her hair done Thursday mornings, so you can even come in for a while."

I could hear the smile in his voice. "Tempting, so tempting, but we won't have time for any entanglements. Not right now."

My curiosity was piqued. "Oh? Why not?"

"You'll see," was all he would say.

In a few minutes we pulled up to the three-decker and walked up to the door. I hesitated for a moment before pushing open the door to my room. My tiny room would undoubtedly seem barren, lacking ... but at last I led us in.

He looked around with interest, his eyes landing on the guitar, the row of books. "Cozy."

I gave a snort. "That's one word for it." I rummaged through the shirts, drawing out a long sleeved green one, a pair of jeans, and the other items I'd need. "I'll be as quick as I can."

"I'll be right here," he promised.

It was hard turning from him, and I probably showered and dressed more quickly than I ever had in my life. When I came back to my room he was standing at the window, staring out into the street, a distant look in his eyes. He turned at my approach, his gaze warming.

"You make it challenging to stay on a timetable," he murmured, stepping forward to put his hands on my hips. "It would be so nice to –"

A grey Subaru Outback eased past the house and turned into the driveway.

I sighed. "And there she is, right on cue."

Sean chuckled, picking up the helmets. "Your chariot awaits, My Lady."

We headed north, up 190, and by the time we turned west on 2 I had settled in for the ride, soaking in the lovely foliage along the twisting, turning road. The sunshine was glorious, bringing out rich orange rusts and deep crimsons from the leaves. At times he'd go off the main road and into smaller nooks, then there were spots where he hit a straightaway and opened her up, the wind blowing back my hair.

And we rode.

Our conversations streamed along with the miles, easy, relaxed, about anything and everything. I learned he adored bread pudding with a caramel-whiskey sauce. He'd always wanted to explore Alaska. He missed his mother and wished he could visit more often.

I told him about life growing up with four older brothers. Three of them were now cops like my father had been, spread out in Miami, Vegas, and Boston. The fourth ran a restaurant near Hartford. My mom was still a teacher, still trying to convince ninth graders that Emily Dickinson and Sylvia Plath had meaning in their lives.

The sun was embellishing the sky with purple spirals and violet whiskers by the time we were near home again and easing down the ramp into Worcester's Shrewsbury Street district. With the area being block after block of delicious food, I wondered where Sean was planning on taking me.

I smiled as he pulled into the parking lot of the Flying Rhino. Out of all the restaurants here, this one definitely had the most personality. Lime green walls, cherry-red chairs, the menu was eclectic and, by all reports, delicious. I'd never been here before. And, best of all, they'd be quite fine with our jeans and motorcycle gear. They took all comers with a smile.

My lobster ravioli was absolutely stunning, soaked in a sherry sauce, and I took another sip of my Riesling. "I won't have room for dessert, at this rate," I teased him.

His eyes gleamed. "No dessert here," he countered. "I have other plans for us."

I smiled, not even asking. I was going to leave everything in his capable hands. So far, this had been one of the best afternoons of my life.

When we were done, we suited up and drove south this time, down 146. In no time at all we had reached an abandoned drive-in. The large, stone archway entrance was cordoned off with a neon-yellow cable. Sean guided the bike around the outside of the arch, through the dense weeds, and we went up the gravel road to the drive-in area itself. The speakers and posts were long gone, but the plant-speckled pavement still had its traditional undulations. The projection house was half caved in, and the large screen had a few missing panels, but in the glowing moonlight there was a romantic, nostalgic feeling to the place.

A thick row of trees shielded us from the noise of 146, and it gave only a soft murmur as cars whooshed past.

He pulled to a stop in a prime viewing location, in front of the looming, pale screen, and I obediently climbed off. He opened up the side bags and laid out a large, dark green blanket for us. Then he brought out a bottle of bubbly, an elegantly-wrapped cheesecake, and a collection of plastic utensils and plates.

I looked at the cheesecake, impressed. "S&S Cheesecake, Bronx, NYC. I've heard about them."

He grinned. "Only the best in the world," he agreed. "Come, have a seat." He undid the wire cage around the cork, wrapped his hand around the top of the cork, and gently eased it off. He winked at me. "Keeps the most bubbles in the wine," he advised me. "Gets you drunk more quickly."

"Oh, does it?" I teased. In a moment he had our glasses poured, and he held his up.

His eyes became serious. "Kay, you are the most amazing woman I've ever met. To you."

I blushed and tapped my glass against his. "Thank you. For everything."

He took a sip, and then a playful look came back into his eyes. "And now for the main feature."

He reached behind him and drew out a large iPad. He arranged the Champagne bottle before us, leaning the iPad against it. Then he pressed a few buttons.

Top Gun began playing, the deep bass notes echoing across the empty field.

I laughed out loud, settling back. "How did you know I liked this movie?"

His eyes twinkled. "Oh, just a guess. Would you like some cheesecake?"

"Absolutely!"

The dessert was as stunning as anticipated, the stars twinkled overhead, and by the time the movie reached its blue-hued sex scene with Tom Cruise bringing Kelly McGillis to new heights of pleasure, Sean and I were right there with them.

Chapter 8

I twined my fingers into Sean's across the bar's counter, content simply being with him. We had talked so much over the past few days that I felt that we could read each other's thoughts. He was everything I could have hoped for in a man. After all the false starts, after all the heartache, life was finally dealing me a hand I could savor.

I wished I could push away the feeling that it was all about to come tumbling down on our heads.

The Cubans had not made a peep after Sean and Seamus's 'visit' two nights ago. I had no idea if this meant that the Cubans accepted the new status quo or if they were gearing up for something even more spectacular. But for now the two bodyguards lounged in boredom by the door, the regulars skittishly glanced around at every odd noise, and Jimmy paced the floor with a cock-sure attitude which seemed unnatural.

I watched him with curiosity. Had he always had this false veneer over him, or had I become more aware of it since talking with his wife about his past? I could see now how he tried to project an aura of self-assuredness, but the twitch in his eyes showed the undercurrent of nerves. Maybe it'd all been brought out by the recent conflict – but I had a sense it had always been in there. Maybe that was part of why he entertained his series of girls. Maybe they helped him feel more a "real man" amongst his peers.

A tinkle sounded at the door. I turned, and a combination of disappointment and resignation coursed through me. At least this one might have been twenty-two or twenty-three rather than barely legal. Her skin was Renaissance-pale, with wavy, red hair shimmering down past her waist. She wore a delicate, pale-blue dress which skimmed her knees. Her handbag was cream, with a Pegasus and a rose on its center, and she clutched it with both hands.

Jimmy's eyes lit up, and he strode forward. "Ah, there you are. I thought you might have gotten lost."

She nudged her head back toward Kelley Square. "Had to make my way across that deathtrap on foot. It took me nearly ten minutes."

Jimmy patted her warmly on the back. "Not to worry, my dear. Come on in the back where we can talk a bit." He wrapped his arm around her shoulder, guiding her into the dim hallway.

My heart sank as they turned the corner. I found myself pulling my phone out of my back pocket, clicking the text app, and sending yet another message off to Eileen.

Sean's voice was low. "No answer from her yet?"

I shook my head, staring at the screen. "It's been over a week since she last wrote. I hope she's OK. I know her grandmother was very ill. Maybe things took a turn for the worse."

He patted my hand reassuringly. "Or maybe she just misplaced her phone or something. I'm sure she'll get back to you soon."

His brow creased. "You know, if you really hate working here that much –"

I stuffed the phone back into my pocket. "I promised Eileen I'd keep things together until she got back. If I quit, and they had to hire another girl, they might not take Eileen on when she came home again. She's been working here for nearly a year now and loves it. She'd never forgive me if I made a mess of things here."

His fingers brushed over mine. "You're very loyal to her."

I gave a wry smile. "She was there for me when I finally wrenched myself away from Derek. I owe it to her."

A shadow crossed his face. "I hate to think of you with that man; the things he did to you."

I squeezed his hand and smiled. "That is all in the past now," I assured him. "I could never trust him; he lied constantly to me." I looked up into those steady eyes. "I know you would never lie to me. I trust my heart to you."

He curled my fingers around his hand, then lowered his head to kiss them.

Time drifted by, our conversation wrapping us in a warm cocoon, and I barely noticed when the red-head slipped out on her way home, or the traffic in the square slowed to just a manageable Twister game. But at last Jimmy emerged from his office, yawning and stretching his arms over his head.

"That's it, boys," he announced to the guys. "Time to head on home." He turned to Sean. "And you, I think you have something to show to that girl of yours."

I looked at Sean in surprise. "You do?"

His eyes sparkled. "I was waiting until you were done for the evening."

Jimmy made a waving motion. "Go on. I'll lock up. You two have fun."

Sean came around and held out my leather jacket for me, then we went out to the back lot. He rolled the Triumph out of the shed. In a moment we were in motion, but not toward my street. Instead we headed south just a few blocks and pulled up alongside a rectangular, three-story brick building.

I looked at it in surprise. "I know this place. Didn't it used to be a schoolhouse?"

He nodded and then guided me in to the back door. He punched in the code, and we started up the stairs. "I've got a studio on the third floor. Jimmy and Seamus are helping me with it, in thanks for my assistance."

A twist went through my stomach at the thought of Sean getting deeply involved with those two. "Are you sure …"

We had reached the door, and he turned to look down at me. "Am I sure what?"

I dropped my eyes. Here he was, trying to get back on his feet, finally in his first new apartment, and I was going to ruin the evening for him. I shook my head and put on a smile. "Nothing. Let's see this new place of yours."

He put the key in the lock, turned the knob, and pushed open the door.

I stepped through, my mouth falling open in surprise. It was stunning. The floor was polished wood, shining in the moonlight. The walls were exposed brick interspersed with white. A bank of windows overlooked the city, edged by white curtains. A large bed was against the far left wall, made with a thick, ivory cover and several large pillows. Small oak tables stood on either side of it. There was also a sturdy oak dresser, an oak table with two chairs against it, and a modern kitchen in white and chrome.

I stepped in, turning in place. "Sean, it is fantastic!"

He smiled, coming to me. "I'm glad you think so."

He had left the lights off, and the moonlight gave a glittery sheen to everything in the room. He shrugged off his leather jacket, took mine, and hung them on hooks by the door.

As my eyes adjusted, I realized that there were large paintings on the walls – squares and rectangles interrupting the steady brick pattern. I approached the one hanging over the black couch. "And what is this poster of?"

As I drew close, I realized it wasn't a poster. It was a black and white photograph – blown up – of his Triumph. It was a side view; the bike's front wheel was tilted slight toward the camera, as if the motorcycle were giving a come-hither look to the viewer. The emotion in it stunned me.

"Did you do this?"

He came up beside me, and the look in his eyes was almost hesitant. "I did. What do you think?"

I looked up at him in amazement. "That is incredible!"

The smile that brightened his face was like a child's at Christmas, and I wrapped him in a hug. I gazed again at the photo. "Do you exhibit these?"

He shook his head, glancing again at the image. "My father said doing art was for pussies, for those who couldn't earn their living properly with their own two hands. One time I brought him a photo I'd taken of a local church. I was so proud of the way the shadows fell across the green." He looked down. "My Dad grabbed it from me and ripped it into confetti. Said I was wasting my time with this nonsense, and should be focusing that energy on practicing my footwork."

I laced my fingers into his. "Well, your dad was a fool, because these are great. I want to see them all."

The next one was a field of rippled white, with just the tops of a pair of Adirondack chairs poking up from the center. I realized this must have been a massive snowstorm to have so thoroughly covered the wooden chairs.

"From a friend's yard, during a blizzard," he explained.

The scene could have been just a simple document of the inches that had fallen, but again Sean had managed to work so much more into it. The two chairs seemed close, like lovers, but the snow had held them apart, had all but covered them up. They were forced to wait, frozen, immobile, until spring came and gently released them.

My breath caught in my throat. My voice was a mere whisper.

"That was us."

He brought his hand up to brush my hair back from my face, his gaze tender. "Oh, Kay –"

He drew me in, and his kiss was gentle, soft, and burrowed deep into my soul. He swept me up in his arms and carried me to his bed. He laid me on the blanket, then stood, gazing down at me. "Wait there for just a moment."

I watched as he moved to a closet, withdrew a medium-sized box, then walked around the room. At each counter and table he placed a pillar candle and lit it. Soon the entire room sparkled with glittering flames.

I gazed around at the effect. "Sean – it's beautiful!"

He stopped by the bureau, leaving the empty box by its side. He set his phone into the Bose speaker unit and pressed a button. In a moment rich cello music, laced with longing and desire, swelled from every corner of the room.

I recognized it at once as one of my favorites. "That's Yo-Yo Ma, playing Bach."

He seemed caught for a moment, lost in time, then he came back to my side, kneeling. His eyes glistened with emotion. "Kay, sweetest Kay, I never thought I would find you."

He drew me to him, and while I had thought the kisses of the past few nights could never be topped, something in the way he held me, he pressed his lips to mine, brought tears to my eyes. I wrapped my arms around him, and his tongue met mine, but not to claim me – to save me.

His hands went to the bottom of my shirt and slowly, tenderly peeled it up my body, as if I were the most precious present he had ever received. His eyes glowed as he removed it over the top of my head, letting my hair cascade back down over my shoulders. He dropped the shirt to the side, his eyes never leaving me, and he drew in a long breath.

"You are stunning. Someday I will photograph you."

I crossed my arms self-consciously over my bra, blushing. "I don't think that's a good idea."

He gently took my hands in his, drawing them back away from my breasts. "I will capture for you how I see you, and then maybe you will understand." His head lowered to nuzzle along my left breast, and fire blazed within it, peaking my nipples, sending waves of desire throughout my body. His lips suckled at the soft flesh, pushing along the edge of the bra, and I craved him with all my being.

He slid down the bed, slowly undoing the button of my jeans, then sliding the zipper down one notch at a time. I could hear each soft click, could feel the liquid flowing in my sex. By the time he slid my jeans down my legs my skin was alive with sensation. Every movement of the fabric felt like a tantalizing caress.

I was now only in my black lace bra and matching panties. He smiled at that, his eyes moving down me. "You are art incarnate," he murmured. "You were made for me."

If before he had been a windstorm, a raging river, tonight he was the steady, inexorable waves of a beautiful tropical seashore.

And he was mine.

I drew up to sitting, putting my hands at his waist. "You are my present, too," I reminded him. "Let me unwrap you."

His eyes sparkled with amusement mixed with something stronger, but he remained still as I slowly, languorously drew the fabric of his shirt along his rippled muscles and up over his thick, well defined biceps. By the time I drew the neck over his head, letting his thick hair fall through it, his gaze had become richer, swirled with passion.

My Saint Michael pendant glistened against his skin, and my heart swelled.

He was mine.

My hands moved to his belt, slowly undoing the buckle, sliding the leather through the loops one rung at a time. By the time the last bit drew clear, the outline of his need for me pressed hard against his jeans.

I slid my hand along the bulge for a moment, and his breath caught. He reached a hand out for me, but I leaned back, shaking my head. I brought my hands down to his button, pulling the fabric apart so the fabric around the button stretched, stretched … and then finally the button popped free.

He groaned.

I slid his zipper down inch by inch, letting each click echo in his body. Finally I reached the end. He lifted his hips, and I slid the jeans off of him with a twisting motion, giving his skin the time to crave even more touch.

His black underwear was tented, and I smiled up at him.

"Maybe you should take a photo of both of us," I murmured.

His gaze was full heat, mixed almost with a sense of wonder. "Yes," he murmured. "Yes."

I eased off the bed and stood between him and the window, so my body would form a silhouette, my shadow falling across him. I slid my right strap off my shoulder, then my left. I put my left arm across my breasts, holding the bra in place, then with my right I undid the back.

His breath was coming in long, slow draws, and his eyes soaked me in like a salmon breathing in the scent of its long lost home.

I lowered my arm, arching my back slightly, and he gave a long groan of desire.

I turned in place, showing my back to him, then hitched a finger on each side of my panties. As I slid them down, I bent over, so that by the time they reached the floor my hair was pooling at the floor by my feet.

I looked around the side of my calf to the bed. His face shone with torment and desire.

His voice was rough. "God, Kay, I need you. I need you."

I turned to slip my hand into his jeans pocket, finding the foil square I knew would be there. I put a corner in my teeth, then went to the bed. Again he raised his hips as I drew his underwear down the length of his lean, muscular legs. I straddled his thighs, ripping the packet open and drawing the condom down the rock-hard length of his shaft.

His hands went to my legs, sliding their way up to cup my ass. He groaned again, his body arching.

I lowered myself, my moist opening finding him by instinct, the pressure of him stretching me, filling me, and I slid until I was fully seated against him. My nipples brushed against his chest, and electricity sizzled through me, racing down into every corner of my being. I slid up again, savoring every moment, then down, more quickly this time.

His groan was louder.

His hands slid to take a firm hold of my hips, I drew my calves tight against his, and then our rhythm grew, built. It echoed between us like ripples building off each other.

Our moans echoed off the brick walls, drowned out the music, soared over the buildings and streets of Worcester County.

And then at last we were exploding, cascading, showering the moonlit world with silver-laced notes of unadulterated release.

Chapter 9

I blinked my eyes open, feeling both exhausted and satiated beyond all reckoning. My breath caught, and I stared at the sight before me.

Sean was asleep. The thick, white comforter was drawn to his waist, and he looked like a Greek God come to life. His six-pack and sculpted form could have been marble, the sensual curve of his bicep a masterpiece created by Michelangelo.

And he was mine.

Sean opened his eyes, and for a long moment we were lost, were connected in a way I had never thought possible. And then time became a distant memory.

It was nearly noon by the time I was sitting at the oak table finishing off a delicious stack of pancakes. He had made us a batch from scratch, complete with strawberries and whipped cream.

I pushed the plate back with a grin. "I could get used to this."

He reached over to sweep the hair from my face, tucking it behind my ear. "I would like that."

His phone buzzed, and he looked down at it. "It's Jimmy – I need to take this."

I waved him away. "Of course. I'll just check up on things." I pulled my own phone over.

He went to the far side of the room, hitting the answer button and talking quietly into it. I checked my email – nothing of note – then went to the Worcester Telegram webpage to see if anything was up in town.

It must have been slow news for a Saturday. The lead story was some blonde curly-headed moppet, age fifteen, who had managed to break a record for sculling. Apparently she was already quite tall for her age, and the reporter expected even greater achievements from her as she grew into her full strength.

Sean came back to me. "They need me for something over at the warehouse for a few minutes. If you want, we can swing by there, then go for a ride before you have to start work tonight."

I smiled. "I'd like that a lot. As long as we leave time after the ride for me to change and have a quick shower, that sounds perfect."

I slipped back into my clothes from yesterday and stood by the door while Sean gathered up his wallet and keys. The photo here was the only color photo in the entire room, and like the others, it held an intense power in it. This one was a close-up of a burning home. It seemed to be a second story window, with glowing crimson flames licking out of the black opening. Thick, ivory smoke billowed up from the eaves of the roof, visible just above. The wooden shingles of the house were buckled and twisting, as if the heat were pushing them out from within. The whole piece gave a sense of power – of intensity – and of imminent collapse.

The feeling hung with me as I climbed onto the back of his bike, as we navigated the hellish doom which was Kelley Square and then headed further into the depths of Worcester. The brick warehouse was down a narrow, back alley, with high buildings on all sides. I could barely make out the blue sky above.

He glanced at the black metal door, then me. He took off his helmet, hanging it on the handlebar. "You stay right here," he stated. "I'll be back in a few minutes, and then we can have that ride." He smiled. "We should have time to make it down to Providence, to ride along the bay for a while. How does that sound?"

I smiled. "It sounds lovely."

He patted me on the arm, and then he turned and went to the door. He knocked, the door was pulled open, and then it swung shut again.

The image of Sean's photo hung before me. The flames were almost alive in their bright, forge-hot glow. I could hear the groaning of the timbers, the whooshing of the air driven by the heat. Time ticked by and I wrapped my arms around my chest. Where was Sean? I wanted to get away, get out onto the open road, where the breeze blew free all worries and concerns. I knew the fresh salt air would shake loose these phantom thoughts.

A scurry of a movement in the side alley made me jump, and I climbed off the bike before I knew I was doing it. I pulled off the helmet and tucked it under one arm. Maybe I would just ask to wait inside with him. Surely they couldn't be much longer.

I went to the door, and a crack of light shone along its edge. I realized that they hadn't closed it fully after he went in. Maybe I could ease in without anybody noticing, and just stay by the door. I was sure they wouldn't mind.

A scratching noise came from the alley, and that settled the issue for me. I pushed the door open slightly and stepped in.

The warehouse was fairly large, about the size of a football field, and all the windows were boarded over from the inside. The area near me was all in darkness and shadows, with stacks of boxes and other random supplies piled in haphazard heaps. A grouping of large lights on stands was at the far end, centered around in a circle. There were low voices and milling people.

Curious, I stepped forward.

I had reached a pyramid of Guinness cases when the scene resolved more clearly for me, and I staggered, leaning against them. It took a minute for my brain to catch up with my eyes, for the meaning of the scene to coalesce into a firm thought.

The lights were all pointed at a large, king-sized bed, done up in black satin sheets with red accent pillows. The Japanese girl from several nights ago was sprawled, naked, across its center, and one hand languidly stroked the shaft of a middle-aged man who stood at the side of the bed. She looked half-bored, half-annoyed.

On the other side of the bed, the Renaissance beauty from yesterday was standing with a crimson robe around her, her face done in bright makeup. Tears were streaming down her cheeks. Mrs. O'Malley was speaking to her through gritted teeth, her voice low, but the emotion evident with every sharp movement of her hand.

Finally she pointed to the bed, reached out her hand, and ripped the robe off of the girl, leaving her pale skin stark naked under the glare of the spotlights.

I spun in place, racing the short distance to the door, slipping through, and closing it carefully behind me. My heart pounded against my ribs as if it wanted to break free and run … run …

I climbed back onto the bike, in complete shock, retreating within my closed visor and my leather jacket. I wrapped my arms around my body, still unable to fully take in what I had seen.

The door opened, and Sean strode out, coming over to the bike with a satisfied look on his face. He slipped on his helmet, closed the visor, and my earpiece crackled into life. "And here we go! Ready for a ride?"

Unable to speak, I tapped him on the leg. He rolled on the throttle, and we eased away from the warehouse, abandoning all those within to their torment.

As he took us up onto the highway, I brought my phone out of my pocket and, with shaking fingers, queued up Mozart's "Requiem". He chuckled as the first notes echoed through our ears.

"In the mood for some music, are we?"

I tapped his leg in confirmation.

I could hear the smile in his voice. "As you wish, my darling." He revved the bike, bringing up the speed, and the world flew by.

I barely knew where we went. The music soared and cried. The landscape turned from rolling hills to ocean waves. And yet all I could see were the streaks of tears on the young woman's face, the hollow shock in her eyes as her robe was stripped from her, as she was exposed to the group. She had not made any move to cover herself. She had seemed trapped, helpless, beyond saving.

I blinked. We had come to a stop on my street, in front of my house. I had lost complete track of time. The sun was easing below the horizon, in deep crimsons and fiery oranges, and they reminded me of the house in Sean's studio apartment, burning, burning, burning.

He turned off the bike's ignition. His voice was cheery. "And here we are!"

My throat closed up. I couldn't think. I didn't know what to do. The thought of going back to the bar turned my stomach, and I swayed.

He half turned. "You OK back there?"

I found my voice. "I'm not feeling well. I think I'm going to call in sick tonight."

His voice took on a note of concern. "It wasn't the pancakes, was it? Could you be allergic to something?"

I shook my head, forcing my tone to be even. "I think my landlady had the flu last week, and maybe I got it from her. I just want to go in and rest."

"I'll come in and –"

I shook my head, climbing off the bike. "I appreciate it, but I'd rather just go in and crash for the night. I'll keep the helmet, and that way when you come get me tomorrow I'll be all good to go."

He drew me into a hug. "If you're sure, but how can I kiss you goodbye?"

"I don't want to get you sick," I murmured. Truth was, I knew if I lifted my visor, and he got a clear look at my face, that he'd know something was wrong. And I doubted I'd get free of him easily after that.

He chuckled. "Sick from a kiss? After how close we were last night, that -"

My voice nearly broke. "Please …"

He stilled. "You really are worn down, you poor thing. You should have said something."

I shrugged, biting my lip. I was afraid I might burst into tears if this went on for any longer.

At last he gently patted the side of my helmet. "You go on in. You seem exhausted. Get some rest. I'll come by in the morning and see if you're feeling better."

I squeezed his hand, and then I turned and walked to my house. Once in my room, I went to my window and waved at him. He waved back, and then his bike eased smoothly down the street and out of view.

I took off the helmet, placed it on my dresser, lay face down on my bed, and sobbed.

Chapter 10

I held on as Sean carefully threaded the bike into the back lot behind the bar, drawing to a stop by the shed's door. I climbed off the back and stood aside as he unlocked the latch. When he pushed in the bike I followed him into the shed, not saying a word. My helmet had been firmly in place when he arrived at my street, and I had barely spoken on our trip over. He had been concerned, but seemed to ascribe my short answers to my flu. More than once he had asked if I wanted to call in sick again, but I had refused.

I wanted to see Jimmy with my own eyes.

How could Jimmy and his wife be involved with this? Surely there was some mistake. It was one thing for him to be overly amorous with every woman who came within reach. But what I had seen yesterday had escalated the situation beyond my worst nightmares. I could still not quite bring it all in. Some part of me hoped it was a mistake – a bizarre hallucination created by a flash fever.

But I knew, deep in my heart, that what I had seen was real.

Sean removed his helmet and put it on a high ledge, then turned to me. "Hand it over," he teased.

I blinked my eyes several times, took in a deep breath, then undid the latch. I slid the helmet up off my head and handed it to him.

He put it on the shelf alongside his, turned back to me – and stopped. He put a hand out to my cheek, his brow furrowing.

"Jesus Christ, Kay."

I flushed. I knew I looked ragged from the long night of crying and lack of sleep, but I had done the best I could with cold washcloths and make-up.

Apparently it had not been enough.

His voice was tight. "You need to go home, Kay. You don't look well at all. You should be in bed."

That's where I wanted to be – curled up beneath the covers, the pillow over my head, the door locked. But I resolutely shook my head.

"I'll be fine," I insisted. "I want to see Jimmy."

Something in my tone of voice caught his attention. He tilted his head slightly, like a hunting dog which has caught the barest hint of a hidden deer. His gaze settled more deeply into mine, and his fingers brushed down my cheek to my shoulder.

His voice steeled with concern and determination. "What is it, Kay? What's wrong?"

I couldn't help it. The exhaustion, the worry, the being apart from him, all coalesced into an ache which delved into my core. I folded against him, his arms automatically came up around me, and tears cascaded from my eyes.

He groaned, drawing me in hard against him. "What is it, Kay? Tell me what it is. Whatever it is, we'll face it together."

At long last he gently pushed me back, looking down into my eyes. His gaze called for me to trust in him. "You can tell me."

My throat closed up, and I could barely get the words out. "I know, Sean. I know the truth. And I don't know what to do."

A ripple of tension moved through him, and he turned for a moment, slipping his phone into the speaker on the shelf. A push of a button, and Beethoven's Moonlight Sonata began playing. Usually the slow, steady notes soothed me, but today they merely drove my panic into stronger waves.

Sean dropped his voice, taking my face between his hands. His gaze held mine with serious focus. "Kay, what do you know?"

I found it hard to even say the words out loud. "Sean, I followed you. I followed you into the warehouse. I saw the girls, and the bed, and then Mrs. O'Malley stripped the robe off that girl …"

I couldn't continue. My tears started fresh, in waterfalls, and my legs could barely hold me up.

His breath left him, and he drew me in again. He ran his hand down my hair, soothing me as if I were a little girl. The music rolled on, rich, aching, and at long last I had run out of tears and my breathing had slowed again.

His voice remained low, and it was hard to read the emotion behind it. "I'm sorry you had to see that, Kay. You shouldn't have to see that warehouse. And I'll get us free of it. I just need a little time. You need to trust me."

My voice cracked. "But that girl …"

He nodded. "Girls get lured into that type of situation every day, because the market demands fresh, new meat. They probably thought they were being recruited for an indie film and were star-struck at the opportunity. Then, with one twist after another, they found themselves under those bright lights."

I looked up at him. "We have to save them."

He kissed me on the forehead. "We should get you home."

I shook my head again. "I'm staying." I brushed at my face. "I want to see Jimmy."

His brow creased in concern. "I don't think that's a good idea."

"I won't attack him," I assured him, although saying the words sent a rush of pleasure through me. "I just want to look at him. Besides, I promised Eileen I'd stay."

As much as I tried to inject enthusiasm into the sentence, a deadness echoed in my heart when I finished. I didn't know if I could do it. Even with all Eileen had done for me, this was asking too much.

His lips drew into a thin line, but at last he nodded. "If you're sure."

I turned and walked to the shed door. He took his phone from the speaker; the music vanished, replaced with a dense silence. We walked together into the bar. I took my normal station behind it, while he settled on a stool. His eyes held on me, dense with a swirl of emotion.

Jimmy was by the pool table, talking with the players, and his eyes lit up as we came into the room. "There you are, my Katie!" he called out, his arms wide. His forehead creased as he drew closer. "Good God, girl, you look like shit. You sure you want to be here?"

I nodded, drawing my eyes over him. Somehow I'd expected him to sprout red-tipped horns from his skull or to have developed razor-sharp canines. But he was the same Jimmy he'd always been, the wide, bright smile and the fluffy body. He was like the friendly uncle that everybody loved at parties.

How could he be involved in what was going on?

Sean reached his hand across the counter, and I twined my fingers into his. His gaze held rich concern.

There was the tinkle of a bell, and my heart constricted in turmoil. I could barely bring myself to turn, to see –

A moppet. A cascade of blonde curls. The girl was tall, perhaps five-feet-nine, but slender, wearing a Worcester Crew aqua t-shirt and long, black sweats. She had a bright, hopeful gleam in her eyes which made my heart ache.

She was fifteen.

Jimmy bounced forward with enthusiasm, drawing his arm around her shoulder, and she flinched. A flare of tension burst through my shoulders, and Sean's fingers tightened on mine. A new level of serious attention was in his gaze, a steel I had not seen etched there before.

Jimmy's voice was bright. "This way, my darling." He ushered her down the hall toward his office.

I took in one deep breath, then two … then I was storming from behind the bar, prepared to –

Sean swept me up from behind, continued walking me down past their office, out the back door, and back into the shed. He shut the door, popped his phone into the cradle, and swiped at it while turning to me.

The soundtrack to Gladiator came on. Normally I adored the power of the piece, the contrast of a choreographed Viennese waltz counterpointed with the brutal efficiency of the Roman Empire war machine.

But in this shadowy shed, with the thought of that innocent fifteen-year-old girl falling into the clutches of Jimmy's predatory hands, the music only fired my determination to do righteous battle.

My voice came out in a hiss. "We have to stop him! Sean, he's in there with her. We have to get her out!"

Sean's face was lost in the darkness. "Kay, we need to take it slow."

My voice rose. "Slow? Sean, she's fifteen! *Fifteen!* She'll be scarred for life! My God, how can you sit here even talking about this?"

He reached to hold my hand, and I yanked it back as if his grasp was red hot. As he moved, the glimmer of silver at his neck caught my eye.

He was wearing my father's medallion.

My anger, frustration, and exhaustion boiled over into a new, lethal combination, one that cored me with iron. I stared at him with cold fury.

"Give me my necklace back."

His hand automatically went up to his chest, and his eyes widened.

His voice was hoarse. "Kay –"

I took a step forward, my hand out. "Give it to me. Now."

He paled, but his hands went behind his neck, and in a moment he was holding out the pendant to me.

I grabbed it from his hands, my eyes welling yet again. This couldn't be happening. I was utterly lost, and there was no way to rewind back to when things were OK.

Things would never be OK again.

I stuffed the pendant into my left back pocket, and then from my right I pulled out my phone. I brought it around to my face. My entire body was solidifying, calcifying, being coated with ice and layered over with feet of snow. I was submerging. Soon I would be drowned.

Sean's voice was distant, a whisper in the wind. "Kay, what are you doing?"

I barely recognized my own voice, its guttural growl. "I am calling the fucking police."

My finger was nearly at the screen when he popped the phone out of my hand. "Kay –"

He was six-feet, one-hundred-eighty pounds of solid muscle, and I stepped up in front of him with clenched fists. "That girl is fifteen, and I am calling the police," I seethed. "And you and I are done."

I reached for the phone, but he held it higher, his gaze pleading with me to trust him. "Kay, just give me –"

I turned, ready to storm straight across Kelley Square and find somewhere – anywhere – with a phone. I didn't want to take one step back into that bar without sirens blaring and lights flashing.

He grabbed at my arm, his strong fingers holding me in place. "Kay, listen to me." His eyes were now swirling with a wealth of emotions I could not even name.

"I trusted you," I spat. "I trusted you, and look what you turned out to be."

His voice was hoarse. "I trust you with my life."

I stared at him, beyond any emotion I could name, beyond anything I had ever felt before.

"Then prove it."

He stared at me for a long moment, the connection between us a sizzling bolt of energy which could have lit up the darkest night.

And then at last, at long last, he spoke, and his words resonated with a kaleidoscope of emotion.

"Kay, that girl is twenty-two."

I gazed at him in disbelief. "You liar! She was in the paper! She's fifteen!"

He shook his head, his gaze locked on mine. "She's a woman, Kay. And she's in there on purpose, to get close to Jimmy."

I stared at him in shock, the world taking on a dream-like state. Lisa Gerrard's ethereal vocals soared around us, but all I could see was the tense line of his shoulders, the hollowed shadows in his eyes.

My voice was barely a whisper. "How could you possibly know that?"

He released my arm, put his hands out to the side, and it was as if he were surrendering himself wholly to me. "Because I'm an undercover cop."

Book 2: A Soul Ajar

A SOUL
AJAR

OPHELIA SIKES

A WORCESTER NIGHTS NOVELLA

Chapter 1

The soul should always stand ajar,
ready to welcome the ecstatic experience.
-- Emily Dickinson

Sean was an undercover cop.

The run-down shed with its rickety shelves faded from view. Lisa Gerrard's soaring vocals drifted into silence. My senses detached, one by one, until all that was left was Sean's face before me, his eyes, the window to his soul.

He was trusting me with his life.

I'd grown up the daughter of a cop. I knew the risks taken by those who went undercover, the violent results which often came about if they were discovered. By sharing his secret with me, Sean had put himself into my hands.

Not only that, but he was risking the life of the blonde who, even now, was in Jimmy's office pretending to be a helpless fifteen-year-old girl.

The world wound up into motion around me as that vision shimmered into my consciousness. She was still in there. Whoever she was, I had no doubt that Sean was serving as some sort of backup for her.

I glanced at the speakers; they filled the air with rich music, masking our conversation. I pitched my voice low. "Later on tonight, you and I are going to have a long talk," I stated, my tone sounding sharper than I'd intended. "However, I imagine right now it's important for you to be in the building."

His brow creased with concern. He half reached for me before allowing his hand to fall back at his side. His voice was tight when he spoke. "Yes, I should be at the bar right now."

He paused for a moment, and his jaw tightened as if he was resisting speaking. Finally, he let out a breath. "Are you sure it wouldn't be better for me to drive you home? You were sick, after all, and they wouldn't question it. That way you wouldn't have to maintain a front."

I shook my head. "I will stay with you, and after closing we will have our talk," I insisted. "I swear I won't put her at risk." I gave a small shrug. "And, besides, as you said, they think I've got some sort of a flu. They'll brush off any oddness on my part as being related to that."

He looked as if he might pursue the issue, but at last he nodded. He took his phone out of its cradle, the shed went silent, and that heavy blanket lay over us as we walked across the small lot and in through the back door of the bar. Jimmy's office was mercifully quiet as we moved past it. In a moment we were back in our usual places – me behind the bar, Sean sitting at a stool before it.

It seemed almost inconceivable that the two pool players traded their quiet jibes as they always had, that Joey took in a long sip of his Bushmills while watching some reality show involving couples trying to choose the prettiest camel. The chaotic whirl of Kelley Square continued unabated on the other side of the row of windows. And yet, somehow, my entire world had been turned sunny side down.

I took up a handful of limes, placed them on the white cutting board, and focused my attention on the dimpled fruits, not on the man who sat before me.

Sunny side down.

But was it, really? I had spent the last two days in torment because of the pornography ring filming in the warehouse, one Jimmy was apparently intimately involved with. I had, only ten minutes ago, been willing to do whatever it took to alert the police.

And here he was.

I knew how delicate an operation like this had to be. I knew about the outstretched tendrils of most criminal organizations, how hastily rounding up the workers could easily let those truly responsible go scot-free. The crime lords would simply lay low for a few months, then set up shop again, larger and more lethal than before.

If Sean was here, submerging himself in their world, law enforcement was undoubtedly looking to excise the entire tumor, not just trim away its edges. He was doing exactly what I had wanted to be done. And he was risking his own life to save those girls.

My eyes moved up to his of their own accord, and the shadowed tangle of emotions deep within his gaze made my breath leave in a long sigh. I put down the lime and knife, stepped over to him, and laid my hand on the table before him.

An easing ripple ran down his shoulder blades, releasing the tension a hair, and he brought his own hand on top of mine. The faintest hint of a smile came to his lips, and he dropped his head, acknowledging me.

There was a movement from the hallway, and we both turned. The moppet's face was wry, apologetic, and she tucked her phone back into her purse. "I'm sorry about my mom calling like that," she sighed as they reached the door. "It's just, with it being a school night and all, she wants me home."

"Of course, of course," reassured Jimmy, patting her on the shoulder. "Still, I have so much to talk with you about.

Maybe if you came by tomorrow, a bit earlier, then we could have more time together."

She bit her lip, giving it some thought. Then at last she nodded. "I could come by right after crew," she agreed. "How does that sound?"

His eyes lit up. "That sounds perfect. It's a date."

Her cheeks tinted pink, and she looked down at her feet. "Sure, if you say so," she murmured. Then she stepped back, turned, and was out through the door.

Jimmy's eyes followed her until she vanished from sight, and then he sighed with pleasure, rolling his shoulders. He stepped jauntily over to the stool, plunking down on it as if he'd just chosen a winning ticket from the MegaMillions. "A Redbreast, my dear."

I turned to the green bottle, wondering at the calmness within me. Surely I should be berating him for his pond-scum morals, or laughing in delight at the impending doom which hovered unseen just over his head. Sean was Jimmy's own personal Sword of Damocles. But somehow I was able to lay the glass before Jimmy, pour out his double, and even offer him a smile as I placed the bottle next to his glass.

He nudged his head toward the glass. "You know your job, Katie."

My hand was rock steady as I picked up the glass and let a trickle of the whiskey coat the back of my throat. Toffee. Honey. I found strength in it, strength in the knowledge that soon he, his wife, and everyone else involved in their despicable operation would be deep behind bars. And I knew well how pedophiles were treated in prison.

I did smile at that.

Jimmy grinned as he took the glass back from me. "There's my Katie," he praised. "I knew you'd feel better after a drink. It makes the world seem brighter." He looked at the glass, then drank it all down in one long pull. Stretching, he stood again. "Well, lass, you know where to find me." In a moment he'd vanished into the darkness of the hall.

I settled against the back of the bar, bringing my eyes determinedly up to the TV. If I looked at Sean, or said anything to him, the floodgates would be hard to keep shut. There was a great deal to say – and it would have to wait until we got on that Triumph of his and made our way to safety.

Chapter 2

The bar had finally been locked up for the night, we had ridden north on 290, and now we were moving along a quiet road in the dead of night. He turned right, taking us up a long driveway lined by dense trees. Up ahead was a large building of some sort.

It wasn't until he switched off the engine in the parking lot that I finally realized where we were. "We're at Tower Hill Botanical Gardens, aren't we?"

He nodded, and I climbed off, removing my helmet. He took off his as well, tucking them to one side. Then he led me along the path. We went around the main building, to the far end of the formal gardens, and then he pulled a flashlight from a pocket.

A distant part of me wondered if I should be worried, going into this quiet wood with him. But one look in his eyes and that flutter of concern faded. He had trusted me with his life, I had come through for him, and I could see in his gaze he was deeply honored.

We took the quiet path up a short distance through the trees. I knew where he was leading me, and even so, as we crested the rise, the vista took my breath away.

Where the orchards we had visited several days ago faced south, toward Worcester, this view stretched northwest over the Wachusett Reservoir. The moonlight was strong, shimmering silver in a clear ebony sky, and an almost magical glow gilded the landscape. We could have been Diana and Verbius, tending with care to our stags and great horned owls.

He turned, his voice strained with tension. "From that first time that we talked all night long at the bar, I have wanted to take you here. If this is to be our last evening together … well, I wanted you to see it in its glory. I wanted to be there with you when you did."

I took a long look at the gorgeous nocturnal landscape, the rippling hills of oak and pine. Then I gently dropped cross-legged onto the grass. I folded my arms across my chest.

"Well, then, this is the ideal backdrop for the truth. Start from the beginning."

He ran his hand through his thick hair, then settled to sit before me.

"I got my degree in criminal justice from Berkeley, then went into the police academy," he began, his gaze on mine. "Spent much of the last six years in vice, deep in the Bronx."

It was still hard for my brain to reconcile these two different views of the man before me. Of course he hadn't been a felon. Of course that had been a cover story. Still, a stab of pain wrenched through my core as I said the words. "So you lied about the raiding of the Italian restaurant?"

He flushed, but nodded. "There was an incident that took place, but I wasn't involved. My support team altered the records in case anyone went digging."

My chest constricted, but I forced myself to continue. "Your aunt? And your mother in Ireland?"

His breath was coming in slow, even draws, as if strong emotions were roiling within him and he was doing his best to remain still. "All of that was true. My father, my childhood, that is all what happened. We figured it was best to stick with the facts as much as possible. There's less to mis-remember that way."

I nodded. I'd heard the same from my own father numerous times. He used to laugh about how criminals would trip themselves up over complex lies.

"So how did you get involved in this operation?"

"The group here is primarily Irish, and the people planning the operation thought someone with a similar background would be more easily accepted. Also, I'm from the Bronx; the chances of me running into someone here who would recognize me would be slim."

"So your plan was ..."

He made a waving motion with his hand. "To hang around the bar for a few weeks, to build a friendship with the staff, and –"

The blood drained from my face. I'd been used. I'd just been a stepping stone for him, a way for him to get to Jimmy. Everything had been fake. The way he'd kissed me, the way he'd touched me –

I was on my feet before I knew what was happening, and he rose with me, his face tense with emotion. "Kay, I didn't mean –"

"You bastard," I snarled. Rage, loss, and despair roiled within me. "You used me, just like Jimmy uses those girls!"

He shook his head, his eyes locked on mine. "My feelings for you are real," he vowed, talking quickly, holding himself back with visible effort. "God, Kay, I will swear it on anything you wish me to. I shouldn't have gotten that close to you. I knew it. But when I saw you across the bar, I –" He ran his hand through his hair, at a loss for a moment, gazing into my eyes as if I held the most precious item in the world within me. "I don't know what it was, Kay. I was completely taken in. From that moment I knew I had to have you."

I remembered that look. I remembered the power that had sizzled between us, how I had been unable to speak, to think.

He took a hesitant step toward me. "The next day, I thought I'd talk with you for a while. I was sure that just a few minutes with you would help snap me out of it – would show me that you were shallow, or married, or *something*." He shook his head, his eyes glowing. "And instead, what I found was that you were just right. You were a woman I had dreamt about for years and had given up hope of ever finding. No girlfriend had ever come close to what you offered."

My throat closed up in panic as fresh thoughts crowded their way in at me. He was undercover. Perhaps he was not even single!

My voice was nearly a screech. "Girlfriend?"

He brought his hand to his chest. "I swear to you, Kay, I am unattached. There is nobody waiting for me back home. That is part of why they sent me."

His breath came in long draws as he held my gaze. Moonbeams drifted across his face, deepening the shadows in his eyes. I could suddenly see clearly just how much he was affected by this conversation.

I thought back over our days together, how quickly we had combusted into our relationship. We had launched at each other like fireworks heading for the finale, without thought, without reason. I had felt that powerful drive, had been caught up in its grasp. He had tried to warn me off, now that I thought about it. He had tried to put on the brakes, several times, and I had overrun his defenses with passionate fervor.

Could I really have expected him to reveal his secret mission, risk the lives of himself and others, after only knowing me for such a short period of time?

How much must he have trusted me, to do so?

I took a step toward him, then two, and then we were clinging to each other as if a tornado might tear through the woods and rip us apart. His hand twined thoroughly into my hair, the other around my waist, and his lips pressed against my forehead. I could hear him murmuring prayers of thankfulness.

His lips kissed their way down my cheek, over to my mouth, and they were gentle, tender, as if I were a fragile statue of immense value.

The kisses spun fiery energy in my body, in my breasts, in my sex. I brought my hands up into his hair and pressed my lips more fully against his, opening my mouth to him, needing far more than he was giving.

He groaned, wrapped me in his arms, then gently lowered me to the grass. He lay alongside me, the length of his body pressing into mine. His kisses became deeper, stronger, and my body melted beneath his, every part of me craving him.

He stripped off my jacket, then my shirt. The boots and jeans came next, and in a moment I was laying under the moonlight, clad only in my bra and panties. The glimmering light reflected off the silver stitchery along the black fabric.

Sean knelt at my side, gazing down at me, his breath coming in long, full draws.

"My God, Kay, you are stunning."

I blushed, but I resisted the urge to cover myself up. Instead I basked in the strength of his perusal, in the heat in his eyes.

He reached his hand forward, slowly sliding one of my bra straps off my shoulder, then the second. My breasts swelled against the fabric, craving his touch.

He smiled at that, then slid his hand under my back and deftly rolled me over onto my stomach. A lift of his arm and I was up on all fours, facing out over the lake.

He knelt behind me, running his fingers along my back, sending shivers down my spine. He traced circles around the bra clasp, and I moaned, wanting him to just release it, to set me free. Instead he slid both hands to the front, cupping my breasts through the fabric, kneading and pinching at the nipples until I could barely breathe. He pressed his hips in against my rear, and I arched back against him, craving him.

His voice murmured hoarsely in my ear. "Look out at your world. Look out at the beauty."

I raised my head, and the shimmering light took my breath away. It was as if a giant had spread a fistful of diamonds across the lake, sending them into a glittering waltz. And then both his hands eased in under the bra, sliding to hold my breasts, and he undid the strap with his mouth. The tension came free, my breasts filled his hands, and I groaned again. His fingers rolled the nipples, pulling them, and I could feel my panties soak through.

"God, please," I moaned.

He slid his hands down the length of my side, to my hips, and then hooked the panties there and drew them down to my knees. There was the sound of a zipper behind me, then a foil pouch, and at last I felt the pressure of his shaft just at my opening. It nudged temptingly against me, tormenting me, and when I arched back toward him he withdrew, tantalizing my soul.

My voice became pleading. "I need you …"

He ran his fingers lightly along the curve of my ass, and I could feel my juices flow down my leg. My voice became a wordless moan of desire

His voice was hoarse. "You want me?"

"Yes, yes, yes." The ache echoed throughout my body, stretching me taut like the bow of a violin. "I want you ... I need you ... God, please ..."

He settled both hands down on my hips, I braced, and then he groaned as his head slowly pressed within me. A tremor ran down his hands, and then whatever restraint had been holding him back slipped loose. His movements became hard, rhythmic, and I rocked back at each stroke to meet him, my cries echoing out across the landscape. The world opened up before me, the moon shone down high above, and each thrust and counter sent me soaring, soaring –

We exploded together, filled with silver and diamonds, wider than the ocean, higher than the scattered stars. And we soared.

At last, at long last, my breath came in longer draws, and I eased myself down onto the grass. He came with me, still within me, lying down at my side. One of his arms served as my pillow, while the other wrapped along my side, his hand resting possessively between my breasts.

I sighed in the deepest of contentment. "Oh, Sean."

He stilled at that, and I turned my head in confusion. I looked up into his eyes and saw the same dark roil of emotion I'd seen the other nights, when –

It suddenly struck me with full force.

His name wasn't Sean.

With his arms around me, and the glow of our lovemaking still resonating, I found that it didn't matter. I knew who he really was. Our connection went beyond names and words. It was something far deeper.

The corner of my mouth turned up in a smile. "So what *is* your name, then?"

"Sean is my middle name," he murmured, holding my eyes. "That way I could react to it fairly automatically. But my full name is Michael Sean Rowan."

I looked into those moss green eyes, rolling the name around in my mind. "Michael …"

My hand moved to my chest, where the pendant had hung for so many years. The spot was now empty. It took me a moment to remember the scene back at the shed, when I had demanded the necklace and jammed it into my jeans pocket. It seemed like eons ago.

I reached over into the pocket and drew it out. I laid the pendant out in my palm for a long moment, gazing at the familiar oval.

His hands moved slowly into my vision. He gently took the clasp in one hand, the chain-end in the other, and he brushed my hair back from my shoulder. He leant forward to bring his hands to meet behind my neck, sealing the clasp. Then he sat back, settling the pendant between my breasts.

He looked at the pendant for a long moment, his eyes shining in the moonlight. Then he brought his gaze up to meet mine.

"Now we will both be looking out for you."

I brought my hand to the pendant, feeling his warmth still on it. The thought that I was wearing his namesake boldly on my chest, proclaiming the name that no others in my world knew, filled me to my core.

He trusted me.

Michael Sean Rowan, deep undercover, trusted me. He was mine, he was watching over me, and nothing would tear us apart again.

Chapter 3

*R*rrrrrring!!

I buried my head deeper beneath the white covers. Late morning sunlight streamed across Sean's loft, creating patchworks of gold against the deeper brown and red. Sean groaned, then pushed the blankets off of him and made his way wearily to the middle of the room where his jeans lay in a heap. He dug the phone out of his pocket and put it to his ear.

"Sean here."

He listened for a minute, said "sure," then hung up and tossed the phone down on top of his jeans. In a moment he was climbing back under the covers, sliding his hand along my hip. My body kindled in delight.

I turned to him, brushing my lips against his. "And who was that?"

His hand cupped my ass, slid down along my thigh, and lifted my leg so it moved up and over his. "Just Jimmy saying he wanted you to take today off. Something about you needing to heal up."

My brow creased in concern. "But if that girl – I mean that woman – is going to be going back –"

He shook his head, trailing kisses down my neck. "She's going to end up busy today," he murmured in my ear. "To stretch this out, so he's forced to just take her to the warehouse untested."

He gave a teasing nibble to my neck and I moaned. "So we have the day to ourselves?"

He sucked harder at my neck, I gasped, and the world spun away.

It was mid-afternoon by the time we pulled up to the stately granite pillars which fronted the Worcester Art Museum. We brought our helmets in with us, checking them in the locker room, and then stepped out to the large atrium with its Roman-era mosaic.

He took my hand in his. "They said there could be rain later today, so riding around wasn't much of an option – and I'm not entirely sure the studio is safe for talking in. I wouldn't have put it past Jimmy and Seamus to have it bugged as a matter of course."

I flushed at the thought of those two miscreants listening in on our lovemaking, but nodded. There were bigger issues at stake here.

Sean gave a wave with his hand, indicating the galleries around us. "Also, I wanted to have you see a few women who have been immortalized over the years, to view how beauty comes in a myriad of forms. That way when I photograph you tonight, you'll feel more at ease."

A hot blush rose to my cheeks, and I glanced around to see if anybody had heard. There seemed to be nobody within hearing distance. Still, I took a step closer to him and dropped my voice. "I don't think I would make a good subject."

His eyes shone, and he ran a hand along my cheek. "Ah, Kay, how can you not see yourself for how you truly are?"

The heat in his eyes coursed through me, and I dropped my gaze lest I be drawn into passionately kissing him right then and there.

He chuckled, then tugged gently on my hand and led me up the stairs.

He drew us to a stop before an oil painting of three young women in Victorian-style white dresses. They were sitting before a rural landscape of quiet trees and water. Each woman had her own way of holding herself, an individual gaze, and I marveled at the piece.

Sean motioned to the placard. "This is Frank Benson's *Portrait of my Daughters*. See how the hair falls against the cheek of the woman on the left? And the line of the shoulders on the one on the right? Each one is beautiful, in her own way. Each one maintains her own uniqueness. And some of that appeal to the viewer comes from the angles, the shadows, the placement of curls against skin."

I could see what he was saying. It was the arrangement which brought a reaction, not simply the forms themselves.

He brought me along to another piece, this one *The Breakfast Room, Winter Morning, 1911* by Childe Hassam. He pointed at the blurry face. "You can't even see the woman clearly here," he commented. "And yet, what sense do you get?"

I gazed at the gossamer turquoise dress she wore, the drifting ivory curtains in the background. "Serenity," I murmured. "She is content and peaceful."

The corner of his mouth tweaked up. "And would you say she is beautiful?"

I thought about it for a long moment, then nodded, a sense of wonder filling me. "Even though I cannot see her clearly, there is definitely a feeling of beauty, created by the textures and surroundings. It is about the atmosphere the painter created, more than a specific detail."

We walked along to another gallery, and he drew to a stop before *The Dance* by Jean-Baptiste Pater. The scene was an outdoor clearing by a river, where a group of elegantly dressed men and women were enjoying a sunny afternoon. Several couples held each other.

Sean's voice was low. "Look at these two, in the lower left. See how he has his arms around her waist, how she rests her own on him. How comfortable they are with each other." He put his own arm around my waist, and butterflies fluttered up against my ribs.

His breath whispered on my ear. "Can you sense what she's feeling?"

I could. I could see it in the small figure's eyes, feel it viscerally from the curve of her body and the glow on her cheeks.

His fingers cinched in against my skin. His voice was a spinning rod, reeling me in, drawing me deep within him. "Do you see her beauty?"

I did. She glowed with it, shone with it. And it was not about a perfect silicone-enhanced body or botox-enriched lips. The beauty came from the emotion expertly brought forth by Pater's brush.

Sean pressed a heated kiss against my neck, and his voice was hoarse. "Let me capture you in my camera. Let me show you what I see."

I nodded, unable to speak.

He took me for lunch to Surya for Indian food. A distant part of my mind knew the food was delicious, and the décor was lovely, but the pakoras and palak paneer could barely be sensed through the blanket of desire he had wrapped around me. Every time he brushed my hand with his, every time he leant over to refill my glass of Shiraz, my craving for him crept to a higher level. By the time I climbed behind him on the Triumph, my embrace around him was more than what safety might have required. My left arm went high, around his chest, but the right delved down, to his thigh, and pressed.

He groaned, revved the throttle, and then we were racing toward home.

We laughed as we ran up the stairs, tumbling into his studio, and he whirled me up in his arms, spinning me around before drawing me into a long kiss. His eyes shone as he held me out for a moment.

"God, Kay, you are simply amazing."

He gently released me, then nudged his head. "All right, you, onto the bed."

Heat flushed even harder down my body, pooling in my sex, and I turned to do as he asked. I reached down to pull off my boot, but he called out, "No, no, not yet."

I looked up, a question in my eyes.

He was bringing a tripod over, and he set it up at the foot of the bed, adjusting it so it was about head level as I sat on the edge. He then brought one of the end tables over next to the tripod. He set his laptop up on it and connected it to the camera with a cable. Then he went over to the speaker on the bureau and put his phone into its cradle. A few presses of buttons, and soft, four-four rhythm classical music began to sing out.

I raised an eyebrow. "Handel's *Io t'Abbraccio?*"

A sparkle lit his eyes.

I chuckled. "Isn't this part where the lovers have their last moment together, before the hero is slated to be executed?"

His grin widened. "I have a different kind of *culmination* in mind for us." He moved back to the laptop, put his finger over a key, and waited for a moment. Then he pressed.

The camera began snapping, rhythmically, in time with the music.

I blinked in surprise. "You have the camera set up to coordinate with the song?"

He came around to the side of the bed, standing alongside me. "That way we know, every fourth beat, that a photo will be taken. We will sense it coming, and we'll be ready for it."

He knelt by my side, sliding a hand along my thigh. "Look into the camera."

I blushed, but did as he asked.

His hand languorously traced up my inner thigh, slowly, maddeningly, and then paused there, creating small circles. Tension build up within me, wanting him …

His fingers flicked, barely brushing my sex.

I gasped in raw desire.

Click

His fingers slid up, toward my jeans button, and lingered there for a moment, tugging slightly at the button-hole. The ache within me blossomed, grew.

The metal circle popped free; I groaned with the release.

Click

He slid down the zipper, and I leant back for a moment so he could pull my jeans and panties down together. He took off my boots and socks all at once, leaving my entire bottom half naked. He put a hand behind my back and drew me back up to sitting, then knelt between my legs. He slid each hand under one of my butt cheeks and spread them slightly for a better grip. Then he eased his face down between my legs, his breath coming hot against my sex.

A wordless moan rolled out of me.

Click

His nose nuzzled, ever so gently, against the soft curls there, exploring, tantalizing.

Click

I wrapped my hands into his hair, groans easing out of me, and I rolled my head up to look at the ceiling.

He squeezed my cheeks and murmured in a gentle scold, "Look at the camera. I want to see. The camera will be my eyes."

I dutifully brought my gaze back down to the small black circle watching me. This was Sean's eye. This was his window into a world he would otherwise be unable to glimpse. His tongue pressed against my clit, warm, tender, and I groaned in delicious agony. He let it flick left, then right.

Click

My fingers twined more tightly into his hair, holding his head in place, my every ounce of attention focused on the movement of that tongue.

Wet, moist, left, right, and I needed him to speed up. I needed him …

Click

His fingers squeezed me more firmly, his tongue built up his rhythm, and I must have been soaking the bed, so rich was the heat that flowed through me. The music wrapped around me, transporting me, and the late afternoon sun glistened golden through the large windows, sending rectangles of shadow and light across us. His tongue was wet, so wet, and the speed was increasing, the ripples like a speedboat skipping across the water, thumping, thumping, launching –

I cried out, wordless, and then my body was taut, arching, and I lost my struggle to stay focused on the camera. I bent back, reaching out, lost completely in the flood of pleasure and sensation which filled every part of me. It seemed to go on for long minutes, the waves of delicious richness, until at last I was collapsed back against the bed, completely spent.

He massaged my rear for a moment, waiting for me to come down fully, and then he drew to his feet, moving around to the side of the bed. He gently rotated me around, then rolled me, so I was on my stomach with my head facing the camera. He stripped off my top and bra. Then he climbed on the bed behind me. He put his hands on my hips and drew me up so I was on my hands and knees.

There was the sound of foil ripping behind me, then he leant forward, his arms on either side of mine. His voice was a murmur in my ear.

"Ribbed ... for her pleasure."

A thrust, and he filled me completely, wholly, fully. I gasped at the suddenness of it, the rich pleasure that tumbled me.

Click

His lips were at my throat, my shoulder, my cheek, as his hips rocked, his pelvis slamming into my rear, the shudder of contact rippling through my body. I braced my body, giving him that solid anvil to hammer against, and one of his hands reached down to slide wetly against my clit. I groaned, the heat of passion bubbling up fresher, hotter, richer within me.

Click

His breath was coming hard now, his groans in time with his thrusts, and my own passions were rising right along with his. The black eye was before us, watching, gazing, and then he thrummed with his fingers and I was spiraling past the stratosphere, as his cries shook every vestige of me away.

Click

I was drifting, soaring, breathing, and he rested his body against mine, our sweat mingling. I could feel his heart pounding against me. At last he wrapped one arm around my chest, holding me close, and he murmured in my ear, "Look up, my love."

Warmth washed through me at the words, a sigh eased out, and I looked up.

Click

Chapter 4

I leant against the back wall behind the bar, holding my phone in my hands, paging again through the photos. Most of them were only safely on the laptop, of course. The ones showing me deep in the throes of passion, or sailing on the edge of ecstasy. I had been stunned with the desire, the emotion, which had glowed off the screen in those images.

But here on the smaller screen were the tamer images which still had the power to take my breath away. My eyes brimming with life. My breath deep and strong.

And then there was the one.

His head was alongside mine, his eyes gazing at me. I was staring full at the camera, my lips parted in joy, my face radiating contentment. In his eyes shone satisfaction – and something deeper.

I looked up at the real Sean sitting before me at the bar, and his eyes held twinkling amusement. "You going to stare at that thing all evening long?"

I blushed, tucking it back into my pocket. "Maybe."

He toasted me with his whiskey. "And here you had resisted the idea."

I gave him a mischievous smile. "Maybe next time we could try –"

Jimmy strode out from the hallway, and I quickly cut off my comment. He scanned the room and blew out his breath. "So, Jessica's not here yet?"

I shook my head, holding in a smile. Sean had only given me a brief summary as we rode over here, but apparently we had to stall for a few more days to let the Boston, Providence, and Hartford groups catch up to Sean's quick progress. Once the others were fully in place, we could let Jimmy bring Jessica over to the warehouse and prepare her for her starring role. That would be the final lynchpin to seal the pornographers' fate.

"Maybe she's just running late," I offered. "Want a drink?"

He looked as if he might say yes, but then he shook his head. "Want to be sharp for today," he murmured. "She's a special one."

My smile brightened. Special was certainly right.

He sighed, then turned. "Well, you know where I am if she shows up." He stalked back into the hallway.

Joey lethargically waved a hand. "Another drink, Kate, please."

I poured his Bushmills and brought it around to him. As I set it before him, I noticed his nose was running again. "Jeez, Joey, haven't you shaken that cold yet?" I went back to the bar and brought him out a box of tissues. "Here you go."

He was transfixed by the basketball game, the Celtics against the Orlando Magic. "Thanks, Kate."

I took up his empty and brought it back around to the bar.

Sean was gazing at me, a crease in his brow. He gave his head a short shake.

I leant in close to him. "What?"

He raised an eyebrow. "A cold?"

My brows drew together. "Yeah, he always has it. His nose is always running."

He shook his head again. "Kay. He does heroin."

I blinked in surprise, then glanced over at Joey. He was slouched on his stool, his eyes glued to the TV, his hand bringing the glass of whiskey to his lips in an automatic motion.

I couldn't quite wrap my mind around it. "Joey?"

He nodded. "Classic symptoms."

My heart twisted. "Wow, I had no idea. I think of heroin as something you hear about in news stories, or read about in books. Like Sherlock Holmes doing heroin when he has no case to work on."

The corner of his mouth quirked up. "Cocaine."

I blinked. "What?"

"Sherlock Holmes did cocaine, not heroin. A seven percent solution."

I chuckled. "You made that up."

His eyes brightened. "Not at all. Sherlock reveals that in *The Sign of Four*. A great story."

I began unloading the dishwasher and placing the glasses on the shelf. "Tell it to me."

A smile grew on his face. "You'd like to hear the story?"

"Absolutely. It'd be much better than the dreck these guys tend to watch on TV."

He sat back, taking a sip of his whiskey. "It would be my pleasure. You ready?"

I grinned. "Ready and waiting."

He gave his drink a swirl. "All right then. We begin our story with Sherlock lounging in a chair, preparing his hypodermic needle of cocaine. He rolls back his sleeve, finds the correct place on his arm, and injects. Watson is watching this, as he has been for many months now, with growing concern for his good friend …"

I glanced over at Joey, lost in his daze, and the thought came to me of how little things changed.

Chapter 5

Sean pulled us into the bar's parking lot right on time for my shift, negotiating the burnt-out Camaro and bulky dumpster with practiced ease. In minutes we had the Triumph safely tucked into its shed. He opened the back door of the bar for me, and we went down the short hallway into the main room.

Mrs. O'Malley was standing there with her husband, her brow creased into furrows. "Well, do you think she'll be ready in two days? We'll have to make other plans for the shoot if she isn't."

His voice was a mutter. "I'm working on it, but she's skittish. It might take some time. We don't want to lose her."

She shook her head in frustration. "Just don't screw it up, like last time. We don't want her popped before –"

She glanced up and saw us coming in; her face morphed into a welcoming smile. "Katie! There you are. I could set my clock by you. And Sean. So good to see you again."

I moved over behind the bar, hanging my jacket on the hook. "It's nice to see you, Mrs. O'Malley."

"Bridgit," she said automatically. She turned back to her husband. "I need to head over there to set some things up. You call if you hear anything."

"Sure, of course," he agreed. He watched as she turned and walked out into the darkening afternoon. Then he sighed and came over to the bar.

"And how are you two love birds doing?" he asked, plunking himself down on a stool. "That lust-crazed glow starting to fade yet?"

I chuckled, glancing over at Sean. "Not quite yet," I teased.

Sean's eyes lit with interest, and the corner of his mouth quirked up. "Not for a long while," he promised.

Jimmy ran a hand through his sparse hair. "That's just depressing," he grumbled. "Gimme a drink."

I pulled out the bottle and glass, poured him his double, and took my sip of it before placing both before him.

He looked at the glass for a moment. "Here's to youth. Treasure it while you have it, because all too soon it'll be gone and you'll be old and dried up." He tilted the glass and drank it down.

Sean's voice was steady. "You hardly seem dried up," he pointed out.

Jimmy turned the glass in place. "Yeah, but you didn't know me when I was twenty-one," he pointed out. "When I used to stride into the local pub, there were always four girls hanging on me. Good lookers, too. Long, flowing hair. High, firm tits. I could have my pick of any one." His eyes shone. "Sometimes, if I was lucky, I got two."

I glanced at Sean in amusement. "Sounds like the life."

Jimmy held out his glass, and I refilled it. He drank some down, then sighed.

"Yeah, it was great, right up until my brother, Liam, and his best friend, Seamus, decided to play hero. Next thing I know they're running guns up to Belfast and making me go along as their driver. I didn't want to get involved; I had a nice job already, doing local meat deliveries. I had a good life. But then they went and …"

He shook his head, looking down. "There was a raid, the cops came, and I saw it all. I saw Liam get gunned down in the street, like a rabid dog. I ran to him, and held him, but there was nothing I could do. The light just faded from his eyes."

I put my hand over his. "I'm so sorry for your loss, Jimmy."

He squeezed my fingers for a moment before taking another drink. "Yeah, and the cops would have swept me up, too, as an accessory, but Bridgit took charge, as she always did. Dragged me here to the states, and Seamus too. We got a fresh start." He looked around the bar. "I thought I could recreate what I had there. Build the bar, fill it full of the same signs, the same whiskey, and the rest would just happen." He downed the rest of his drink. "But it's all gone. Everything I had, it's all gone. And there's just wreck left."

I wasn't sure if he meant the place or himself. Maybe he encompassed all of life in that statement.

Jimmy gave himself a shake, then stood. "I'll be in my office. Oh, and Katie, if you need Thanksgiving off, just let me know. I'm sure we can work out some coverage for you." He turned and vanished down the hall.

Thanksgiving.

I glanced at Sean, my mind whirling. I hadn't even thought about Thanksgiving. How could I bring Sean down with me, and introduce him to the family as an ex-felon who had served seven years in prison? I doubted he wanted to risk spreading his true identity any further than it had to, especially with the net pulling close. Or could he even get away for a day? Waterbury was only two hours south, but maybe he wouldn't want to risk the time.

I flushed. Maybe he wouldn't want to go at all.

He looked at me with steady eyes. "You always go home for Thanksgiving?"

I nodded. "I've never missed one. Sometimes one of my brothers can't make it, depending what his case load is, but we all make that effort to be together."

He was quiet for a long moment. "Would you want –"

"We'll stay here," I decided, wrapping my hand in his. "I want to be with you, and here is easiest. We'll have Thanksgiving, just you and me, in the studio."

His brow creased. "Are you sure?"

I nodded. "Absolutely. I'll make us a turkey and gravy, home-made mashed potatoes, and even the yam circles in brown sugar."

His eyes lit up. "That sounds delicious."

I grinned. "Oh, they are. Quite tasty. And some Grand Marnier adds the flavor boost."

He brought my hand up for a kiss. "It sounds like a perfect Thanksgiving."

His phone rang, and he released my hand to draw the phone out of his pocket. "Sean here."

He listened for a moment, then nodded. "Sure, Seamus. I'll be there in ten minutes."

He tucked the phone back into his pocket. "They need me for something over at the warehouse. I should just be a half hour or so."

I gave his hand a squeeze. "I'll be planning out the shopping list," I teased.

He leant over the bar to give me a long kiss on the lips. By the time he drew back my heart was thumping against my ribs.

His voice was a low murmur. "I'll plan the dessert," he promised. From the look in his eyes, I didn't think he just meant apple pie.

"I think I'm going to like this Thanksgiving," I chuckled.

He winked, then he had turned and headed out the back hall.

I busied myself cutting lemons and limes, wiping down the tables, but it was surprising how used I had gotten to his presence in the bar. Even with the six regulars going through the usual motions of pool-playing and TV-watching, the place felt hollow, empty. It was as if robotic replicas of humans were going through the motions of activity, and I was the only real person in there.

Finally the counters were clean, the dishwasher was run and emptied again, and I looked around for something to do. The recycle bin was half full, but it was worth getting that cleared. I turned to Joey.

"Joey, I'm –"

He waved his hand at me, not taking his eyes from the TV. "Yeah, yeah."

My shoulders slumped. I grabbed up the plastic bin and went down the hall, wedging the bin against the wall in order to get the door pulled open.

Night's shadows had thoroughly overtaken the lot, and I had to let my eyes adjust before I could see the bin to dump the glassware into. When I turned, I realized the shed door was half open. My eyes lit up with delight. Sean was back. If I was lucky – truly lucky – we might get some close-and-personal time in before heading back into the bar. My body warmed with the thought, and I snuck toward the opening. Maybe I could catch him by surprise.

I got to the edge of the door, my heart pounding, a wide smile on my lips. I peered around the edge.

WHAM.

Something heavy and blunt struck me on my right temple. The world tilted, swung, and went sideways, coming up to hit me in my left shoulder.

Walking toward me at an impossible angle was a sumo wrestler, bald, thick, with a tattoo on one bicep.

The world stuttered, rewound, and turned off.

Chapter 6

I blinked my eyes in agonized confusion. Someone had drilled a hole in my head, and it ached with a power which staggered me. Not only that, but a hive's worth of honey bees had moved into the drilled-out location, buzzing and vibrating. I moved my hand to massage the spot.

Or I tried to raise my hand – it stayed resolutely in place. Another tug, and I realized it was tied in place with some sort of a rough rope. A quick flailing informed me that my other wrist and both ankles were tied as well, apparently to a wooden chair.

I forced my eyes open wider, struggling to focus in the shadows.

I was in some sort of an office without windows, and it was probably nearly dawn, judging by the low glimmer of light coming through a doorway to another, larger room. There was a desk to one side, filing cabinets to another, and an elegant painting of a bullfighter on a far wall.

There was motion at the doorway, and a man stepped into the opening, moving his hand to flick on the lights. They blinded me, and I groaned, shutting the lids against the pain.

The man's voice was deep, with a heavy Cuban accent. "*Mierda*, Raul, what in God's name have you done?"

I forced my eyes open, enduring the pain with long breaths. The bald man came in behind the first, shrugging. "Just what you said, boss. I found us a hostage."

The first man came forward, and I could see him more clearly now. He looked just like the man from the Dos

Equis commercials, the Most-Interesting-Man-In-The-World. He had that same kindly look to him, along with the casual assurance that he could get anything he wanted. I could almost imagine him looking down at me, saying, "I don't always take hostages, but when I do, I make sure they're innocent, young women with a penchant for poetry."

I held in my giggles and wondered just how bad my concussion was.

He shook his head, looking me over. "My dear, I'm sorry you've been caught up in this. My name is Javier. I'll see to it that you're not hurt." A flicker of concern danced in his gaze. "Hurt more than you have been already," he amended.

I looked down myself. Apparently I'd fallen against something sharp at the shed. My jeans leg had been ripped in a long jag, and crusted blood coated the edges of the opening. Smears of blood led to me across the hard wood floor.

Javier's voice was soft, encouraging. "What is your name, my dear?"

I didn't see any harm in him knowing it. Perhaps it would help Sean and the others negotiate more quickly for my release. "I'm Kate."

Javier nodded. "Don't worry, Kate. This is simply a business transaction. We'll have you back where you belong soon enough." He looked behind him into the other room. "Aymee, come in here. I want you to go up to the bedroom with Kate and get her cleaned up."

He turned to Raul. "You carry her up there, so she doesn't have to walk on that leg." He looked around at the blood-smeared floor. "And get the cleaners in here to take care of this mess." His gaze darkened. "After that, you and I are going to have a little chat."

Raul's lips curled down, but he nodded and moved toward me. He pulled a black-handled knife from his back pocket, swung it open, and cut loose the rope ties. Then he slung me over his shoulder as if I were a futon mattress. He went out the door and up a narrow flight of stairs. The door at the top was open, and we went in. He flicked on the switch.

The small room smelled faintly of lemon-spearmint cleaning detergent. There was a single peony-painted lamp on a small table by the bed in the corner. The pair of windows opposite were boarded over with planks and half-covered by long burgundy drapes. A large painting on one wall showed a Hispanic woman in a long, elaborate black dress with red roses. A door in the far wall led to a bathroom.

He plunked me down on the thick, dark brown blanket and scowled at me. "You're more trouble than you're worth," he snapped.

A young, elegant woman in a tight black dress stepped into the doorway, and she sniffed dismissively. "Go on, Raul. Go to your master."

Raul's fingers clenched in anger, but he turned and headed back down the stairs.

The woman closed the door behind her, then turned with a smile. Her high heels clicked on the wooden floor as she crossed to me. "And now, my dear, Kate, is it? I am Aymee. Not to worry. I'm sure Javier will take care of everything." She pouted her perfect lips as she looked me over. "But you are definitely a mess. First thing we need to do is get you cleaned up."

She put out a hand, and I carefully got to my feet. It seemed the floor was moving, that we were aboard a ship at sea. She put an arm around my waist and helped me into the bathroom. It was a simple white-décor space, with a small mirror over the porcelain sink and a shower stall surrounded on two sides by frosted glass.

She smiled encouragingly at me. "I'll bring you a nightgown. You get yourself washed up. There's soap and shampoo in there, and you can use that towel – it's clean. I'll be right outside when you're done." She released me to sit on the closed lid of the toilet, then stepped out and shut the door.

I immediately reached for my phone in my pocket – but it wasn't there. I had no watch, nothing else on me but my clothes. And my head was throbbing as if an L. A. rave had burst to life within its walls.

Wearily I pulled off my clothes and tried to examine the injury on my leg. With the matted blood it was hard to see how bad it was. At least it seemed that nothing else had gotten hurt in the process. I carefully pressed myself up to standing and went over to the mirror. My eyes were ringed with black shadows, and there was a sizeable lump on my right temple, but nothing else seemed affected.

I tried to peer into my own eyes in the reflection. Was one pupil larger than the other? It seemed like it might be. I would not be surprised if I did have a concussion, with the way a woodpecker was hammering its way into my skull. I would have to try to hang on until rescue came. I had no doubt that at this very moment Sean, Jimmy, Seamus, and all the rest were doing everything in their power to find me.

I moved carefully to the shower and turned on the blast. It took a few minutes for the hot water to come fully through, and then I stepped into the stream. I groaned in a sublime mixture of pleasure and pain. Somehow they melded into a sensation I found it hard to put a name to. I simply stood there for a long while, soaking in it. Then at last I began the routine of shampoo and soap.

Under careful ministrations I was able to work my way through the brown-red mess of my leg and get to the underlying skin. It wasn't as bad as I had thought. There were three jagged stripes, but they didn't go deep. I gently washed them, making sure there was no debris embedded in the wounds. Finally I rinsed thoroughly and came out to towel myself dry. I then wrapped the towel around my middle.

I went to the bathroom door and opened it the tiniest amount. "Aymee? Are you out there?"

There was a movement by the door, and a long, thick, white cotton nightgown was pressed into my hands. "About time," she teased. "I thought you had drowned in there. Here you go."

I closed the door, put my panties back on, then pulled the fabric over my head. It felt heavenly, wrapped around me. I gathered up the rest of my items and stepped back out into the bedroom.

She took my clothes out of my arms. "I'll get these washed for you. In the meantime, you look like Hell. Get some sleep."

I didn't protest. My lids were already closing of their own accord, and I could barely stand. I wobbled my way over to the bed and climbed under the heavy covers. From below came the steady whirr-thump, whirr-thump of the cleaners and their equipment, washing away all trace of me.

The sound was soothing, mesmerizing, and the world fell away.

Chapter 7

I lost all sense of time. I woke up shivering, in the middle of the day, judging by the streaming light shafting through stripes between the boards. I had tossed off my blanket at some point in my sleep. I pulled it back on me, burrowed deep beneath it, and sunk back into oblivion.

Aymee came by later, fed me a bowl of chicken broth, and I could barely stay awake for it.

My dreams were dark, tangled, and laced with dread. I was deep in a gothic forest of twisted evergreens, my feet sliding in the mud, crows calling high overhead. I was searching for something, but had no idea for what. My clothes kept catching on the brambles around me.

The sharp thump of a closing door shook me into wakefulness.

The room was pitch dark. I had no idea if it was late evening or nearly dawn. What I did know was there was a presence in the room.

I bit down the scream which launched from my core. I clenched my hands into the blankets and sat up, moving my back into the corner. Was this friend or foe?

The steps cautiously moved forward toward the bed. I strained in the darkness, searching, striving …

A twisting motion, and a thick rag was brought across my mouth, solid hands tying it behind my head. I cried out in agony at the pressure, but the sound was muffled by the dense fabric. I bunched myself up into a ball, pressing hard into the corner, but a beefy hand latched onto my upper arm and flung me face down onto the bed.

Raul's rough voice growled in my ear. "You've been trouble since I first saw you at that bar, you *puta*. And now you'll get what you deserve."

He grabbed for the bottom of my nightgown. I scrambled to find the lamp, or anything at all, to use against him. He snarled and threw me back onto the bed, the motion sending my head pounding. A wave of nausea swept over me, and my focus zoomed in on not getting sick. If I threw up with this rag in my mouth I could choke to death. I had no doubt Raul would gladly let that happen.

His hands were back at my nightgown, and I kicked out backwards, still striving to drag in long, deep breaths to ease the rocking of my head. He grabbed my calf and slammed it into the mattress, kneeling across it with a heavy pressure. The other leg was quickly similarly pinned.

He slid his hands along my thighs, his breath coming in harsh draws. My eyes filled with tears, and I shook them away. The action sent a fresh wave of nausea and vertigo through me, and I was lost. I collapsed down against the bed. Raul's fingers slid higher, and one thought shone through the madness. One thought glowed like a beacon in the blackest of nights.

Sean.

I focused on that, released everything else, and shut my eyes.

Crash!

Remnants of board showered over me, peppering me with tiny pinpoints of sensation. Raul launched to his feet, a growl of frustration and anger filling the room.

A dark shadow was framed in the broken-in window. When he stepped forward, the light came around him to highlight his face.

It was Sean. His face was shadowed, carved in marble, and I had never seen anyone as handsome or determined in my entire life.

Raul launched at him like a charging bull, and they were in motion. I could barely make out the swings and blocks, the dodges and counter-punches. The dense shadows, my blurry vision, and the speed at which the men moved made it an impressionist painting which had sprung to violent life. I could hear their grunts of pain, the solid, sickening sounds of fist impacting flesh. But neither man called out for help. Neither could afford the attention that rushing feet would bring.

There was a massive crunch, a pause, and then the solid thud of a body hitting back against the door. It was followed by a sliding sound as the body settled down against the floor.

Then silence.

My heart frantically sought to escape the walls of my ribs. Was that Raul laying there unconscious – or Sean? If it was Sean, what came next could be far worse than I could possibly imagine. I wrapped my arms around my legs, barely able to breathe, and there were footsteps …

A pair of steadfast eyes blinked in front of me. Sean's voice came, low, hoarse, tinged with pain and exhaustion. "Kay?"

I flung myself at him, wrapping my arms around him. A heavy shudder of agony shook through him, but he returned my embrace with a grateful groan. "Oh, Kay, Kay …"

He swept me up in his arms, drawing carefully to his feet, then moved over to the window. He sat on the edge of the sill, and I could see we were on a quiet side street of some sort, with three-deckers all along both sides. There was a man on the street below, holding a rope. The rope went up to a hook which was sunk into the side of the window frame. A carabiner there held the rope in a loop, and the rope's other end held a harness.

Sean quickly slipped me into the harness, then waved to the man below. I was slowly, carefully lowered down. When I was sitting on the ground the man braced, gave a nod, and Sean grabbed a hold of the rope. He slid down the length, coming to a stop at my side.

The other man knelt at my side the moment Sean had touched ground. "Kay – my God. Are you all right?"

I blinked in surprise. I couldn't see his face in the darkness, but I would know that voice anywhere. "Evan? Is that you?"

My eldest brother drew me into a bear hug. His presence there let loose the last, tenuous hold I had on my emotions. I burst into tears.

He wrapped me up in his arms, drew up to standing, and in a moment the two men were striding side by side down the sidewalk. Around the corner, under a streetlight was parked a car I knew well – Evan's Caspian Blue '65 Mustang. He carefully slid me into the back seat, then the two men hopped into the front. A roar of the engine, and we were off.

The world drifted in and out, I was being carried again, and then Sean's white comforter was being laid over me. I looked up to see the two men's faces over me, side by side, furrowed with weary relief.

I was safe.

I let the world go.

Chapter 8

Someone was using my head as a Taiko Dojo drum, pounding it with steady rhythm, and I made a shooing motion with my hand, trying to ward them off. Strong hands clasped my fingers, and Sean's voice came in warm relief. "There you are. How are you feeling?"

I blinked my eyes open. It was probably late afternoon, judging by the streaming light, and the familiar brick walls filled me with a sense of sturdy safety. I looked into Sean's eyes, as he knelt by the bed, and then drew him into a tight embrace.

His voice was thick with emotion. "You're all right. You're home now."

I kept my mouth right by his ear, and spoke in a low whisper. "Is Evan gone?"

He nodded against me. "He wanted to stay, but –"

"I know, he's a cop. It could complicate things."

"Our story will be that he stopped by to talk about Thanksgiving plans, and when he heard you were missing, he joined in the hunt."

I pressed a kiss on his cheek, then pulled back. Sean was right – the closer we kept to the truth, the better. Someone could easily have seen Evan's car in the parking lot, and it was not exactly a common model. I had no doubt that the moment I went missing and Sean let his handlers know, the blue grapevine had sprung into action and Evan had been alerted.

My mouth quirked into a smile. "Did he happen to stop by a few hours after I'd gone missing?"

He ran a hand tenderly down my hair, and his eyes sparkled. "More like ninety minutes," he corrected. "I hear that his Mustang can do one-twenty if it's opened up."

I twined my fingers into his. "And I suppose my darling brother now wants me to go down to Mom's to heal up."

His eyes shadowed. "Absolutely. As do I. You've been through a traumatic event, and you probably have a mild concussion. We should get you into the hospital to be sure."

I shook my head, then closed my eyes as a wave of nausea swept through me. "I'll be stuck sitting in a waiting room for five hours while all manner of contagious people cough on me," I argued. "In the end, they'll just tell me to rest and take it easy."

His mouth quirked up into a wry smile. "Evan said you'd say that," he countered. "So we have a doctor friend of his coming by in about an hour to look at you."

He gave my hands a squeeze. "In the meantime, how'd you like some Campbell's Chicken and Stars soup?"

I chuckled. "You and Evan have been busy chatting, I see. Sure, I'd love some."

The soup was just the comfort food I needed. I napped, and then the doctor was there to check me over. After poking, prodding, and inserting objects into orifices, he pronounced me quite fine with a minor concussion. His recommendation was simply to rest for a week and take over-the-counter medication for the pain.

I looked over at Sean after he'd left. "See, what did I tell you?"

He smiled, coming to sit on the edge of the bed. "It's always best to be sure," he advised. "Just in case it had been something worse."

He ran his fingers down the side of my face, and his look shadowed. "Oh, Kay, this is all my fault. I should have been there. I should have looked out for you."

I brought my fingers over his. "You can't watch me twenty-four hours a day," I pointed out. "And we thought that whole Cuban thing was in the past."

He hesitated for a moment, his jaw tightening, and then he asked, "Did they … did they hurt you?"

I squeezed his fingers. "They did not," I reassured him. "Raul intended to, but you got there in time."

Relief eased the tension in his body, and he pressed a tender kiss onto my forehead.

Sean's phone rang, and he sighed, pulling back. He drew the phone from his pocket. "Sean here."

He looked over at me as he listened. "I'll ask her."

He hit the mute button on the phone, then put his head in close to mine. "Seamus and Jimmy want to come talk with you about what happened. Are you up to it?"

My brow creased with worry. "What should I say?"

His gaze held mine. "As much as possible, the truth. We don't know what they saw or heard. For Evan, he stopped by to chat about Thanksgiving."

I nodded, and he clicked the phone back to life. "Yes, she's awake. As long as you keep it short. The doctor said she should rest."

It seemed only minutes later before Seamus and Jimmy were pulling chairs over to the side of the bed, their eyes dark and serious. Jimmy patted my hand. "We'll get the focking bastards," he swore, his brogue coming on heavier than usual. "We'll string the Cubes up by their balls."

Seamus pinned me with his gaze. "You tell us exactly what happened, from the beginning. Everything you can remember."

And so I did. I told them about being in the back lot, and how Raul had hit me with something. I told them about the office where the Most Interesting Man in the World looked me over. I explained how Aymee had tended to me. And, with Sean holding my hand, I described how Raul had almost raped me.

Jimmy and Seamus were silent through it all, letting me tell my story at my own pace. Their gaze darkened as I went, and by the end I could see the anger tightening their jaws.

Seamus looked over at Sean. "I'll have my sister come and sit with her. The three of us need to talk about what happens next."

Sean turned to me. "Will you be all right?"

I nodded. "I'm sleepy anyway. I wouldn't even know you're here. You do what you need to do."

He leant forward to kiss me on the cheek. "You get some sleep."

I didn't need a second urging – it seemed that the moment I closed my eyes, darkness sucked me in.

Chapter 9

I sat at the table, enjoying my final bite of the chocolate chip pancakes. "These are delicious."

His mouth quirked up in a smile. "Evan said they were your favorite."

I chuckled. "Seems like you two hit it off."

His gaze shadowed. "I wouldn't say he's too pleased with me," he countered, "but we have an agreement. He'll come by tomorrow evening to bring you down to your mother's, once you're up for the drive."

I shook my head, and, thankfully, the pain of the past two days had faded, due in equal parts to the rest and the Tylenol I'd been taking. "I'm feeling fine, really. And my mom is busy enough, getting all her final exams and grading done before the Thanksgiving holiday. The last thing she needs is me underfoot right now."

He took my hands in his. "Kay, you really should go."

I squeezed his fingers, then stood, picking up my plate and cutlery and moving to the sink. "I'm fine, and I'm staying." I grinned at him. "You'll find that I can be quite stubborn when I want to be." I rinsed off the items and put them into the dishwasher.

He came over next to me. "But I need to go in to the bar and –"

"And I'm going with you," I finished up for him. "I'm fine. Really. I can certainly stand behind a bar and pour drinks. It's not the Sago coal mines."

His brow furrowed. "The doctor said rest."

I nodded. "I can put a chair behind the bar. At least you'll be there to talk to. If I stay here, I'll be all alone. Didn't the doctor say someone should be with me for the next few days?"

He pressed his lips together, but at last he nodded. "We'll get Ethan to take us over. I don't want you on the bike right now, until you're fully healed."

I sighed, but took the concession. "I'll be ready in a half hour."

When I walked into the bar, you'd have thought I'd been gone for years on a death-defying mission to defuse land mines in Burundi. Everyone crowded around me, talking at once, offering me hugs and support. It was a few minutes before I could take my place behind the bar, sitting on one of the stools.

Jimmy and Seamus came out of the back room, and Seamus shook his head. "You should be home, resting."

Jimmy clapped me heartily on the shoulder. "She's a fighter, this one," he praised. "Tough as nails."

Seamus looked over to Jimmy. "In any case, we'll delve into this later. You come by the house after you lock up, and we'll figure it out."

Sean looked up. "You want me to come by?"

Seamus shook his head. "You keep an eye on Kate. Get her home safely."

Sean nodded. "Of course." I could see in his eyes that he was frustrated by the exclusion, but he quickly brought on a smile to hide that.

Seamus gave Jimmy a final glance, and then he turned and left. Jimmy took a seat at the bar. Without being asked I turned, grabbed the bottle, and poured him his drink.

His brow creased as he looked at it. "I guess you can't have any, at least for this week. Jesus, Katie, to think of what those bastards did to you."

I looked again at Sean for a moment. Maybe I could be some help in drawing out what Seamus and Jimmy were up to. I leant forward to Jimmy. "I did go through a lot," I murmured in a low voice. "It was Hell. So I want to know what you and Seamus are planning."

Jimmy glanced around. "I'm not really supposed to –"

I gripped his arm. "Jimmy, that bastard nearly raped me. I deserve to know."

He held my gaze for a moment, and at last he nodded. He drank down his whiskey, and I poured him a fresh glass. "You're right. You're the one who suffered, and you deserve to know what we're going to do about it."

He drew his head in closer, and Sean and I matched his move. His voice was low. "When Javier contacted Seamus with the ransom demands, he was ... precise ... in the business arrangements he wanted to set up with us. Too precise. It didn't make sense. We need to figure out how they got that information."

My brow creased. "You think they have someone spying on you?"

Jimmy shrugged. "We don't know. But we need to figure that out." His gaze darkened. "And, of course, we need to teach them a lesson. Apparently our previous one wasn't strong enough."

My brow creased. "Aymee was kind to me. I wouldn't want to see her hurt."

He smiled, patting my hand. "You have a good heart, Katie. Don't you worry about any of that. We'll take care of it. We'll get them to stop."

Joey's voice called from his stool. "Some Bushmills, please?"

Sean began to stand, but I waved him down. "I've got this," I assured him. "My legs were beginning to cramp anyway." I stood and reached for the full bottle of whiskey.

The world tilted, twirled like the Sugar-Plum Fairy on a Sugar-Plum High, and the bottle went flying. It smashed into the far wall, missing the TV by mere inches, and whiskey and glass showered the room.

I fell against the bar, holding on for dear life.

Sean was around at my side in an instant. "Kay! Are you all right?"

I shook my head, carefully standing up again. The spinning settled down, and I looked across at the mess I had created. "I'm so sorry! Is everyone OK?"

The men stood, shaking themselves off, picking bits of glass off of shirts. One by one they indicated that they were fine.

I turned to Jimmy. "I'll clean it up. I can't believe I did that. I could have really hurt someone."

He smiled reassuringly at me. "It's just a spilled bottle. I'll get Trai Hok and his wife to come right over. Hand me the phone."

I passed it over, and sure enough within fifteen minutes the pair of middle-aged Vietnamese were carefully gathering up the glass shards with gloved hands. The woman used a spray bottle on the wall, the scent brightening the room. Trai brought in a floor cleaning machine which looked sort of like the popcorn-push-toy I had as a toddler – a circular base with a long stick. They cleared the tables and chairs to the side of the pool table, and then he began methodically doing passes on the wood floor, the whirr-thump soothing me.

Jimmy patted my hand. "It'll all be fine, Katie. Just you wait and see."

Chapter 10

*B*rrrring!

I dove my head deeper under the covers. Good God Almighty. If they were going to call early, at least they could wait until it was light out. There wasn't even the glimmer of morning yet coming through the windows. What time was it?

Sean groaned, then climbed out of bed, padding his way over to his jeans. He pulled the phone from his pocket and put it to his ear. "Yeah?"

He listened for a minute, and when he spoke again, his voice was sharp, attentive. "Sure thing. Be there in ten minutes."

I looked over. "What is it?"

Sean was pulling on his jeans. "Sounds like they're nailing down the details of what they're going to do to the Cubans. I need to be there."

I nodded. "Of course."

He pulled on his shirt, then came over to kiss me. "You'll be safe enough in here. Keep the door locked, and don't leave until I get back. I shouldn't be too long."

I smiled at him. "I'll keep the bed warm for you."

His gaze kindled, and he ran his fingers down my face. "You feeling ready for that kind of activity?"

My grin widened. "If we take it slow."

He chuckled. "I can do slow."

My body warmed at the thought. "Hurry back, then."

He gave me another kiss, and then he was out the door. Sleep swept back in on me.

The sun was strong and warm by the time I awoke again. I made myself a fried egg and bacon, enjoying it with coffee while I surfed the web on Sean's laptop. Then I added the mug and plate to the dishwasher and started it up.

I was reading how nine applicants were attempting to open pot dispensaries in Worcester when an odd thumping noise began coming from the dishwasher. I went over and opened it up. One of the spatulas had turned into an angled position and was interfering with the spinning water jet. I rearranged the spatula and reset it, and it went back to its usual low hum.

Thumping.

I remembered, suddenly, my first night at the Cuban place. How I had fallen to sleep to the whirr-thump of the cleaners scrubbing my bloody tracks from the office below. The sounds were overlaid with the whirr-thump of Trai Hok's machine as he undid the aftermath of the exploding Bushmills bottle.

Could Trai Hok be the mole that was passing information to the Cubans?

The man certainly had access to the full run of the bar, and could spend as much time as he wanted in Jimmy's office without causing any suspicion. I would bet he was also the one they used to clean the warehouse.

I googled "floor cleaning machine" and quickly found the one I was after – blue base, long silver handle. There were several videos on YouTube of the scrubber in motion. In every video the sound of the machine was smooth, even, and without any thumps.

It had to be Hok. His machine was old, worn down, and had some sort of a mechanical flaw.

Was his wife involved, too?

I thought again of her cleaning the walls with that spray – it was fresh and lemony-spearminty. Just like the scent in the bedroom I'd been held in. Chances seemed slim that both of those fairly unique traits – the specific aroma and the unusual sound – would be in both locations together like that.

I reached for my phone, pushing Sean's icon, and my heart pounded as I waited for him to pick up. The phone rang … rang …

"You've reached the phone of -"

I hung up in frustration. I needed to warn him. For all I knew, Trok was there at the warehouse, "innocently" cleaning while the plans were made. The Cubans could lay an ambush which would seriously hurt Sean – or worse.

I scrolled through my icons and pressed the one for Ethan. He picked up on the second ring. "Hey there, Kate. Need a ride?"

"Yes, to the warehouse. When can you be here?"

"Ten minutes."

"Great, see you soon."

I threw on some clothes and was down waiting for him by the time he pulled up. The ride over to the warehouse seemed to take forever, and I already had the money in my hands by the time he pulled up.

He waved me off. "No need, Kate. Jimmy covers my tab for you, including tips."

I didn't waste time arguing. "All right, then. Thanks!" I hopped out and strode over to the door. I rapped sharply on it.

It was about a half minute before Jimmy pulled it open. He shook his head, looking at me. "Ethan said you were coming. Seamus wants me to turn you away, but I think you're strong enough to take it. You've got a feistiness to you, Katie. So I'm going to let you in."

I nodded, following in behind him. Undoubtedly there was filming going on today, and he didn't want me to be shocked by the goings on. I readied myself to show the appropriate amount of surprise at the scene. Indeed, the lights were set up and lit at the far end of the warehouse.

Jimmy walked along at my side. He put his arm around my waist, not in a suggestive way, but in the way a paramedic would support someone who was near collapse. "This might be tough to see, Katie. I'm here for you. You know that, right?"

My brow creased. Jimmy seemed awfully concerned. A twisting sickness ran through me. Did they have young girls involved in the filming today? Was that why Jimmy was so worried? I fervently hoped not.

We drew closer to the lights, and I realized in confusion that the lights were not circled around the large bed. The bed had been pushed over against the far wall. Instead, the lights ringed around a man slumped on a wooden chair. His arms were tied behind him, and his ankles were fastened to two of the legs. Blood oozed out of deep gashes in his arms.

He wearily raised his head at our approach, his face bruised and battered.

It was Sean.

I gasped, swayed, and it was only Jimmy's arm around my waist which held me upright. His voice was a soothing murmur. "Hang in there, Katie. You have the right to know."

Seamus stepped forward from the ring of men, his face hard, angular.

"He's a cop, Kate. He's a fockin' rat." His eyes were cold marbles. "And once we're through finding out what he knows, he's getting exterminated."

Book 3: A Song of Soul and Hope

Chapter 1

"Hope" is the thing with feathers—
That perches in the soul—
And sings the tune without the words –
And never stops – at all –
-- Emily Dickinson

Seamus and Jimmy knew that Sean was an undercover cop.

Jimmy's arm around me was all that kept me from collapsing at Sean's feet. Sean's eyes were on me, blackened, closing, and I could see the fire of determination which blazed within them. No matter what they did to him, no matter the pain his body suffered, he would never reveal that I knew the truth. His message to me was as clear as if he'd shouted it, full throttle, with his very last breath.

Get to safety.

I looked around the ring of hardened criminals. Seamus stood before me, stocky, muscular, his grim face telling me that he meant his threat. Once they were sure they had wrung from Sean every last kernel of information he could divulge, they would dump his broken body in a dark corner of the Quabbin where it would never again see the light of day.

I was not about to let that happen.

I closed my eyes, narrowing my focus with pinpoint precision to the cards in my hand. These men had been criminals for so long that their view of the world had calcified. Case in point – they assumed that I would go along with Sean's execution without blinking an eye. A steady Irish girl backed up her clan, no matter what. She ruthlessly eliminated any threats. She did what had to be done.

Mrs. O'Malley sprang to mind – Seamus's sister, Jimmy's wife. Both men clearly respected the woman. If I could show them I was as tough as Bridgit – and at the same time prove that Sean was a loyal soldier – we might just come through this alive.

Steel flowed through my veins, and I opened my eyes again.

Sean's brow creased with confusion, and then his face went pale. He tried to reach for me, but the ropes held him secure.

I drew myself to standing, stepping apart from Jimmy. I turned to face Jimmy and Seamus, bringing harsh disdain to my face. These men thrived on a no-nonsense approach. I would give it to them with both barrels.

"What is this, some sort of a hazing ritual? Are we ivy-league frat boys just weaning ourselves off a mother's tit?" I waved a hand in Sean's direction. "A little punching bag action, to prove your fists don't shatter like glass?"

Seamus's eyes narrowed, but he glanced at Jimmy, a hint of doubt flickering behind his small eyes. "Kate, Sean is an undercover cop. He's been using you. He's been fucking you as part of his play-acting."

I held back the flush of heat which threatened to brighten my face at the echo of the words that, only a few days ago, I myself had thrown at Sean. I gave a scoffing laugh. "I know when a man is screwing me without emotion," I informed them. "Sean was in prison for *years.*

A woman can feel that kind of a thing when they're in bed with a man. Believe me. He's no cop."

Jimmy glanced nervously at Sean before meeting my gaze again. "But it all fits, Katie. He shows up out of nowhere. Suddenly he's climbing into bed with you. And practically at the same time we've got *rafters* breaking up the bar and the Cubes know our inside workings." He gave a barking laugh. "Or are you going to tell me that Mexican-Mud-head Joey is to blame?"

I pinned him with my gaze. "Joey couldn't change the channel on a TV without help," I snapped. "Are these flimsy circumstances really all you have on Sean?" I bit sharply on the inside of my lip to keep the bright surge of hope from shining in my eyes. We might just get out of this.

Seamus's face still held a hard edge to it. "There's his phone, Kate. He's made several calls to Evan – that man who helped him rescue you."

I threw my hands in the air. "That's because Evan's my eldest brother! And, yes, Evan is a cop. Like my father was. You guys knew that." I laced a growl into my voice. "And you also know that my father was shot and killed." My eyes swung to Jimmy. "Just like your brother, Liam, was shot and killed. You know what that's like. You know how it changes you."

I turned to Seamus. "Liam was your best friend. You know about the soul-deep itch that brutal murder gives you. Like it's time not to trust others. That you have to take things into your own hands."

I steeled my gaze. "My dad was a cop, and when he was killed, they couldn't even figure out who did it. My brothers and I were left on our own, with just our mother trying to hold things together. We relied on ourselves and nobody else. Certainly not the police." I brought a tone of disgust into my voice. "When, after all we'd been through, my brother *became* one of them, I washed my hands of him. Completely."

Seamus nodded, a note of respect coming into his eyes. He nudged his head at Sean. "So why was Sean talking to Evan?"

I crossed my arms in front of my chest. "Evan, that bastard, was trying to get me away from Sean. Thought Sean was a bad influence on me. Wanted me to move back home with my mommy, as if I was eight years old."

Seamus turned to stare down at Sean. "Is this true?"

Sean nodded, and his voice was hoarse as he spoke. "Said I was a fucking bastard for letting Kay work at the bar." His gaze shadowed. "Told me, if he had his way, I'd never get within a hundred miles of his sister again."

Seamus looked into his eyes for a long moment, then nodded, a hint of surprise coming to his face. "I think I believe you."

I brought an edge of harshness into my voice. "Well, you should, because it's the truth." I took a step toward Seamus. "Not only that, but I know who the real mole is."

That got the attention of every man in the room. They swung to stare at me. Seamus's gaze narrowed. "Well, who is it?"

I waved a hand at the room around us. "Who comes and goes without any restrictions? Who walks into Jimmy's office, into these rooms here at the warehouse, and you don't question his presence at all?"

Seamus pointed a finger at Sean. "This man here."

I shook my head. "On the contrary, you immediately suspected Sean, because he was a newcomer. How stupid would he have to be, to show up and then have the Cubans cause trouble only a day or two later? Surely, if his presence was part of some master plan, he'd invest more time in building up his friendship with you before he launched into the conflict stage."

Seamus slowly nodded. "All right, then - who?"

I put my hands on my hips. "When I was with the Cubans, being held hostage, there were a few odd things I noticed. The lemon cleaning scent in the bedroom had a certain bright spearmint zest to it. Also, as I was falling asleep, the cleaners were downstairs. Their machine made a whirr-thump noise."

Seamus crossed his thick arms. "And?"

I looked at Jimmy. "When I spilled some liquor at the bar the other day, Jimmy called in Trai Hok and his wife to clean it up. They used the exact same scent to clean the walls. Their scrubber made the exact same whirr-thump noise."

Jimmy's brow creased. "I suppose it does make that noise, but heck, Katie, maybe those scrubbers all do."

I shook my head. "I looked up the equipment on Google. I found video after video of those things in operation. *None* of them make that noise when they are healthy. Trai's is old, failing, and it's got a specific, distinctive hiccup to it. It's got to be him."

I looked between the two men. "Trai comes and goes when he wants. He goes into all of your offices. He could read anything and everything. He's probably in the background during half of your meetings."

Seamus glanced at Jimmy. His fingers drummed on his arm as he considered it. "She could actually be right."

I took a step to come up before him. "I *know* I am right," I corrected him. "And not only that, but I know how we can prove it."

Chapter 2

Sean was now spread-eagled on the bed, tied in place, and I resolutely kept my eyes from him, from the bruising on his face, from the gashes in his arms which still leaked a slow, steady stream of blood. I knew I would see, in his eyes, a fervent pleading for me to get as far away from this warehouse as possible.

I would not leave him.

Jimmy held his phone to his ear while he walked a circle around the thick spatters of blood on the floor. "Thank you so much, Trai. I appreciate it. We use this area for filming, you know, and we want to get this mess cleaned up before it leaves a permanent stain. Ten minutes sounds great." He clicked off.

Seamus glanced at Sean for a moment, then looked at me again. "You know it might not be Trai, right, Kate? It could still be Sean, playing us all for fools. Using us."

I stepped up to Seamus, staring him directly in the eyes, pouring my fury with him and all his perverted cronies into my gaze. "If Sean is a fucking rat, then I swear I will shoot him myself."

Seamus gave a small smile at that and looked over to Jimmy. "She reminds me of Bridgit, when Bridgit was her age. You didn't tell me Kate had this kind of steel within her."

Jimmy grinned, coming over and putting an arm around me. "She's my girl, all right."

I held in the shiver of repulsion which strove to tremor through my body, instead focusing on Sean lying helpless on the bed. If Sean could have endured that beating, I could certainly handle Jimmy's lecherous touch.

Brrrrring!

A familiar ring came from an aluminum frame table against the side wall. I looked over in surprise. Sean's phone was laying there, along with his keys and various other items. One of the thugs glanced down at it. "It's Evan," he reported.

A thought kindled in my mind, and I stalked over to the phone, filling my face with raw anger. "Evan? That bastard? Let me have a word with him."

The soldier looked to Seamus for orders, and Seamus's eyes lit up with interest. "Sure, let Kate have a chat with her brother. This could be fun."

I grabbed up the phone, taking a deep breath. I had to be cautious with this. One wrong word and I could be joining Sean in the Quabbin's soulless depths.

I hit the answer button. Before I could speak, Evan's voice burst out of the phone, raw with fury. "Where the hell have you been, Sean? I told you I'd be out later today to take Kate back home, where she belongs, and that you and I needed to settle something first. Settle it *permanently.*"

Seamus's grin brightened. "Put him on speaker."

Trepidation hammered in my heart, but I pushed the button and held the phone out before me. Then I filled my voice with the same rage which had just blasted from the phone like an avenging angel's trumpet.

"And who the hell do you think you are, to order me around? I'm an adult, Evan. I've got a college degree. I don't need you to act as my nanny. God knows you did more than your share of that over the past ten years."

There was a sputter from the phone, and Evan's voice was even richer with fury when he spoke again. "Sean put you on the phone? He's a coward in addition to a bastard! He should never have let you stay in that bar!"

"Nobody *lets* me do anything," I harshly corrected him. "I *choose* for myself what I will do."

"Like when you *chose* to date that bastard, Derek?"

Righteous indignation flared through me, and I didn't need to act my anger any more. It spewed like a pyroclastic surge billowing from an erupting volcano. "I wouldn't have made that bad decision if you'd let me date back in high school, to have even some experience in handling relationships," I shot back. "You muffled me up like an Eskimo papoose on a cradle board! I couldn't go out with friends, I couldn't even go out and get a job!"

His tone heated. "Right, so now your brilliant *choice* of a job is being a bartender at that tacky, seedy, hell-hole of a bar which deserves to be burnt down and ploughed under?"

There was a growl from the men around me, and Evan's voice became sharp. "What the hell was that?"

It was the opening I'd been seeking. I let satisfaction ring in my voice. "Well, I'll tell you, Evan. I have you on speakerphone right now, and I'm with the men from that very *hell-hole*. These are my friends. This is my group. And you know what, this is the life I've chosen. Starting from this very moment, you and your damned cub-scout ideals can take a flying leap."

Jimmy slapped Seamus on the shoulder in delight. "What did I tell you?"

There was a pause from the phone, and when Evan spoke again his voice had a tone of careful attention to it. "And what about Sean?"

I couldn't help it. My eyes automatically moved to lock on to Sean's, where he lay tied to the bed. His gaze was shadowed, exhausted – and held a steel core of absolute loyalty. Whatever path I chose, he would follow me down it.

I held Sean's gaze as I spoke into the phone. "Evan, Sean's an ex-felon. His father was a drunk. He's probably been in more fights than Floyd Mayweather." My throat went tight, and I added in a lower tone, "He certainly looks it right now."

Evan's voice layered with that trace of awareness that I knew so well, that I had been seeking. "Kay?"

I took in a breath. "Evan, I love him. Whatever he faces in life, I will stay by his side."

Sean's eyes shone, and for a moment the creases of pain eased in his forehead.

There was another long pause from the phone, and this time when Evan spoke I could hear the tension. I could imagine his fingers gripping his phone, turning white.

"Then what do you want from me, Kay?"

Here it was. A ring of eyes was watching my every movement, hanging on every word. Sean's life hung in the balance, and probably my own as well. Even if I called in the cavalry, Seamus could easily shoot us both before the doors were breached.

If I played my cards right, we could have it all. We could nail the group not only for the pornography, but also for multiple counts of attempted murder. I had no doubt that Trai and his wife would go on the short list the moment it was proven that they were the leaks.

I looked down into the phone in my hand. "Evan, I don't want to see you again until you are wholeheartedly ready to support Sean and me. I want to see dedicated effort from you to prove you are taking me seriously. And don't try enlisting our brothers or friends, either. This is between you and me."

The phone went silent, and I held my breath. He could refuse, of course. He could think it too risky to go it alone and insist on bringing in the entire eastern seaboard. He could do a thousand different things.

And Sean could die.

At last I heard his sigh, almost a groan. When he spoke, his voice was low and rich with emotion. "Kay, I love you. If this is what you want, what you truly want, then I'll support you in your choice."

A click, and he had hung up.

For a long, long moment, the world hung motionless. There was only Sean's gaze on me, deep, fathomless, and so full of emotion that I thought it would spill over and drown us both.

Life spun back up into activity. Jimmy bounced over to me, drawing me into an enthusiastic hug. "Jesus, Mary, and Joseph, you really let him have it! I'm glad you're on our side, Katie."

Seamus came over to me, holding out his hand. I passed over the phone. He gave an approving smile. "We need more women like you around here, Kate. Makes me feel like I'm home again."

There was a call from the front door. "Boss, Trai's here."

Seamus turned, a gleam in his eye. "Send him on in."

Jimmy still had an arm around my waist, and he drew me over to the side. The splotches of blood in the center of the room had almost a Jackson Pollock quality to them – angular, sharp, interlaced with the dark, smooth brown of the boards.

Trai barely glanced at Sean or the blood as he set up the scrubber. He took up the power cord and began walking toward the far wall.

Seamus turned to me, pitching his voice to carry. "So, Kate, what was that again that your cop-brother told you about those Cubans?"

I stilled, the suddenness of his question intruding on the carefully constructed conversation I had just finished with Evan. It took me a moment to remember the purpose of Trai's visit here, of the trap we were setting.

"Oh, right," I stated, catching back up with the present. "My brother had information about Javier and Raul."

Trai slowed in his motions, his head turning slightly toward us.

Seamus nodded. "It's almost a shame we won't be able to take those Cubes down ourselves, but, you know, if they're all going to be in prison, that's good enough for me."

Trai fumbled with the plug, taking a moment to re-seat it in his hand.

I shrugged. "Well, from what the cops say, the Cubans have no idea that every phone in their system is bugged. Not a word goes in or out of that group without the Feds listening in on it. With everything the team has gotten on them up until now, it'll be an easy case to lock them all up for life." I rolled my shoulders. "It's almost a shame that Massachusetts did away with the death penalty back in eighty-two. But life in prison should be good enough."

Seamus grinned. "Good news for us, that's for sure. We'll be able to waltz in and take over their entire territory without a peep."

Trai turned back to us, an apologetic look on his face. His voice was soft and clipped with his Vietnamese accent. "I'm so sorry, but I forgot some of the cleaning supplies. I'll be back in a short while."

Seamus nodded. "Just don't take too long," he commented dryly. "If this blood sets into the boards, it'll be hell to scrub out."

"Not to worry, I'll be back soon." Trai didn't even bother to move the scrubber. He just dropped the coils of the plug next to the unit, then scurried out the door.

Jimmy winked at us, then he was in motion, slipping out the door after Trai.

Seamus grinned, stretching. "About time Jimmy put those driving skills of his to good use. You should have known him when he was younger. Best wheel man I've ever seen. A real talent there." He pulled his phone from his pocket. "Kate, that was a touch of brilliance on your part, to tell him that their phones were bugged. It means Trai can't just call them to warn them. He has to go in person."

Seamus's phone rang. He hit the answer button, then the speakerphone. "You're on, Jimmy. You got him?"

Jimmy's voice held more excitement than I'd heard in it during my entire time at the bar. "He's flying, Seamus. I was worried I'd have to hang back so he didn't spot the tail, but Trai barely sees the red lights in front of him. Nearly took out an old woman at the corner by the post office."

Seamus was calmness personified. "Just stay on him, Jimmy. If anybody can do it, you can."

Jimmy let out a chortle of glee. "Hah! Nearly had her on two wheels that time. I've still got it!"

"You do indeed. You keep on his ass. Is he –"

"He's slowing down," interrupted Jimmy, his voice bright. "Same place Katie was held at. They haven't even fixed the window yet. He's nearly taken out the garage door, he skidded so hard, and now he's raced in the front door."

"You're sure they didn't see you?"

Jimmy scoffed. "He didn't look around once. He was in such a panic that he barely saw the cars crossing him. He nearly took out a family of four."

Seamus nodded in satisfaction. "Good, good. Come on back home, Jimmy. You did well."

I could hear the pride puff up Jimmy's voice. "I did, didn't I. I'll be back soon."

Seamus clicked off the phone, then stared at it in consideration for a long moment. He carefully tucked it in his back pocket before raising his gaze to look at Sean. His eyes were considering, flat.

He walked over to stand at the side of the bed. I hung back, not wanting to intrude on this moment. The situation still hung in tense balance. Seamus might decide Sean wasn't the risk to keep around. Sean had been badly beaten – would he carry a grudge? Would he end up being a canker which ate into Seamus's organization?

Seamus pressed his lips together. "What we did was good business sense," he stated. "We had a serious issue, and you were the most likely candidate."

Sean nodded his head. "I know. If I were in your position I would have done the same thing."

Seamus's gaze drilled into Sean. "We beat you pretty good," he pointed out.

Sean gave a wry chuckle. "You haven't seen my father," he countered. "What you did here, my father would have called that his warm-up. There's a reason my mother sent me out of country."

Seamus nodded. "So we're good?"

Sean held his gaze. "I have no problems from my side. I'm a soldier. I do what you tell me, and I accept the risks."

Seamus raised an eyebrow. "And the Cubans? You'll follow my orders on that, too, and not go blasting solo on some hot-headed quest for revenge?"

Sean's jaw tightened. "*Tiocfaidh ár lá.*"

Seamus's eyes brightened, and for a moment he stood straighter. "*Tiocfaidh ár lá.* Our day will come."

Sean nodded again. "I trust in you to lead us. To make the plan, to utilize our resources, and to wipe those cockroaches from the face of the earth."

Seamus's face gained an inner glow, as if his skin had been dark before and something within him had caught alight. "It's been a long while since I've had something like that to tackle," he murmured. "All this shit that goes on here, I'd never have thought, twenty years ago, that this would be my life. I had such plans to better the world." He looked down at Sean. "You and I, we are going to better our world. We are going to eradicate those vermin and make our city safe for decent folk again." He glanced over at me. "Safe for the women, the children."

Sean's face was steady. "Just tell me what to do."

Seamus stepped forward, pulled a knife from his back pocket, and with quick, expert moves he cut the rope from Sean's wrists and ankles. Sean groaned as he brought his arms and legs in. Seamus stepped back, giving Sean room to climb to his feet.

Seamus nodded to Sean. "I'll tell you what to do first. You go home with that woman of yours, and get some rest. Rest well, because a few days from now we're going to have a special event."

Sean's face stilled. "You're going to move on the Cubans that quickly?"

Seamus's eyes glinted with amusement, and he shook his head. "No, no, that operation is going to be much larger this time. Larger and more final. So we're going to have a gathering of all the heads and their most trusted captains. I'll call them in, and we'll meet here. With our combined might, we will pulverize them into the earth. It'll be the Romans at Carthage."

Sean's gaze lit, and I could see the effort it took for him to keep his voice steady. "You'll have all the families together, here?"

Seamus reached into his back pocket and pulled out his wallet, thick black leather. He flipped it open and began pulling out one-hundred dollar bills. When he had taken fifteen of them, he folded the wallet back up and returned it to its home. Then he held the money out to Sean. "And you're getting a promotion."

Sean's gaze went from the money to Seamus. "A promotion?"

Seamus tucked the money into Sean's hand. "You're now a captain. You'll get that every week. It'll be enough for you to take good care of Kate there."

Seamus turned to me for a moment, nodding in approval. "Kate, you're a hell of a woman. You are just like Bridgit was when she was your age. I thought they didn't make women like that over here in the states. They're too soft, too unwilling to do what needs to be done. But you've proven otherwise. If I were twenty years younger …" He shook his head, and looked back to Sean. "You take care of her, and you treasure her. She's a special woman."

Sean's eyes glowed with emotion. "I know it."

Seamus clapped him hard on the shoulder, and I could see the tremor of pain which Sean held in. Seamus grinned. "Well then, you two get on back home and rest up. Ethan's waiting outside, he can take you. Just make sure you both clear your calendars for Saturday night."

Sean glanced at me. "You want Kate there, too?"

Seamus creased his brow. "Why wouldn't she be? She's been instrumental in all of this. She deserves to be recognized for her achievements." His brow narrowed. "Or do you think she's less worthy just because she's a woman?"

Sean shook his head. "Not at all."

Seamus nodded. "Then it's settled. The both of you will be the guests of honor at our celebration." He waved a hand to the door. "Let me walk you out."

Every ounce of me wanted to slip my arm under Sean's shoulder and support him, but I knew it would lessen him in Seamus's eyes, and that Sean himself would never allow it. So I just walked alongside him as he slowly, carefully made his way across the warehouse floor. Seamus pushed the door open for us, and indeed Ethan was parked right alongside the building. Sean pulled open the door for me and made sure I was safely inside before climbing in after me.

Seamus lent over into the cab's doorway. "See you in a few days," he grinned. Then he closed the door and hit the top of the cab. Ethan pressed on the gas, and we slid away from the curb.

Sean put his hand over mine, but I didn't turn. I knew if I looked into his eyes that I would lose it. We just had to make it away from Ethan's attentive ears, and I knew we could figure something out.

Together.

Chapter 3

Ethan rolled down his window as we headed up the steps. "Sure you don't need a hand?"

Sean waved him off. "I'm fine, really. You head on back. Seamus might have some other work for you."

"Always does," replied Ethan with a smile. He waved his hand, then he was off.

The moment Ethan turned the corner, Sean slumped against the brick frame of the building. I carefully looped my arm under him, trying to be as gentle as I could.

His voice was hoarse. "Let's get inside." He stepped forward, unlocking the main, outer door. When we got to the steps up, he grimaced, then took each one carefully, holding onto the rail. There was sweat on his brow by the time we reached his door. When we got through it he locked it behind us, throwing the bolt as well. He went straight for the speaker cradle for his phone, dropping it in. He pushed a few buttons. In a moment the soaring vocals of Charlotte Church's "Ave Maria" billowed from the speaker, filling the room, echoing off the brick walls.

He turned, groaned, and collapsed onto the bed. I went around to the other side, climbing in, bringing my face up close to his.

His hand shakily traced down my face, his eyes looking into mine as if we'd been parted for long years. "My God, Kay, you could have been killed. You shouldn't have done it. You should have left and called your brother."

I shook my head with determination. "By the time anybody got in to you, you could have been dead. Seamus wasn't playing around."

"I know he was serious, Kay – and you walked right into his maw! One wrong word from Evan, one mis-step, and your fate could have been worse than mine." His face paled. "God, Kay, they run a sex trade. They could have put you into some twisted hell-hole, and you'd never have gotten free."

I gave a wry smile. "If that had been me, tied to the bed, would you have left me behind?"

His gaze became lost in mine. "Never. I would never leave you."

I leant forward to give him a gentle kiss on the cheek. He flinched, and I looked down his length, at the wounds which were slowly crusting over. "We need to get you looked at. I assume you don't want to go to a hospital?"

He shook his head. "It's not that bad. Really. You should have seen some of the men my father fought against. I don't think anything is broken."

"Best we find out," I advised him. "You just lie here for a minute. I'll go get some washcloths, and we'll see how you are doing."

His gaze sparkled. "Yes, Mistress."

I grinned. "Oh, we're going to be that way, are we?" I went to the bathroom, moistening some washcloths, then grabbed up two towels and some bandages. I swung by the kitchen to get him a glass of water. He had sat up in bed by the time I got back, and I handed him the glass while I sat down at his side. He drank half of it in a long swallow, sighing.

I began with his shoes and socks. Those came off easily, and luckily his thick, leather boots seemed to have kept that part of him from harm. Thank God for motorcycling gear.

Next, I took the bottom of his shirt in my hands and carefully eased it up over his torso. The rippled muscles that I loved so well were criss-crossed with cuts and welts. The arms were the worst, so I began there, gently wiping away at the dirt and debris which had encrusted into the blood. Sean was right – they really weren't that bad, when they were cleaned up. They had been made with careful precision, designed to inflict pain rather than cause damage. I imagine Seamus had wanted to keep Sean alive for as long as possible, to make sure all secrets had been pried out of him before he was killed.

My hand stilled at that, and Sean's hand came over mine. "I'm all right," he murmured. "Everything is going to be all right."

I focused my attention on the bandage, wrapping it carefully around the larger wound and sealing it in place. "You almost weren't," I replied. "You were almost taken from me."

He brought his hands to either side of my face, turning my head to look at him. His eyes were dark, steady, with smoky passion rising in them. "I'm not going anywhere."

I leant forward, pressing my lips to his, and he groaned in pain, but he drew me in anyway, twining his fingers in my hair. Our lips sighed … opened … danced …

It was a long while before I could detangle myself, rising up from him. "We still have to check the rest of you over," I reminded him, my breath coming heavy.

He reached for me, and I shook my head. "No you don't. You lay still. I need to get those pants off."

His eyes darkened with desire, and the bulge in his jeans told me that he had something more than innocent bandaging in mind.

I knelt across his hips, carefully undoing his buckle, pulling the tongue of leather slowly, inch by inch, out of the metal. He groaned, but this time it didn't seem to be from pain. At last the belt was free, and I put my hands to the button. I eased the button out of the hole, then inched the zipper down. He raised his hips up off the bed so I could slide the jeans down. In a moment I had tossed them on the floor.

I started from his toes, working my way up inch by inch along his body, kissing and massaging as I went. He was less injured here, with only the occasional purpling bruise to show where an impact had been made. By the time I reached his briefs, his erection pressed, hard and strong, against the black fabric.

I slid my hand up its length. "Weren't you telling me just this morning that we should take it slow?"

His eyes became distant. "Was that only this morning? It seems like eons ago."

I moved my mouth down to the bulging fabric. "A lifetime," I agreed. I put my mouth around the knob, in its cotton wrapping, and gently pressed my lips closed.

He groaned with desire, his hips rising up, and I firmly pressed them back down. "Uh, uh," I scolded. "You just have to lie still."

His breath was coming in longer draws, and I could see the ripple of effort it took for him to lay in place. I smiled, kneeling over his waist. With slow, languorous movements, I brought my fingers to my waist, drawing my top up and over my breasts, then my head. I tossed the top to the side, on top of his jeans. Then I arched my shoulders back, resting my hands on my ankles, my breasts cupped by my bra and stretching.

He was transfixed by me as I stepped off him. I stood next to him, sliding my hands down to my hips, then around to the button. I leant forward, then popped the button from its hole. Slowly I slid the zipper down, revealing my black, lacy panties beneath. I gave my hips an undulating movement as I eased the jeans down my legs. I bent over, my breasts on display before his eyes, as I removed my boots, then my socks. I slid the jeans free, then stood before him again.

His gaze was all I could have hoped for. His desire for me radiated from him, but he remained on the bed, watching, waiting.

I knelt back over him, smiling down at him. "I suppose you want some of this," I purred, sliding my hands up to my breasts and running my fingers around their curve. "You want …" I pulled at the nipples through the thin fabric, and they hardened, pressing out against the material. A soft moan shuddered through me as I squeezed the sensitive tips.

Sean rocked beneath me, and I gave him a gentle slap on the hip. "Quiet, now," I advised him. "You are still healing."

I reached behind my back, undoing the clasp, then slid one arm up to cover my bra-cupped breasts. I slid one arm out of a strap, then overlaid my arms and did the second. I wiggled so the bra fell free, leaving me with only my arms covering my breasts from Sean's view.

I adjusted my hands so each one fully covered a nipple. I pressed my breasts into each other, relishing the sensation, then allowed the nipples to poke through my fingers, rolling them and pinching them. Waves of pleasure coursed through me, sending sparks through my breasts and rich desire in my sex.

Sean's shaft was now throbbing against me, and I rubbed my pelvis along it as I kneaded, throwing my head back with the pleasure of it. His hands were stretched out over his head, and it seemed to be taking all his willpower to keep them in place.

I put one hand down on the bed next to his chest, using it to support myself, and I leant over, dangling my breasts near his mouth. His lips parted of their own accord, and I let the left nipple just reach his outstretched tongue. The contact sent a shaft of fire through me, of hot desire, and I shuddered. I rose up, separating us, then swung so the other breast was lowered. Again he stretched, and this time I let the whole nipple be taken in by his hot lips, by his questing tongue, and I could feel my panties soak through in response.

I slid back onto his pelvis, and his groan was deeper this time, his cock rock-hard. I moved my hand to his face, caressing it for a moment, then slipping my finger into his mouth. It was warm, wet, and a craving came over me to plunge my mouth onto his, to roll with him and let him take me, plunder me. But I held onto my sanity by the thinnest of leashes. This was my turn to pleasure him, to show him a taste of what he had been doing to me.

I withdrew my wet finger from his mouth, then trailed it down the center of my chest, down into the dense curls of my sex. My finger was drawn as if by a magnet to the hard nub there, and my clit danced with sensation at even the first, brief touch. I gasped, my body arching with it.

Sean's breath was coming in deep heaves now. "God, Kay, let me –"

"You stay still," I scolded him again. "I'm busy right now." I swirled my finger, my thighs shuddering against Sean, and it took every ounce of self-restraint I had to go slowly, tantalizing, drawing out the pleasure that seemed a tidal wave, unstoppable. My hips rocked against his of their own accord, and a long shudder went through him. His biceps bulged with the effort of staying in place.

My finger picked up tempo, and my other hand went to my breast, rolling the nipple, pulling at it, and my breaths came in quick pants. My pelvis thrust out against my hand, my back arched, and it took every ounce of effort for me to bring my eyes back down to Sean, to keep them open under the deluge of pleasure which was soaking into my every pore.

I could barely get the words out. "This is for you, my love. This is … This … Oh … God …" My body burst, skyrocketed, and I was crying out, gasping in breaths, as waves of ecstasy lost all sense of place and time.

It seemed eons before I could focus again, before I lowered myself down, resting on both hands above Sean.

His gaze was deep black, intense with passion and desire. He could barely get the words out. "Kay, you are torture."

I brushed my lips against his, then slid down his length, hooking his underwear in my teeth as I went. He raised up his hips, and soon he was completely naked on the bed. I slid down my own panties and grabbed a condom from the side table. I slowly, tantalizingly rolled it down the length of his shaft. He quivered with my motion, and I half expected him to lose control right there. But he held on, and I smiled as I climbed back on him.

I tilted my hips so I hovered just over his shaft. "Is this what you want?"

His voice was throaty. "Yes, God, Yes."

I lowered myself so just the barest ring of pressure rested against his knob. "Something like this?"

He could barely speak. "Please …"

I gave a soft twist with my hips. "What do you want?"

His cock twitched with desire, and I knew he was riding the edge. "I want you."

"And what do you want me to do?" Another twist.

The shudder ran through his whole body. "I want you to fuck me."

My breasts were tingling back into awareness again, and I squeezed tight my vaginal muscles. His head rolled back with desire, and his breath left him in a gasp. "God, Kay, I'm – I don't know if –"

My voice was a purr, as I lowered myself just a millimeter further down his shaft. "When do you want me?"

His response was half groan, half plea. "Now … Now … Now …"

I slammed my hip down into his, taking him deep into me, and his body solidly sealed with mine. His cry filled the room, reverberating off the large windows. My motions were hard, quick, and then he exploded within me, the throbs sending me over the edge. I joined him in the kaleidoscope of colors, our bodies soaked in sweat, the contact coming forceful, passionate, until finally I collapsed down against him, completely spent.

His arms, at long last, came up around me, wrapping around me as if he would never let me go. He twined his hand into my hair, holding my head in place against his chest. His voice, when he spoke, held an ache which seemed to rise from his very soul.

"Kay, I love you."

Warmth pooled in my chest, flowed outward, and filled every finger and toe. I could feel the whorls on my fingertips expand and radiate light.

I pressed a soft kiss against his chest, and his heart beneath.

"I love you too, Sean."

Chapter 4

I was just thinking about detangling myself from Sean's embrace and getting us some glasses of water when a gentle knocking came from the door. Sean instantly rolled on top of me, shielding me with his body, staring with fixed attention at the door. Without moving, he shouted, "Who is it?"

The voice on the other side was muffled and faint, but I'd know him anywhere. Evan's reply was, "Let me in."

Sean's face went still, but after a moment he climbed up out of bed and pulled on his clothes. I did the same, trying to bring a semblance of order to my hair. I was at Sean's side when he gazed through the peephole and then undid the locks. He pulled the door open.

Evan was standing there in black sweats and a black gym t-shirt, his lean, muscular body soaked with sweat. I wondered if he'd just finished working out when he made that call. And then he was pulling me hard into a hug, and I wrapped my arms around him. It was a long moment before he released me enough to look over at Sean.

His gaze ran down Sean's body, at the bandages on his arms and the bruises on his face. At last he nodded. "You hung in there."

"I always will," promised Sean, his eyes serious.

Evan glanced behind us into the room, then nudged his head toward the hallway. "Interested in dinner? I hear you actually still have a Friendly's left here in Worcester." The corner of his mouth quirked up into a smile, and he looked at Sean. "That soft ice cream might be just what you need for that jaw."

Sean and I gathered up our items, and then we headed down the stairs, Evan before me, Sean behind. Evan led us over to his Mustang and waited until we were both in the back seat before getting into the front and starting it up.

He looked in the rear view mirror as we eased out onto the main road. His brow furrowed. "Kay, you took a hell of a chance."

Sean's voice held an edge to it. "And you took your own sweet time coming out here," he retorted. "What if something had gone wrong? What if she'd needed you?"

Evan's voice glimmered with amusement. "Oh, I was at your place by the time Ethan dropped you off," he corrected. "I have a duplicate building key now. But when I got to your studio you seemed ... occupied ... so I figured I'd give you some time."

My cheeks heated with the thought of my brother hearing our lovemaking, but I pushed it away.

Evan looked over at Sean. "So, fill me in."

Sean went through the events, step by step, and by the time we pulled in at the Friendly's parking lot Evan was shaking his head. He came around to open the door for me, and when I stepped out he pulled me into another hug, longer this time, pressing a kiss on my forehead.

"The brother in me says you should have left and gotten to safety. But, aside from that, I am so, so proud of you," he murmured. "You are an amazing woman."

Sean came up to my side, lacing his fingers into mine. "Yes, she is."

The waitress was blonde, perky, and when Evan indicated we wanted the empty booth in the far back, away from the other patrons, she didn't blink an eye. She walked us over to the table, handed us our menus, then looked again at the two men. She leant over to me and said in a low voice, "Honey, you decide you don't want one of them, just let me know."

I grinned as she left to fetch us our waters. My brother had always been handsome, and maturing had only added a rugged quality to his good looks. And Sean ...

I sighed as I looked at him sitting next to me. Even battered, he had a quality to him that could take my breath away. If anything, the bruises gave him that aura of taking on all comers.

The waitress came, went, and in short order we had our meals. True to Evan's suggestion, Sean settled with watermelon sherbet for now, his mouth making gentle ripples in the scoops. I tried to keep my gaze on my tuna melt. The man could make anything seem sexy.

Evan took a bite of his burger, looked around, and then said in a low voice, "Well, I assume, given her performance in the warehouse, that when I suggest that Kay high-tail it down to Waterbury that she's going to refuse."

I looked steadily at him. "You bet I will."

He sighed. "You know that would be the safest thing, Kay."

"Seamus deliberately asked for me to be there, at this big event," I pointed out. "The event where the entire mess of them could be quickly and easily rounded up. Their whole operation could be brought to a crashing, permanent end."

"We could still do that without you, Kay."

"You know how easily Seamus could spook," I responded. "Heck, he had the glimmer of an idea that they had a mole in the organization, and Sean was beaten half to death. What's he going to think when I suddenly 'get the flu' right on the day that everybody's in one place?"

Evan's lips drew into a line. "Still, it's worth the risk."

I leant forward. "How about the risk of the lives of all the officers and detectives who are charging in there? How about the lives of all the innocent girls which will be destroyed if we don't do this right?"

Evan looked down for a moment. "But, Kay –"

"I won't even be in danger, really," I interrupted. "As far as they know, I'm just a member of their group. Sean will be right there next to me. The cops come in, I get rounded up with the rest, and then somewhere along the way you guys set me loose as not knowing anything. They'd understand that."

Evan looked at Sean in concern. "You wouldn't make her testify?"

Sean shook his head. "Definitely not. We have more than enough evidence without involving her. As far as everybody's concerned, she never knew anything. She's just a bartender minding her own business."

I looked over at him, worry sweeping over me. "But they'll know you were undercover? Won't that make you a prime target?"

Evan growled. "And with Kay being your *known associate*, she becomes someone they might use to get to you."

Sean shook his head. "I've thought of that, and I've talked to my handlers. They're setting everything up so we have independent recordings and videos. I won't need to testify, and if all goes well, my identity stays a secret. We'll stay safe."

Evan's lips drew into a line. "She'd *better* stay safe," he agreed.

Sean's gaze became serious. "I would have let them beat me to death, rather than say one word to jeopardize Kay," he swore. He turned to look at me. "I love her. I will do everything in my power to protect her."

I leant forward to press a kiss to his lips. "And I love you. I will stay by your side, and see this through to the end. This group needs to be taken down." I turned to pin Evan with my eyes. "They were trying to seduce a fifteen-year-old girl. They wanted to film her rape. Can you imagine what that would have done to her? To know that thousands of men out there were watching and rewatching her violation?"

Evan's eyes shadowed. "I know. This group is beyond foul. I just wish you didn't have to be involved."

"It's too late for that," I replied. "I *am* involved. And now I will make sure it gets dismantled down to the nuts and bolts."

The corner of his mouth turned up. "You sound like Dad."

I reached forward to put my hand over his. "He would have wanted us to work together, to do whatever it took to get these bastards behind bars."

Evan's brow furrowed. "He would have wanted us to stay safe."

I raised an eyebrow. "Stay safe? Remember the time we were all barreling down the streets on our bikes, trying to jump over tin cans, and he came out to help us build a bigger ramp?"

Evan's lips spread into a smile. "And then I hit it at full tilt, spun the bike, and broke my arm?"

"And Dad scolded you, the whole way to the hospital, about how you should have taken the lift-off at a sharper angle, to account for the nails!"

We both grinned, and Sean's arm came around my shoulders. I knew, between the three of us, that somehow we'd find a way. We'd take down the pornographers, save the victims, and come out safely on the other side.

Chapter 5

Not a word was mentioned about Sean's injuries when he and I arrived at the bar the next day. I was curious just what kind of a story Jimmy had told the others. There were edgewise glances at Sean, and Joey seemed a little jittery, but they went about their normal business of lining up pool shots and staring at the TV as if it were about to reveal the next five commandments.

Jimmy came out from his office, glancing at the door in desolation. "She can't come again, today," he grumbled. "Too much algebra homework. I offered to tutor her, but she said her Dad was going to do that."

I raised an eyebrow. "You are good at algebra?"

He chuckled. "Not exactly. But I was hoping I could distract her before she realized that."

His hand half reached for the phone in his pocket before he sighed. "And the thought of calling one of my other … friends … just doesn't seem appealing." His mouth turned down in a frown. "I hope Jessica realizes everything I'm giving up for her. The sacrifices I'm making."

I kept my tone even. "I'm sure she will learn that all soon enough."

His eyes glimmered. "Yes, she will," he agreed. He turned and headed back into his office.

I refilled Sean's drink, running my fingers along his hand before turning to put the bottle in its place. In a way, knowing our every word could be overheard made us much more in tune with the subtler things – the way we looked at each other, the touch of our fingers, the subtle nuances in the way we said things. It was almost as if we had a hidden language, all our own.

I turned to look at him, and his eyes drew down me. A slow smile came to his lips. I knew that gaze. Warmth swirled within me, sinking lower, and I glanced automatically at the clock. It was only ten.

The corner of his mouth turned up at that, and he flicked his eyes toward the hall – and to the shed beyond.

My body flared into awareness, and my lips parted.

Sean called over to Joey without turning. "Joey, I think I left my phone on my bike. Kate's gonna come help me find it for a few minutes."

Joey waved a hand. "Take your time. My glass is full."

Sean held his hand out to me, and the texture of his fingers against mine sent swirls of energy circling my nipples, moistening my sex. I gave him an answering squeeze as we took the steps to move into the back lot.

The shed had a bright, new padlock on it, replacing the one the Cubans had cut from it just under a week ago. The thought of that made me pull up, and Sean turned to me, his brow creasing.

"If you'd rather not –"

I stepped forward, fisting my hand in his hair, pulling his warm lips down onto mine. He groaned, then pulled back, glancing around. He quickly undid the lock and led us in.

The moment the door closed behind us, he turned me, pressing me against the wall, his lips on mine, hot with need. I moaned as his tongue darted in my mouth, pulsing, making me want that sensation on my nipples, on my clit. Every part of my body sang out with need for him.

There was a noise from outside, and we froze.

I recognized the voice. It was Zeke, one of the pool players – the tall one with scraggly hair and a Fu Manchu beard. He was whining, apparently into his phone. "But Maaaa, Thanksgiving isn't for another week and a half. I don't want to drive all the way up to Bah Hahbah and freeze my ass off so we can watch Jeopardy all night long. Get that dead-beat sistah of mine to ..."

Sean slid his hand up under my shirt, reaching my nipple, and gave it a firm squeeze.

I bit down on the moan which threatened to fill the shed. His eyes sparkled in the shadows, and he moved his lips next to my ear.

"Ssshhhhhhh."

He squeezed again, and I melted against the wall, my every focus on holding in the sounds which craved release. A faint corner of my mind whispered that this silence had been all I had known with Derek. My ex had insisted on a lack of sound, and I had barely minded, because most of the time the sound I would have made was a sigh of disappointment.

But when Sean slid my shirt and bra up, releasing my breasts, and then brought his moist mouth to suckle at one, pulling, pulling, it was all I could do to rein in the deep-seated groans which seemed to have a life of their own.

His mouth moved to the other, his fingers gently twirling the moistened one, and I could feel wetness soaking my panties. I arched my back, pressing my breasts against him, craving him with all my soul.

He released my nipple from his mouth, grinned, then pulled my top and bra off. He quickly undid my jeans, sliding them and my panties down to my knees. He turned me in place, and I pressed my hands against the wall, my breath coming quickly, eager for what I knew would follow.

There was a zipping noise, and then a moment later his hard cock, lubricated with saliva, was sliding against my butt, moving between the firm folds of my cheeks. His hands pressed the cheeks in tighter, and he leant against me, his mouth near my ear. His voice was a low whisper. "God, Kay, you feel amazing."

My nipples were screaming for attention, and I reached one hand down toward them. He gave the side of my cheek a gentle swat. "Uh, uh," he scolded. "Yesterday you made me wait while you pleasured yourself, using my body however you wanted. Now it's time for you to see what it's like."

My juices seeped down my leg at his words, and I tried to raise my hips so his cock would miss its angle and slide into me, deep and hard. I knew once I had him in me that he would be unable to leave. But he swatted me again, pulled my hips down, then tilted them for a better angle. He groaned, low and soft, a sound for my ears alone. They soaked me through, and my body was in agony. My breasts craved him, my sex needed him, and I could barely breathe. All I could feel was the amazing sensation of his cock moving against me. His breath in my ear was coming faster and faster, interspersed with groans as he squeezed and released my cheeks.

His voice was hoarse with need. "God, Kay, you are so amazing. I could pleasure myself with you every morning and still be hot for you before lunch. I could climb on you at sunset, ride you all night long, and still want more when dawn came around. You are … God, you are … God, Kay …"

I could feel his climax coming, and my body craved it, wanted it … it took every ounce of my energy to keep my hands against the wall, not to bring one down, not to give that faint touch to my clit which would send me soaring with him. My body brimmed with golden energy, with desperate desire, and then he stuttered, pressed, and warm jolts of cum cascaded on my back, flowing like a life-bringing river.

My breath was coming in heaves now, and I balanced on the edge, wanting him, wanting his hand or mouth or I didn't care what to come around and finish the job.

His cock was still pressed against me, the throbbing gentling, and his breath in my ear began to settle. He reached to a rag on a shelf and wiped down my back.

I half turned my head. "Sean –"

He smiled, putting a finger to his lip. "Shhhhh." He turned me around, looking me over as if deciding what to do next. Then he knelt on one knee before me. My body quivered in anticipation as his hands moved forward to –

He hooked my panties, sliding them slowly, attentively back into place.

My heart pounded in confusion. "What are you -"

"Shhhh," he said again, his grin growing.

He slid my jeans up next, and the motion of the zipper against my pubic area nearly sent me over the edge. He gave a slight tug as he buttoned the button, and I groaned, sinking back against the wall. My nipples hardened even further, craving him, craving –

He reached down and picked up the bra, sliding the straps on my arms, then clicking the closure in place. My nipples pressed hard against the fabric, trying to impale their way through it.

My top was drawn on next, and I felt as if I had been swaddled in my clothes, so tight did they seem. I wanted to burst out of them, to shred them, to climb on top of Sean and find my release.

Zeke's voice came as a weary sigh from outside. "Yeah, yeah, Ma. I love ya too." There was silence for a moment, then the noise of the bar's door opening and closing.

Sean did up his own pants, then went to the door, opening it for me. I glared at him while I stepped through, every motion sending new waves of longing through me. He locked the shed back up, then guided me through the bar door. The regulars barely looked up as we returned to our spots. It didn't look as if Joey had even moved.

I leant over the bar at Sean. I pitched my voice low, but the hoarseness made my throat tight. "I will get you."

He moved his hand, reaching for mine, but as it went the edge of it skimmed the edge of my breast. I bit down on the groan which shuddered through me. My whole body was teetering on the edge of an explosion.

His eyes sparkled, and he lifted my hand to his lips. He turned my hand palm side up, and brought the delicate skin of my inner wrist to his mouth. Slowly his tongue traced at the soft skin there.

I was lucky I was leaning against the bar. The sensations he created made the room whirl. My lips parted, and my breath came in shallow draws. I glanced around the room. The others hadn't noticed in the least. Their attention was still glued to the pool table and the TV.

Sean glanced at my free hand, and then down, to my waist.

I flushed with heat. Surely he couldn't be serious? Not

—

His tongue moved, and now he had my finger in his mouth, slowly sucking on it. My eyes nearly rolled back in my head at the intense pleasure. It took every ounce of self control I possessed to soften the groan of pleasure into a silent exhale of breath. My breasts were swelling out of my bra, craving even the gentle slide of the fabric against them.

My other hand went to my jeans button of its own accord, releasing it, and my sex throbbed with hot desire. I undid the zipper, then eased the jeans a bit down my hips.

Sean's voice was a low command. "Look at me."

I brought my gaze to his, and his look was dark, full of passion, a deep craving that could never be filled. I could feel its echo within my own soul.

My finger slipped into my panties.

His voice was hoarse. "Not yet."

My heart nearly pounded through my ribs. My finger was so close, only an inch away, nestled in the thick, moist curls. I could feel my juices soaking my thighs. Every part of my body tingled with want and need and a deep-seated craving that I could never have imagined.

He ran his teeth along my finger, and the sensation nearly undid me. My voice was a strained whisper. "God, Sean, let me –"

Jimmy came around the corner, putting on his coat, his eyes focused on the front door. My heart hammered against my ribs as Sean released my finger from his mouth, as Jimmy passed behind him, his eyes on the door, on Kelley Square beyond. "I'm going for some pizza," Jimmy stated to the world at large. "Be back in about a half hour."

Sean's voice was even. "Sure thing, Jimmy, we'll hold down the fort."

Jimmy didn't even bother to respond, beyond a grunt, before he pushed his way out into the dark night.

Sean swung his eyes back to mine, his gaze clouding with hot passion. "And where were we?" He took my hand up in his. "Ah, something like this." He held my hand palm-side down, brought it to his lips, and then danced his tongue along the delicate webbing between my third and fourth finger.

I nearly lost control of my moan, of my ability to stand, of everything. I wanted him, I wanted him, and nothing else mattered.

Joey's voice was lethargic. "I'm out of Bushmills."

Sean's eyes danced with amusement. "I'll get that for you, Joey." He released my hand and moved around behind the bar. As he reached for the bottle with one hand, the other slid down within my panties, along my ass, his finger easing forward to just tease the edge of my dripping opening. My body flared with heat, and I arched, desperate to have him within me. He grinned, stepping away, bringing the bottle over to pour Joey's glass full again. As he turned to walk back toward me, he put his finger into his mouth, sucking on it, his eyes shining.

My body was aflame. I watched as he slowly put the bottle of Bushmills back into its place, watched the interplay of the strong muscles of his arm, the sleek, lean ripple of his stomach. I wanted him. I wanted every inch of him, and any second now I would push him up against the wall and ride him, ride him …

He stepped forward, looked at me for a long moment which seared my soul, and then with a quick motion he put his mouth hard on top of mine, driving his tongue into me. At the same time he drove his fingers into my panties, pushing my hand aside, his fingers landing exactly on the spot I had been craving, needing, desperately calling for.

The pleasure shook away all sense of time and place. I knew my body wanted to arch, to buck, but his firm muscles held me in place, sandwiched me between him and the bar. His mouth swallowed my cries, swallowed my breathing, and he took me in fully, absorbing my tremors, inhaling my passion. There were only his fingers releasing me, his body becoming my world, his mouth my air.

And I was gone.

Bit by bit, atom by atom, my consciousness drifted down from the ceiling, coalesced, drew together to reform my mortal shape. My clothes shimmered to fit again, my throbbing settled into a heartbeat, one that sung in tune with his.

His hand still cupped around my sex, possessively, and he looked into my eyes. His voice came low against my ear. "Are you ready for the main course?" His finger slid, and it pressed deep within me.

If he hadn't been pressed against me, I would have slid down the bar. I couldn't speak.

He chuckled, then withdrew his finger, holding his hand there for a moment before slowly sliding it from my panties. He did up my jeans, sealing the button, then brought the finger to my mouth. The taste of myself, the look in his eyes, took my breath away.

He withdrew his finger, then stepped back, his eyes swirled with passion. "Only a few more hours until you're home in bed," he murmured. And then he stepped around the bar, moving back to his stool. His gaze drew to my breasts, to my sex, and then back to my eyes again.

I groaned. It was going to be a long, long shift.

Chapter 6

I had dark rings around my eyes when we walked into the bar the next day. I'd barely gotten an hour of sleep - but it had been well worth it. I had never even dreamt of half the things we did, and the other half seemed transported far beyond our mere mortal world.

Sean was a god.

He grinned at me as he slid onto his stool, and I swear the man looked as fresh as if he'd slept soundly all night long. His eyes glinted with energy, with a look that clearly indicated what he'd like to be doing to me right now.

I turned around, reaching for his whiskey. My body was being pummeled by warring factions, and the lustful part of me was billowing into wakefulness. With the sleepy state of my mind, I couldn't afford that. Who knew what my lack of inhibitions would allow.

I poured him his glass, my voice low against his ear. "You behave yourself tonight. I am past exhaustion."

His mouth quirked into a grin. "I wonder why."

I gave him a playful swat on the hand, then returned the bottle.

My phone rang in my pocket, and I pulled it out in curiosity. I rarely got calls and practically never during working hours. The phone number seemed odd, and I didn't recognize it. Maybe it was a wrong number. I answered and put it to my ear. "Hello?"

A woman's voice with a trace of an Irish accent spoke. "Hello, Kate?"

My brow creased in confusion. "Yes, this is Kate. Who is this?"

There was a long pause, and her voice was almost hesitant. "It's … it's me, Kate. It's Eileen."

My lips broadened into a smile; I leant back against the bar. "Eileen! It's great to hear from you! I'd given up hope of you ever responding to me. How's Ireland? How's your grandmother?"

"Oh, she's fine. She's out getting us some *neeps* for tonight's dinner."

"Oh, so she recovered?"

Her voice echoed with confusion. "Recov – oh! Yes, right. Yes, she's fine."

I pursed my lips. "But I thought she –"

Eileen interrupted me. "Kate, Jimmy hasn't … hasn't … come on to you, or anything, has he?"

I blinked at the change of topic. "No, not at all, Eileen. He's treated me like a daughter."

Relief echoed in her voice. "That's good. I was worried, but I didn't know if I should call. I knew you could hold your own against him, if he did. Which, of course, he wouldn't. He said he wouldn't."

I furrowed my brow. "Eileen, are you all right?"

"I'm … yes, well … no, not really … I'm …" A gulp, and the sound of soft sobs.

I held the phone closer to my ear. "Eileen, it's OK. I'm here. You were right by my side when I had to face Derek. I'm here for you, no matter what it is. Don't worry about me and Jimmy. There hasn't been any trouble at all. I've been fine. Just tell me what's wrong."

She spoke between her sobs. "Oh, Kate, my grandmother wasn't sick. I just had to get away. I was so confused. Jimmy was sweet, and I know he's married. But his wife is like a Mack truck! Poor Jimmy, he's so tender, and gentle, and did you know he likes Irish poetry?"

She gulped. "Oh Kate, he would whisper, '*Bid adieu, adieu, adieu*' and, God, Kate …"

The blood drained from my face. My fingers turned white against the phone in my hand. I could barely breathe.

My voice was a rasp. "What happened, Eileen?"

Her voice dropped low, as if she was whispering. "He treated me like a princess, Kate. Like a movie star. He told me that he could immortalize me, that he knew this place that was all set up but was empty after hours. We would go there, just him and me. He would set up the cameras, and, God, Kate, it was amazing. *He* was amazing. We were going to run away together, go live in Carrigaline, or Crosshaven, or even Cobb. Somewhere on the water, somewhere with live music and dart bars and fish-and-chips from the truck."

I leant against the back of the bar. "And then what happened?"

"I … I … Kate, I'm pregnant."

I closed my eyes for a long moment. "How far along?"

"About three months. Kate, I haven't told him. I couldn't. I didn't know what to do. So I came out here to think, to talk to my grandmother, and to get my head on straight. I needed some time alone."

I drew in a deep breath. "Have you decided something?"

"I think … I think I'm going to keep it, Kate. Whether Jimmy wants to acknowledge it, or be with me, or any of it." Her voice became soft. "I can feel the baby growing inside me, Kate. My little son or daughter. And I love him or her. My grandmother says I can stay with her, and we can take care of my child together."

Her voice calmed. "But I think Jimmy has a right to know. Kay, I think it's time for me to come home."

My eyes flared in panic, and I turned to stare at Sean with shock on my face. His brow was wreathed in confusion, and he mouthed *What?*

I shook my head at him. Into the phone I said, "Eileen, we're heading into the holidays. This would be a really bad time to have this kind of a serious conversation. Plus, your grandmother would miss having you around during these times of family. I think you should stay there through Christmas. Let the new year come; let things quiet down. Then, when you come to talk with Jimmy, everything will be even keel. You'll be able to have his full attention and focus."

Her voice sounded unsure. "That makes sense, Kate. It just seems like I've been away from him for so long. He must be missing me terribly."

I held in a shudder. "I'm sure he is," I assured her. "But he's busy now, with all the holiday preparations, the bar, and everything else. He wouldn't be able to give you the time you need. The time you deserve. Just wait the few weeks. That way he can be solely focused on you when you arrive."

"Oh, Kate, you are always the voice of reason. I should have called you sooner, but I was afraid. I wasn't sure how you'd react. You're always so calm and steady."

I thought of what I'd been doing in this very spot behind the bar just twenty-four hours ago, and I blushed. "We all get wild sometimes, Eileen," I reassured her. "It will all sort out. I promise it will. But you need to stay put for now. It's really best for everyone."

"All right," she agreed. "But please don't tell Jimmy anything about this call. I want to tell him myself, in person, when the time is right."

"Of course, Eileen, that is the way it should be. You should tell him face-to-face when you come to see him."

A jangling noise came down the phone line, and Eileen said, "Oh, that's my grandmother. I have to go. I'll talk to you soon, Kate."

"Sure thing. You take care of yourself. Take your vitamins and drink lots of water."

She gave a merry laugh. "Yeah, yeah, I get that from my grandmother all day long. Don't worry, I'm taking good care of myself."

"All right, then. Bye, sweetie."

"Bye." The phone went dead.

Sean's eyes were on me, attentively curious. "What was that all about? I take it that was Eileen? She's doing all right?"

I leant forward, putting my mouth to his ear. "She's pregnant. With Jimmy's child."

His body stilled, and it was a long moment before he brought his eyes up to mine. "And she wants to come home?"

I nodded, returning my phone to my pocket. "I talked her out of it. If she can stay put until after the holidays, hopefully everything will have settled down a bit."

He put his hand out, holding mine. "It's going to be rough on her."

I nodded. "She got me through what I endured with Derek. I'll be there for her through this."

He gave a soft smile. "You're a good person, Kay."

I brought his hand to my lips, running my tongue along his finger. "Take me home, and I'll show you how good."

His groan was all I could have hoped for.

Chapter 7

I gave Sean a playful swat as we strolled into the bar, turning to hang my jacket on the hook. It was definitely getting chilly out there. It was a week-and-a-day until Thanksgiving, and while winter was still officially over a month away, the crisp winds were giving us a taste of what was to come. I swore I could see frost on the edges of the windows.

I blinked as I looked through them. Heading into the roiling chaos of Kelley Square was a black Escalade which I knew well. Seamus guided the car with deft hands, slicing across the middle of the eight-sided tangle as a shark slides through a school of minnows. The car pulled up along the curb in front of the bar.

Mrs. O'Malley stepped out, her sturdy form unmistakable in the dark night, and she pushed open the door. The bell above made its traditional tinkling noise.

Jimmy came bounding out of the back hall, his face glowing with anticipation – and he stumbled to a stop on seeing his wife standing there. He drew his gaze down her burgundy pant-suit, and his face sagged into desolation.

Mrs. O'Malley's lips drew down. "Good to see you too, Jimmy. Anyway, Seamus needs you both. He wants to finalize the plans for security for the event on Saturday. It's only four days away now. He wants to ensure the warehouse is buttoned up tight."

Sean nodded, rising from his stool. "Of course." He leant over the bar to draw me into a warm kiss. His voice became a murmur. "I'll be back soon. You stay inside until I return, just in case."

I smiled at him. "I'll be fine," I promised. "And, besides, you guys are in talks with the Cubans. They'll behave while they think you are negotiating in good faith."

Jimmy's brow drew together. "They'd better."

I thought again of Javier, the leader of the Cubans, The Most Interesting Man in the World. I wondered if he fell into using the meme-famous phrasing when he had his talks with Seamus.

I whispered in Sean's ear. "I don't always negotiate for rights to a porno operation, but when I do, I insist my girls have limes in their mouths."

He gave me a playful swat on the rear. "That's Corona," he corrected me with a grin.

Jimmy was watching our lighthearted exchange with a distant look. He glanced at his wife, and his shoulders slumped. He turned to the door. "All right, Sean, let's get this over with." In a moment, the two men had climbed into the Escalade, and it slipped slowly into the dark ocean of the night.

Mrs. O'Malley settled her bulk onto one of the stools fronting the bar. She turned to eye Joey for a minute. Her voice was gentle. "Hey there, Joey, you climbed off that horse yet?"

Joey looked myopically over in her direction. "Hey there, Mrs. O."

She sighed, turning back to me. She waved a hand up at the Redbreast. "Two glasses, Katie. I think it's time we had a talk."

I paled, but I turned, drawing down the bottle, selecting out a pair of glasses and setting them out. I filled both and put the bottle to the side.

Mrs. O'Malley raised her glass to me. "*Sláinte.*" She pronounced it with the same inflection one would say "It's a lawn chair"; somehow the "t" in the word became a "ch". I'd been around the Irish language in tiny bits since I was young, and more fully in the past month, but it still baffled me.

I met her glass with mine, and we both drank. She smiled at the flavor, stared at her glass for a moment, then settled it down onto a coaster and looked up at me.

She leant forward conspiratorially. "So, who would have thought it, about Sean?"

My heart hammered in my chest. "Thought what?"

She nudged my arm. "You saw it right away, I'd bet. But he had the rest of us fooled."

My voice was almost a squeak. "Fooled?"

She winked at me. "The ex-felon. Living in that rat-hole. And come to find out … he's really not that at all."

I focused my breath, drawing in, releasing out. What would Mrs. O'Malley do with her knowledge?

She grinned widely. "A captain! Can you believe it? And so quickly, too. You have a right to be proud of him, Katie. I never would have guessed he had that in him."

Relief poured through me, and I drank down half of my whiskey in one long swallow. When I finished, I looked up at her. "It took me a little while to see it, too," I admitted. "I judged him based on his outer appearances, on his situation. I didn't give him a chance to prove through actions what type of a man he really was."

She stretched in satisfaction. "Good thing he revealed himself before we kicked him out permanently. He'll be a good addition to the team. Solid. Dependable. A soldier." She gave her shoulders a roll. "Soon you two will have a nice little house with a yard out back. Who knows, you could have a little boy running around, shooting down enemies with his toy gun."

I flushed, looking down at my glass. "I think it's a bit too soon to talk about that," I murmured.

She took a sip of her whiskey. "Youth slips away, my girl. Take advantage while you can. Before you know it, the months turn into years, and it's all lost."

Eileen's conversation from yesterday rang in my ears, and I turned my glass in my fingers. I kept my tone even. "Did you ever think about having kids?"

Her voice became distant. "Sure I did, all the time. We were going to have twelve of them, Liam and I. An even dozen. Six boys and six girls. Our own little army. Had all the names picked out, knew how early we'd get them started on pellet guns. Had plans for a firing range out in back of my parents' house. They had plenty of land for us to build right next to them." Her face became wistful. "It would have been perfect. Just perfect. And what a father he'd have been. Stern, but patient."

She seemed lost in her vision of the past, probably baking up traditional soda bread while she packed bullets on the counter. An ideal daydream of domestic bliss.

I sipped my whiskey. "How about you and Jimmy?"

She gave a snort, looking up. "Jimmy? Sure, the sap talks about kids all the time. How he'd take the boy out to ball games and let the girl take ballet classes." She rolled her eyes. "What kind of a role model would he be? Whoring all day and staring at the TV all night? Can you imagine what any of his spawn would be like?" She pressed her lips into a line. "No. I will not bring any of his like into this world. And he'd damn better not get any of those sluts pregnant, either. That's the one thing I insist on."

I flushed, my face glowing with heat.

She nodded at me. "Oh, yes, I know all about his activities with the girls. How he *softens them up* for their roles." She shrugged. "It's fine with me. It gets them more comfortable for when we put the lights on them. Sometimes they even think they're doing it *for him*." She snorted. "As if he cares for any of them. Another one comes along and he's like a hyperactive terrier, leaping into every new crotch to sniff at it."

I thought again of Eileen, and I flushed. Had she been used and discarded like that? I admitted that I had some small hope that Jimmy had been honestly touched by her, that even from prison he might provide some support for her. But it seemed unlikely. Then again, if he truly craved kids, this might be his one chance to pass down his line.

Mrs. O'Malley took up the bottle and poured her glass full again, then topped off mine. Her face seemed shadowed, and I wondered just how cavalier she truly was about her husband's activities. In her mind, she had lost everything she had once dreamed of. She had hoped for a second chance at love when she married Jimmy, and he had let her down in every way possible. Surely that must have carved a hole into her.

She tapped her glass against mine, then took a long sip. "Let me give you some words of advice, Katie. Men are lions. They're stallions. Heck, they're rams. It's in their nature to go after every woman within range. It's built into their brains." She took down a swallow. "I'm sure you've seen it, in clubs. A hot woman saunters in in a red dress, and every guy turns his head. Doesn't matter if he's married or single, his dick gets hard. His body is built to want her."

I flushed. "Surely they can control the urge, though."

She raised an eyebrow. "You know what it's like when that urge powers through you, nearly submerges you with its force. You can barely think. And for us women, we're trained to be careful. After all, we get knocked up, we have to care for the brat for years. But the guy, he moves on to the next opportunity. It's in his best interest to mount everything that moves."

I looked down into my drink. "Maybe back in caveman days …"

She gave a wry grin. "Same brain, Katie. Same cock swinging between their legs. When that little head takes control, not much they can do but go along for the ride." She took down another swallow. "Liam tried to explain it to me one time. It's like being addicted to chocolate, and being in a chocolate factory tour. Someone's standing right in front of you, with the most delicious chocolate bar you've ever smelled. They bring it up to your lips. They rub it along the skin there, and your entire body craves it. All you have to do is part your lips. That's all, and it's yours." She gave a soft shrug. "There's only so long they can hold out."

My stomach twisted at the vision. "Surely some guys do hold out," I pointed out.

She gave a shrug, leaning on the bar. "Oh, sure, if they work nine to five in an accounting firm, where they never leave their cubicle. If they come straight home and plunk in front of the TV to watch SportsCenter all night long. There's no chocolate bars. There's hardly anything to tempt them."

She nudged her head toward Jimmy's office. "But in our world? With the women sauntering through every day, eager to prove their tits and ass are the best ever seen? Where the hot young thing wants nothing more than to pop her mouth over the guy's cock so she can get her big break? How many times do you think the guy says no before he finally sits back and lets her?"

I flushed, glancing toward the door. I wondered how long it would be before Sean got back.

She nodded at my look. "You're strong, Katie. I heard about you at the warehouse. You have fire in you. That's why I know you can make it through this. It's part of why Seamus decided to make Sean a captain – he knew you'd be at his side to be his rock. A man needs that in his life if he's going to succeed. Seamus has me. Sean has you." Her lips pressed together. "But you have to come to terms with this, Katie. It's going to happen. You have to be ready."

She looked down into her glass. "It'll hurt the first time. I won't lie to you. You'll convince yourself that somehow your guy will be different. He'll be the one to beat the odds and resist everything that makes him male." She shrugged. "But that's the point. He *is* male and this is part of it. We like them being male – and that has both bad and good with it. On the good side, of course is the sex." Her eyes went distant for a moment. "I can still remember the way Liam's lips tasted, and the feel of his body on top of me. God, Katie, the man was …" Her voice drifted away.

She gave herself a shake. "But there's a bad side to that drive, of course. That drive means they're a rooster in a barnyard of hens. They're a rutting dog in a kennel of bitches in heat. They just can't help it. They're driven to fuck, and they do it. Repeatedly."

My throat was tight, and I found I could only nod.

She finished off her second whiskey, then climbed from her stool. "Anyway, Katie, if you ever need to talk, I'm here for you. I've been through it all and came through fine on the other side. You'll do fine, too." She moved around the bar, pulling out the cutting board, sliding the knife from the block. "Pass me the limes, would you?"

Chapter 8

Sean glanced at me as he settled my helmet onto its shelf in the shed. Daylight was just fading through the open door, tracing shadows across his face. "You were quiet the whole way over here, Kay. Are you still stuck on what Bridgit said yesterday?"

I sighed, bringing a smile on my face. "I know. It's silly. And you were kind to listen to me for half the night. It just … she seemed so caught up in it all. It made me sorry for her."

He put his arm around me, leading me from the shed. "Well, if you're lucky, she'll be here again, and you two can commiserate."

I bumped him with my hip, and we walked through the door and down the hallway. I stepped into the room –

Sigh.

Mrs. O'Malley was sitting at the bar, her olive green dress making her look like a bulky sack of potatoes. Seamus was standing near the doorway talking to Jimmy, and both looked up as we came in. Seamus spoke up. "There you are, Sean. Got some errands for you to run." He stepped forward and handed Sean a piece of paper. "Stop by and pick these up from Thomas, then meet us at the warehouse in about an hour. Got to do our sweep; make sure the place is clean."

Sean took the list from him, nodding. "Sure thing, Seamus." He came back to me, giving me a long kiss. "We'll talk later," he promised. "Everything will be fine. Trust me."

I nodded, and he slipped down the back hallway.

Seamus turned to Mrs. O'Malley, and he nodded at his sister. "You call me if you need me."

Her voice held a hint of warmth in it that I rarely heard from her. "Sure thing, Seamus. You take care of yourself."

She glanced at Jimmy, then turned her gaze back to the limes before her. Her knife moved through them with quick efficiency.

Jimmy's shoulders slumped, and then he and Seamus were pushing their way through the door.

I came around to join Mrs. O'Malley. "So, we're getting close, huh? Tomorrow's Friday, and then the big day is here."

She glanced up at me, as if something had struck her. "Do you have a dress?"

I thought to my meager closet in the three-decker that I barely visited any more. "Well, there's the blue knit one I wore to my graduation party, and then there's this short, black one –"

She shook her head. "No, no, this is a formal event," she explained as if I were a toddler waddling up in my diapers. "The men will be in tuxes. Surely Jimmy –" She sighed, rolling her eyes, and dug her phone out of her purse. She pressed a button. "Seamus, Bridge here. Yeah, Katie didn't know about the formal dress. Probably means Jimmy didn't tell Sean either. Could you ... yeah ... OK, thanks." She hung up.

She looked me up and down. Her voice was flat. "Well, no way you're fitting into one of my dresses. I'll watch the bar tomorrow so Sean can take you out to Natick, to the mall. The Lord and Taylor there has some nice options. You'll see what strikes your fancy."

I knew what type of ending Saturday's event would actually bring, but still, a flare of interest rose in me. An elegant dress? Sean in a tux? Maybe we could at least enjoy the preparation, and a little of the party, before it all came to a crashing end.

She chuckled at the smile on my lips. "I know. Nothing quite like the sight of a man in a tux, right?" She sighed. "You should have seen Liam, when my cousin got married. He was the best man. God, he was handsome. I had on this hot number in emerald green – I was slim back then – and when he got me in that back room …" Her voice faded away.

Joey's voice was a slur. "Hey there, Kate –"

I nodded, grabbing the Bushmills and going around to his glass. I filled it back up and gave him a pat on the shoulder. He barely seemed to notice, his eyes glued to the set.

I came back around to behind the bar and began emptying the dishwasher. Bridgit picked up the phone and punched a button. "Yeah, it's me. I'm ready. OK, five minutes." She hung up again.

By the time I had finished settling the last glasses in their places, Ethan's taxi came to a stop before the bar. He gave a quick honk.

Mrs. O'Malley nudged her head toward the door. "That's for you, Katie." Her eyes shadowed for a moment. "I know you are strong. You're steel inside. Steel and diamond, like a tennis bracelet that can never be scratched or bent. You'll be fine."

I looked at her in confusion. "What do you mean?"

"Ethan's going to take you over to Sean's studio. He'll wait for you in the parking lot. I'll be here to talk, when you get back."

My brain could make no sense of her words. "You want me to go home?"

She gently pushed me toward my coat, and held it out for me. "It's like a band-aid, Katie. It's best to rip it off all at once, so you can get through it. Just remember, I'm here waiting for you."

A tumble of bees began whirling in the pit of my stomach, and I pulled on the jacket, walking across the bar and out the door. I climbed into the cab and Ethan pulled away from the curb without speaking. Surely this was all some sort of a mistake. Mrs. O'Malley's paranoias were reaching new levels, and now she was sure every man around her would cheat at the drop of a hat. Or maybe she was testing me.

I brightened, and I clung to the idea with both hands. Of course. That had to be it. She wanted to make sure I was steady and reliable before they brought us fully into the group. She wanted to make sure I wouldn't fold under pressure, or babble under stress. How I behaved would reflect on Sean, and would determine if the group did in fact get together on Saturday.

I laced my fingers in my lap, setting my shoulders. I could get through it. Whatever this test entailed, I would pass it with flying colors.

Ethan turned into our driveway and pulled to a stop in front of the stairs. He turned back to look at me. His elderly eyes seemed shadowed. "I'll be right here."

I gave him a smile. "Thanks, Ethan." I stepped out of the car into the cold dusk and crossed to the stairs. I turned my key in the lock and started up the stairs. I got to the second floor and turned the corner.

There was a noise up ahead, and I froze, flattening myself against the wall. I could see the edge of Sean's door at the opening to the third floor. There was a thump, and a giggle, and then it opened.

She was statuesque, curvaceous, built like a woman that men would risk kingdoms for. Her dress was crimson, the neckline dipping low into her cleavage, hugging her ample breasts. A golden key nestled deep within. The fabric caressed her down to her waist, then swept out over the curves of her hips.

She bent over to slip a matching high heel onto her foot. She turned to look back behind her, giving her ass a wiggle. "Out of time for more, eh, sweetie? That's all right, I'll see you again soon enough. Ciao." She blew a kiss into the studio, then turned to walk toward the stairs.

I couldn't move. I couldn't breathe. This couldn't be true. Not my Sean, not the man who had pledged his love to me, who trusted me with his life. Not the man I had risked everything for.

She sauntered to the stairs, taking the flight down as if it was a catwalk for a Maxim photo shoot. She glanced at me dismissively as she approached – and then she looked over again. Her mouth grew into a glistening smile.

"Why, you must be Katie! I recognize you now. Sean's told me all about you, of course. What a darling little thing! It's nice to finally meet you." She held out a perfectly manicured hand.

I took it, and shook it, my mind a blank.

Her grin grew rapturous, and she looked down at me with glowing eyes. "My, but aren't you a sweet thing. Those jeans must be just the item for hanging around at that bar. Such a pain to wear, though." She ran a hand down the silk of her dress. "I prefer something I can slide right out of, when the time is tight."

My throat constricted, and I leant against the wall.

She leant forward, dropping her voice. "But you know what I mean, don't you. Sean's like some sort of a god. He just looks at you, and your body flares to life. You can't help it. He's like chocolate dosed with every other aphrodisiac known to mankind."

Chocolate. My mind flailed to find some reason – any reason – that would explain this all. Maybe Mrs. O'Malley had set this all up. She'd sent this slut up to hang around Sean's room as if she'd been with him. It was all a setup.

She hadn't been, of course. This was a test.

My breathing slowed a bit, and my heart stepped down its speed from Monaco Grand Prix level to simply racing on the Mass Pike. I strove to keep my voice steady. "I don't think I caught your name."

Her grin deepened, showing sharp canines. "Francesca. I'm surprised Sean hasn't mentioned me to you. He's a naughty boy."

A flare of jealousy coursed through me, but I tamped it down with deliberate effort. This was all a hoax. I just had to get through it. "I'm sure he is," I agreed.

She leant forward, dropping her voice. "I can think of the ideal punishment. Get him into that bed of his and make him pleasure you all night long. You know he can do it. And then the next morning he's as fresh as an alpha wolf. Up and eager for more."

I gripped the bannister behind me. The O'Malleys listened in on us, of course. That's how they knew this, to test me. She'd been briefed well.

Francesca's eyes gleamed. "And that trio of freckles, on his hip – they're like an arrow. Pointing straight down at his cock. I swear, there are few men hung like Sean."

My heart was racing faster again, and it was all I could do to keep my breathing steady. Somehow she knew that. Maybe Seamus had spotted it during their beating of him. Sure, he'd still had his shirt and jeans on when I'd found him, but –

She gave a low laugh. "And, of course, there's his love of photography."

I closed my eyes. It couldn't be true. Had I been stupid this entire time? What did I really know about him? With all these hot girls coming and going, maybe it was natural for him to take what was offered, to give in when one of them leant forward and offered a rosy nipple on an ample bosom. Maybe –

I shook my head, clinging to a tiny thread of sanity. This was all a test. Sean wasn't even up there. I just had to make it through this, report back to Mrs. O'Malley, and Saturday's final event would go on as planned. Sean and his crew would round up the entire pornography ring. We could move on.

I took in a deep breath.

There was a creak from above us.

Sean's head poked out from the door, and I stepped down a stair so he couldn't see me. He called out, "Francesca, you still there?"

Her face brightened with satisfaction, and she glanced at me before replying. "I'm here, sweetie."

"Remember about tomorrow night. I need you ready for me on time."

"Of course, darling. See you then."

The door swung shut with a click.

I leaned against the bannister, the world weaving.

She gave me a wink. "Well, I'm off. Lots to do before Friday. I'm sure we'll run into each other again soon.

Ciao!" She turned with a swirl of crimson, her hips swaying as she moved into the shadows.

The click of her heels faded into the distance, and all I could hear was the deep inhales, the shaky exhales. The world still ebbed and flowed; the bannister was slick beneath my sweaty palms. Time became lost.

There was a thump from above, and I realized in a panic that Sean could be leaving at any moment. He couldn't find me here. Not now, not when my mind was such a chaotic whirl. I scampered down the stairs, nearly tripping, and when I came out Ethan was waiting for me, the taxi still running. I yanked open the door and tumbled into the back seat.

The moment I closed the door he eased away from the curb. We rode in silence for a minute. When he spoke, his voice was low and gentle. "I'm sorry, Katie. I saw the woman come out. She was … well, I see why Sean gave in."

The words wrenched a hole in my heart, and I twined my fingers together. I would not cry. I would not cry.

I blinked, and we'd pulled up in front of the bar. I knew I should reach for the door handle, but I couldn't bring myself to do it. Sean would be coming back here soon. He'd walk in, and I'd look into his eyes, and …

Ethan gave a quick honk on the horn and waved his hand when Mrs. O'Malley looked up. She immediately strode around the bar. She pointed at Joey, said something, pointed at the counter, and then she was stepping through the door. She went around the other side and slid into the seat next to me. Ethan pulled out into the traffic without a word.

Mrs. O'Malley put out a beefy arm to draw me in, and I collapsed against her bulk, breathing in that jasmine-and-orange scent of hers. I couldn't think. Nothing made sense. I was lost, and the world was closing in around me, shrinking down to a mote of dust.

The taxi drew to a stop, and I looked out. It was the O'Malley's house. Mrs. O'Malley stepped out of the taxi, came around to my door, and helped me out. She waved to Ethan, and then she guided me up to the front door. In a moment, I was settled onto the dark green tapestry couch. She went into the kitchen for a moment, then returned with a pair of thick, oversized highball glasses. Each glass held a single, large, round ice cube about the size of a baseball.

I stared at mine as she returned to the kitchen again. It was like a crystal ball, with delicate fissures and bubbles within its frozen water body. It held my fortune within it. And what could that be? After all I had gone through, had I trusted in a man who was untrustworthy?

A nervous giggle ran through me. I was trusting in a professional liar. His whole purpose in life was to deceive people, to convince them he was something he was not. Why should I be any different? With that kind of a talent, surely he could have any woman he wanted, and convince each one that she was the most important thing in his life. He could live the male fantasy – a new girl every night, a continual rotation of fresh, nubile bodies, there for him to use and enjoy.

Tears slid down my cheeks, and Mrs. O'Malley stepped in front of me. She poured my glass full – perhaps a third of the bottle. Then she filled her own glass. She put the bottle down onto the oak coffee table, then leant over to tap her glass against mine. "Men are pigs," she offered. "Us women always have to stick together against them. Always been like that, always will be."

She took a long drink, and I mirrored her action. The thick whiskey coursed through me, sturdied me, and I took in a deep breath.

Her voice was steady and warm. "We've all been there, Katie. Sean's just a guy – and there's many who are far worse. Look at Roman Polanski. He was in his mid-forties when he raped a thirteen year old girl. Thirteen! He flees to France, where they all fuck anything that moves, and he's still praised as a great man. Sure, he fucked a girl barely into puberty. That's OK, he's a guy. Guys do those sorts of things."

She took another drink. "How about Woody Allen? When he was fifty-six, he started sleeping with the girl who he had raised as his stepdaughter. There he is, a father figure, someone she looks up to and trusts, and when she turns nineteen he's sucking her tits. But that's all right, of course, because he's a famous guy. It's what guys do. They like to touch young girls, and we cheer them on. Heck, it's in their nature."

I took another drink of my whiskey. I felt sick. Soul-deep sick.

My phone rang, and I pulled it out. It was Sean. I hit the "reject" button.

Mrs. O'Malley patted my arm. "It'll get better, honey. I know it seems dark right now, but a few days will put it into perspective. It's why I thought you should get through it sooner rather than later. Give you time to build up your skin. He's still the same Sean he's always been. He's just a man. It's what they are."

She gave a snort. "Look at Allen. He's been praised for staying with his step-daughter for so long. Praised! As if continuing to sleep with the girl who wholly trusted him was an admirable thing? 'What a good guy, he's still

willing to climb on top of that sexy young daughter of his.'
She couldn't even *drink* yet, when he started sticking his
cock into her."

My phone rang again, and I pressed hard on the OFF
button. The noise cut off into silence.

Mrs. O'Malley ran her thumb over her ice ball, giving it
a spin. "Life can suck for a woman. Look at Demi Moore.
She marries Freddie Moore when she's eighteen. The guy
is twelve years older than her and had already been
fucking her a while. Nobody blinks an eye. It's just what
guys do, fuck under-age girls." Her gaze darkened. "Later
on, she is interested is Ashton Kutcher. He's twenty-five,
so far from a child. But she's older than him." She downed
another gulp. "And the world goes mad! How could she!
She's older than him! He can't know what he's doing!
She's using him!"

Her phone burst into life, and she looked down at it for
a moment before hitting a button and bringing it to her ear.
"Yeah, Seamus?"

She listened for a long moment, nodding. She glanced
over at me. "Yeah, she's here. We're fine."

Another murmur of talk, and she pursed her lips. "Hold
on." She hit the mute button. "Sean wants to talk with you.
Make sure you're OK."

I huddled back into the couch. "I don't want him here."

She gave me a pat. "I know, sweetie. But you know
how these guys are. If he thinks you're not OK, he's liable
to come storming over to make sure I'm not holding you
hostage or something."

I flushed. That would be just like Sean, too. I put my
glass down on the table.

She looked at me carefully. "You sure you can talk to
him calmly?"

I nodded, taking in a deep breath. "I'll get rid of him."

She gazed at me for another moment, then nodded. "You're a good girl." She hit the mute button again to deactivate it. "All right, put him on." She handed the phone over.

Sean's voice was tense with worry. "Kay? Are you there?"

My throat tightened at hearing his voice. Overlaid with it was the sound of his voice calling out of his studio after Francesca.

He'd slept with her.

In our bed.

I forced a coolness into my voice that I wouldn't have thought possible. "I'm here Sean. I'm fine. Mrs. O'Malley and I are just chatting about the party on Saturday."

There was a pause, and his voice seemed to ease slightly when he spoke again. "I can be by in about ten –"

"No, no, that's all right," I assured him. "I'm enjoying our chat. I think I'll spend the night. A girl's night out, that sort of thing."

His voice was still laced with worry. "Are you sure? It'd be no trouble at all."

"We're having fun, drinking and talking. I really shouldn't be on a bike like this. I'll sleep it off here."

I looked over at Mrs. O'Malley, then said into the phone. "Oh, I have to go. Talk to you later."

"All right … if you're sure … I'm here for you, Kay, so call if you need me."

"Sure. Bye." I hung up the phone and handed it back.

Mrs. O'Malley nodded with satisfaction. "I knew you had it in you, Katie. I knew you'd be able to handle the truth. We need more people like you on our team, Katie. Women are tougher than men, you know. We have to be. We shoulder the burdens, and they just fuck themselves out of thinking about things. We're the one left to pick up the pieces and make it work."

I stared into my drink. "You're right, Mrs. O'Malley. Pick up the pieces."

She patted me on the shoulder. "Call me Bridgit, lass."

I nodded. She was my friend. She was the only one who told it like it was. "Bridgit," I agreed.

She reached over to the stereo on the side wall, and hit the on button. Another click, and the Dubliners burst out of the speakers, filling the room with lively, rich music.

As I was goin' over the far famed Kerry mountains,

I met with Captain Farrell, and his money he was counting.

I first produced me pistol and I then produced me rapier,

Saying: "Stand and deliver, for you are a bold deceiver!"

Bridgit nudged her head at the speakers. "There you have it. Men lusting for adventure, for glory, for that rush. It's what they do. In our modern world they can't go out and slay dragons. So all they have left to prove their manhood is the conquest of women. The younger, the better."

She patted my hand. "Just make the best of it you can, lass. Enjoy the time you have. Don't fuss too much when he goes out. It's for the best. Really."

I blinked away the tears which were starting up afresh, and drowned myself in my whiskey.

Chapter 9

I groaned, pulling the covers higher over my head. It was pitch black in the room, but it felt as if blindingly bright lightning was streaming through my veins. Thunder growled in an iron ball rolling from one ear to the other. Surely I'd been kidnapped and put onto some sort of a slaver's ship, heading around Cape Horn. I needed to sleep for another twenty-four hours. Maybe then I'd be capable of standing.

Had we really finished the entire bottle?

A tapping noise wiggled its way through the swirling chaos of my mind. I wearily pried my eyes open, looking at the door. The clock on the stand read two a.m. Good God.

The tapping came again, from the other wall.

I turned – and nearly filled the room with a piercing scream. It took every ounce of effort to bite down on the sound, to bury my mouth in the blanket before me.

A man was looking in from the other side of my window.

My heart beat in a frenzy, and I shook my head in disbelief. Big mistake. The world swirled and spun, and I nearly emptied the contents of my stomach right there. It took me a moment to remember that my room overlooked the attached garage. Undoubtedly whoever it was was standing on that garage's roof.

And I had no doubt who it was.

Sean's face was tense with concern. He dropped onto one knee, then pointed at the latch on the window.

I pulled the blanket against my chest. I didn't want him in here. I just wanted to curl up and let the world go away again.

His brows creased.

I realized, if I didn't do something, that he might decide to take action. I probably wouldn't like his choice. I had to get him to go away.

I pulled the blanket around me like a queen's cloak and carefully climbed out of bed. The floor tilted beneath me. I lurched, holding onto the bed for a long moment. When I'd gotten a sense of the angle of attack, I made my way unsteadily over to the window. I leaned my forehead against the cool glass for a moment.

That felt good.

There was a tapping, and my eyes popped open. When had I closed them? I looked up, and Sean's gaze was there before me. He now looked more amused than worried.

A coursing of anger flowed through me. How dare he think this was funny! I reached up to pop the latch open, then stepped back.

He slid up the window, eased in through the opening, then shut it behind him. He turned with a smile, then stepped toward me with his arms out.

I stepped back, pulling the blanket tighter around me.

His eyes focused on my face. "Kay? I think you might have had a little too much to drink."

The words tumbled out of me before I could rein them in. "Where were you this afternoon?"

He paused, and his tone was more careful when he spoke again. "You were at the bar when we discussed it. I went with Seamus and Jimmy to the warehouse. We were working on preparations for the whole evening."

Bitterness coursed through me, and my tone grew hard. "You mean you never went back to the studio?"

He stilled. "How did you know I was there?"

The outrageousness of his question burst through me like a spark in a powder house. My voice rose into a shriek. "How do I know? Is it really that fucking important how I know?"

There was a thump down the hall, and the padding of footsteps, then a knock came at the door. Bridgit's voice was steady. "Katie, dear, are you all right?"

I took in a deep breath, willing myself to be calm. I would get through this, and get him out. "I'm fine, Bridgit. Just having a brief chat with Sean. He'll leave in a minute."

There was support in Bridgit's voice. "That's all right, Katie. You call me if you need me." The footsteps faded back toward her room.

I turned again to Sean, reining in my volume. The anger still flared from every word.

"I saw her, Sean. I saw *Francesca*."

He flinched at the name, then glanced at the door. His gaze hardened for a moment. I giggled to myself. Apparently the man had figured out who my guardian angel was, who had warned me of his evil ways. Not that it would do *him* any good. He was in trouble now, boy!

The world tilted left, sashayed right, and settled at an oblique angle.

Sean's gaze gentled as he brought it back to me. "Look, Kay, I can explain."

I hunched my blankets closer over my shoulders. "I'm waiting."

"She's … she's my parole officer, Kay."

I blew out my breath. "Jesus, is that the best you can come up with?"

He glanced again at the door. "I swear it, Kay. She's my parole officer. Remember, I'm an ex-felon? I have to meet with a parole officer as part of my conditions. I have to be available for random checks."

I snorted. "And she just happens to look like a high class hooker?"

He flushed. "Francesca is … well …"

I took a step toward him. I didn't want to know. I didn't want to know. Despite my best efforts, the words skidded through my mind, flaring sparks as they went, and burst through my lips.

"Did you sleep with her?"

His gaze was dark, shadowed, and for a long moment time hung still.

His voice was hoarse. "Kay –"

I stumbled back against the bed. Somehow, even in my most desolate depths, I had still held out hope that this was an elaborate ruse of some sort. Surely it was a convoluted plot by Seamus and Bridgit to test my loyalty.

Apparently there was no need to invent the test material.

Sean reached for me again, and I pulled back from him as if he were a red-hot poker. My voice was a hiss. "Don't you touch me."

He dropped to a knee, his tone rough. "It was only one time, Kay. Before you and I had met. I had just arrived here, she was assigned to me, and we went out for drinks. I was single, she was eager, and … it just happened, Kay. The next morning I knew it was wrong, and I told her that, in no uncertain terms. But she …" He sighed, running a hand through his hair. "She's having trouble accepting that."

His gaze grew focused, and he stared up at me. "I swear to you, Kay, that from the moment you came into my life, there has been nobody else. Francesca means nothing to me. She's there in an official capacity – nothing more."

I crossed my arms. "And I'm sure you're just so sad to have her visiting you all the time."

His lips pressed into a line. "Kay, if I could have switched to someone else, I would have. But with everything that's going on ..." He glanced again toward the door.

I thought of Jimmy and Bridgit on the other side of that door, of the pornography ring that stretched across many states. I thought of all the girls and women who relied on us to see this through.

The heated energy faded from me, dwindling like a cigarette snuffed in a bed of sand. I slumped back to sit on the bed.

Sean's voice was hoarse. "Kay, I swear it on my mother. I swear it on my aunt. I'll swear on anything you wish. There was only that one, foolish, drunken night with Francesca. From the moment I've met you, I've been true to you."

I looked down at my hands. He seemed sincere. And I'd known he'd had girlfriends before me. Heck, I had been with Derek for several years, which was certainly more serious than a one-night fling. Would I expect Sean to get wildly jealous if we ran into Derek some evening? Or would I expect him to trust in me, to know that Derek was simply a man from my past, a man who could no longer impact what Sean and I shared?

My stomach tumbled, roiled, and Sean swept me up, carrying me over to the window. He got the window up and my head over the ledge just in time for the contents of my stomach to empty. The spasms shook me for long minutes, and he held my hair back, soothing me. When at last I was done he propped me against the window for a moment, stepping through the door and into the bathroom. He came back with a moist washcloth, using it to wipe down my face and mouth.

He put the washcloth down on the bureau, then came back to stand before me. His gaze held tension in it.

"Kay, I know I should have told you about Francesca. And I'm sorry. She's just so … volatile. I didn't know what she'd say or do. I thought, if I could just keep her away from you for a little while, until we got settled, that I could get transferred away from her. You wouldn't ever have to deal with her."

I held his gaze. "You chose to lie to me."

He blanched. "I was trying to protect –"

I took a step forward. "I'm an adult," I pointed out. "I can choose for myself how to handle issues. But if you're going to lie to me, this isn't going to work."

He took in a long breath, then let it out. "You're right. Of course. I'm sorry, Kay. I'm so sorry. I was trying to keep you from being hurt, not to hurt you even further."

He took a step, coming in front of me. He raised a hand toward my face, then stopped, hesitant. "Tell me what to do, Kay. Tell me how I can make this better." His voice grew hoarse. "I love you, Kay. I don't want to lose you. What should I do?"

I looked up into his eyes, into the tangle of emotions which lay there. At their core shone through a steady, golden glow of love. The warmth of it eased through my tired body, soothed the aches in my muscles.

My voice whispered out of me. "I want to go home."

A sigh eased out of him, then his arms were drawing me in against his chest. I went passively, resting against his sturdy muscles. His embrace was like granite, like immovable walls, and I was safe within their protection.

Time faded away.

At last he wrapped an arm around my waist and moved me to the door. We stepped through into the hallway. There was a noise, and Bridgit was standing in her bedroom doorway, a paisley robe wrapped around her body. Her eyes were gleams in the dark night.

"Katie, are you sure you want to go?"

I nodded. "I'm sure, Bridgit. Thank you for everything. I appreciate it a lot."

She pursed her lips. "All right, lass. You change your mind, the room's all ready for you."

Sean helped me down the stairs, bringing me over to sit on the couch. He slid each of my boots on. Then he took up the jacket which was laid over the arm of the couch. After he zipped it up, he drew me to my feet, then pressed open the front door. His Triumph was parked immediately in front of the house.

He looked at the bike, then at me. "Are you all right to ride? I can call a cab, if you'd rather."

I shook my head. "It's not far. I'll be fine."

He kept his gaze on me for a moment longer, then nodded. We put on our helmets, climbed onto the bike, and in a moment we were drifting through the dark streets of Worcester.

It seemed the blink of an eye before I was back on those stairs, back at the spot where only hours before I'd been confronted by Helen of Troy, by the goddess who drove men to madness. My stomach tilted, and Sean steadied me, helping me up the remaining steps.

I stumbled into the apartment, and he helped me with my jacket, locking the door behind us. I looked over at the bed and a shudder coursed through me. "You didn't –"

"No," he responded shortly. "We went to her apartment. And this was before I even got the studio. Today was the only time she's been here."

I drew my eyes to the photographs on the walls, and my mind went back to the session we'd had, to the connection which had transcended words. My mouth went dry. "And did you –"

"No," he stated again, stepping to me. "You're the only one I've ever done that with. I'd never felt inspired like that with anybody else. My photos were all of still lifes – the Adirondack chairs, the Triumph, even the burning building in its way." He gazed at me with that look which could melt me. "And then you came into my life." He reached out a hand to trace it down my cheek. "God, Kay, I would never do anything to hurt you."

My throat tightened up. "But Bridgit said … she said that for men it's like being in a chocolate factory, and the most delicious chocolate bar is being pressed right up against your lips. All you have to do is open your mouth. How long can you resist that?"

The corner of his mouth quirked up, and he shook his head. "Ah, Kay, it's not like that for me at all." He drew me in so my body pressed against his, his arms securely around me. He gazed down into my eyes.

"We are a team, Kay. We rely on each other. We are like a pair of tightrope walkers, walking on parallel lines stretching across the Grand Canyon. It's a long way to go, and we are holding hands. It's our holding of hands which is keeping us in balance."

He pressed a gentle kiss to my cheek. "If I let go, Kay, to turn to someone else, I hurt us both. You can fall. I can fall. My attention is no longer fully, wholly, on our relationship. I could easily damage it beyond all salvation."

He gave a wry smile. "Some might think that an affair doesn't hurt the main couple. That it's somehow separate from the core relationship. But how could it be? We all only have a finite amount of energy. We have a finite amount of waking hours. The time and attention paid to the extra partner is all time and attention not invested in the main relationship. That can't be gotten back."

His gaze held mine. "And surely you deserve a man who is there for you wholly. Someone whose loyalties aren't divided, whose thoughts aren't distracted." His gaze stilled, settled. "I swear to you, Kay, I am that man."

He swept me up in his arms and carried me over to the bed, gently laying me onto it. He pulled off my boots, then removed his own. He climbed into bed next to me, laying on his side, just gazing at me.

His voice was hoarse. "I will never let go of your hand, Kay."

I closed my eyes, and the world swirled away.

Chapter 10

I smiled in sheer joy as we pulled into the parking lot at the Natick Mall. The weather was stunning, with drifting white clouds dancing across a robin's-egg-blue sky. The ride down the Mass Pike had been fantastic. Now we were going to go shopping for an elegant gown. Life couldn't get much better.

We parked the bike, tucked away our helmets, then walked hand-in-hand into the mall. I blushed, feeling like a high schooler on her first date. We had been immersed in the seedy bar for so long, in the slime and filth of all it encompassed, that to be out strolling in a mall felt almost sublime.

He looked over at the Macy's sign. "Let's try there first, shall we?"

I went willingly. Spending the day shopping for dresses with the most handsome man I'd ever met suited me to a T. I grinned at a pink-and-green ruffly thing he held up, then rolled my eyes at a pumpkin-orange outfit which barely covered my rear.

I gave him a teasing grin. "Looks like something *Francesca* would wear."

He took my hand. "Kay, I'm sorry you had to meet her like that. When I arrived in Worcester, I was briefed by the vice group here. She latched onto me immediately and volunteered to be my point of contact. She'd pose as my parole officer so we could pass information back and forth. Things got … a bit out of hand that first night."

I waved the orange dress in front of his eyes. "Seems she's become rather fond of some of those *roles* she's playing during her undercover vice stings."

His gaze shadowed. "I've seen it before, Kay. It's a hard line to navigate, playing at being a prostitute. The woman has to be convincing. It's not too long before she's affected by the filth of that world. Men constantly groping at her ... treating her like an object, not a person ... it's very damaging. Over time she often does what real prostitutes tend to do – she finds a way to see herself as the one with power."

"Oh? And how is that?"

"She looks at the interaction as one where she is in control. She shows more cleavage, and the guy is eating out of her hand. She lets him look, and he'll do anything she wants. She finds a way to view the situation as one where she's the person pulling the strings, and he's just a crude animal."

I nodded. "I guess I can see that. But surely the brass doesn't normally let the vice cops get that emotionally damaged?"

"You're right. The police are very aware that this can happen. It's why they keep rotations short, so women aren't sunk in that world for long periods of time." He pressed his lips into a line. "Apparently every time they try to transfer Francesca out, she makes a fuss. Talks about all the connections she has. I think she's been in too long. It's got a grip on her that she can't shake. And I think, over time, that the fallout on her world view will only get worse."

I put the orange dress back onto its rack. "Well, I hope she can get out soon. It sounds like a rough place to be."

I nudged my head toward the main mall, giving myself a shake. "In any case, these outfits clearly aren't right for what you have planned. Let's move on, and see what we can find for *our* little undercover work. So that we can finish it – and get out – as soon as possible."

I indulged him while we tried another few stores, but I knew where I'd find my choice. It would either be Lord & Taylor or Neiman Marcus. I'd spent the morning paging through their websites and salivating over the options. Now to see what they had in stock in my size, and how I looked in them.

We stepped into Lord & Taylor first, making our way into the formal wear area. A crimson dress with black lace overlay caught my eye, and I stepped forward to it, running my hand along the fabric.

A woman's voice, dripping with disapproval, sounded from over my shoulder. "Can I help you with something?"

I turned. Her hair was brownish-orange, in tight curls around her head, and her navy blue suit jacket gave her a stiff, formal carriage. Her grey eyes pierced through me as she took in my leather jacket, jeans, and boots.

Her sigh could probably be heard throughout the mall. "Window shopping, I assume?"

I bit down my annoyance. "I was wondering if this dress came in –"

She shook her head. "I don't think so, dearie. You'll probably find things your style down in Sears."

Sean slid his arm around my waist. He flashed me a smile. "That's all right, honey. This dress here is only three-sixty. Seamus said we should get you something costing at least five hundred, so you aren't trumped by those women from Boston or Providence. I'm sure Neiman Marcus can offer a better selection in that price range."

The saleswoman's grey eyes popped open, then glistened with greed. "I think I have just the thing –"

Sean shook his head genially. "I'm sure you have many far more important things to do. Have a nice day." He gave her a smile, then turned me and guided me out into the hallway.

I grinned at him as we made our way down the main strip. "Seamus didn't really say that, did he?"

He gave me a gentle kiss. "Seamus said you should get whatever you wanted. He's footing the bill for the whole party, as the host. It is completely up to you what you wear, my darling. With everything you've been through, you deserve this dress." His voice grew hoarse. "You deserve far more, but we'll start with the dress."

We reached Neiman Marcus, and in a moment we were in their formal gown area. I looked around in pleasure. It was like being in a dream world. There were flowing dresses in ebony and lace, shimmering concoctions in soft ivory, gathered-bodice creations in sea green, and any other combination I could imagine.

"I want to try them all," I breathed in wonder.

A woman with soft blonde curls skimming her shoulders, in a rose colored dress, stepped forward. "Looking forward to a big day, I see! I'm here to help in any way I can. What did you have in mind?"

A strapless black dress with a lace overlay caught my eye. "That one, I think."

Another was the softest of pink, with embroidered designs all along its length. "And that one …"

Then there was the rich burgundy, almost violet, with intricate beading. I sighed, looking at it. "Ohhhhh."

I peered at the price tag, and then flushed. It was far beyond the five hundred dollar mark. "On the other hand – "

Sean put his hand over mine, smiling. "We'll try that one, too."

I glowed with excitement as she led us over to a private dressing room. There was a carpeted pedestal in the middle of the area, and mirrors surrounded me on three sides. I felt like a princess preparing for my wedding day. The blonde hung each dress on its own hook on the back wall, then looked between us. "Did you need any help with the fittings?"

Sean flashed her a smile. "Oh, I think we'll be all set."

Her cheeks pinkened. "Well, you just call if you need anything." She stepped back and closed the door.

I flushed as Sean took a step toward me. I pitched my voice low. "You can't be thinking …"

He nudged his head at the pedestal. "Up where you belong," he murmured. "Let's do this right."

I stepped obediently onto the round. He came up behind me, then stepped slightly to the side so I could see his eyes. He ran a hand along the curve of my ass, and his gaze went smoky, passion building within it.

His voice was thick. "The jacket first."

I brought my fingers to the zipper, easing the metal down slowly, my movements reflected all around me in the mirrors. His hand squeezed my ass, then slid around to caress my inner thigh. I moaned softly, arching at the sensation, then I slid the jacket off my arms, dropping it on the floor behind me.

He continued to stroke my inner thigh. "Next your top."

My top was violet, clingy, and I had to peel it up and over me. When I could see again, there were reflections of me in my black lace bra on all sides. Sean's gaze moved from angle to angle, then back to the real me. "God, you are beautiful, Kay."

I flushed with the praise, my body glowing under his perusal.

He motioned with his head. "Now the jeans."

I removed my boots first, balancing on one foot to pull off the other, then switching. For the jeans I slid them slowly down my legs, watching the motion from all sides. By the time they reached the ground Sean's bulge was quite evident. I reached out a hand. "Maybe it's time –"

He slid his hand up against my sex, giving me a long stroke, and words failed me. I wondered if he could feel my moisture soaking through my panties to his fingers, calling to him.

He stepped away from me, winking. "It's time for dress number one," he commented. "Perhaps this black lace one."

I drew in a deep breath, my breasts swelling out against my bra, as he brought over the dress and held the bottom hem of it out for me. I slid it down over my head, letting him ease the fabric into position, and then I turned.

It was beautiful.

The lace was off-shoulder, coming together to a beautifully decorated bodice area. It drew in at the waist, then cascaded in tumbling waterfalls to my feet.

I turned around in awe, staring at myself from all sides. "Sean, it's amazing!"

His eyes were steady on me. "*You* are amazing," he corrected. "This brings out what was already within you." He drew his eyes up to mine. "So you like?"

I nodded. "I like, definitely."

He stepped forward. "One down, two to go."

I put up my hands, and he drew the fabric carefully over my head. He hung the dress up on the hook, then came back over to me.

"Look into your eyes," he whispered.

I did as he requested, taking in their deep brown color, the flecks of gold within them.

He stepped up against my back, slid his hand around to the top of my panties, and then two fingers delved in, moving easily through the slick moistness to slide against my clit.

My eyes went wide with surprise, then smoky with heated desire. The moan nearly erupted out of me before I swallowed it. I leant back against him. "Oh, Sean, I …"

He stepped back, smiling at me. Then he moved over to the pale pink dress.

The fabric sliding down my body, his hands guiding it, sent tremors through every part of my soul. I was being caressed, desired, wanted, and it seemed that we were going the wrong way. I wanted the clothes coming off!

He chuckled as he settled the fabric in place. "Soon," he murmured. The movement of his lips, reflected in all those mirrors, sent my nipples peaking into hardness against my bra.

The dress was somehow more stunning than the first. The pale color shimmered against my skin, and the embroidery was exquisite. I turned in a full circle, awestruck by the beauty. "I didn't realize dresses like this even existed," I sighed.

"So you like it?"

"Yes, yes."

"Right then." He stepped forward and bent down, his hands starting at my ankles, caressing the skin there. They slid up, and I wanted those hands to leave off with the fabric, get on with the much more important things in life.

But they only skimmed my hips, slid along my sides, and brought the dress over my head. He hung it on its hanger, then replaced it in its position on the wall.

"And the final one," he commented, bringing over the burgundy dress.

It was almost too much to take, his fingers along my neck, their tracery down my back, their gentle caress of my ass as he clothed me. I wanted to be unclothed, untamed, undone …

Then the fabric was over my head and I looked.

Words failed me.

The other two dresses had been beautiful – spectacular, even. But in this, the woman in the mirror was a goddess. The burgundy color shimmered and changed with the angle of light. The fabric clung to me with gentle tenderness, curling in at my waist, swelling out around my breasts. The beadwork was beyond compare. I had never seen the like, not even in those art museum paintings, not in any movie.

Sean's eyes shone. "This one, I think."

I nodded mutely. I couldn't even turn. I could only stare at the reflection, not even fully aware that was me.

Sean nodded in satisfaction. "Stay right there."

He moved to the door, opening it slightly and calling out. "Excuse me, miss?"

The blonde was with us in just a moment. Her eyes widened as she came into the room, and she walked around me, nodding in approval. "Yes, that's it. That's just the one. Look how it brings out the color in her lips, her cheeks. It's perfect."

Sean ran a hand along my hip, and I held back the tremor of need which coursed through me.

His lips quirked into a smile. "I'll be in a full tuxedo, of course. Do you have a bowtie in a matching color?"

She nodded. "Of course, sir. Just a moment." She hurried off, and sure enough, she returned with the perfect item.

He pulled out his wallet, then handed her a credit card. "We'll take all three dresses, plus the bowtie."

I turned in surprise. "Sean, no! I couldn't!"

He looked up at me. "You can, and you will. Seamus is putting all expenses for the party on his corporate card. The more you spend, the less he has left to hire his sharks."

I looked at the dresses hanging behind me, then back at the one caressing my form. It was too much to take in.

Sean looked to the saleswoman. "Take your time in running up the charge – we might be a while in getting dressed again."

The blonde's eyes twinkled, and she nodded. "Just come out when you're ready." She turned and left the room, closing the door behind her.

I shook my head, looking down at the elegant material. "But Sean, where would I even wear them?"

He stepped behind me, starting his hands at my ankles, slowly sliding his fingers along my delicate flesh, up to the tender spot behind my knees. "Oh, I don't know. We could set up a photo shoot …"

A thrill of desire coursed through me. His hands rose higher, sliding over my thighs, curving around my ass.

I let out a shuddering moan.

He tsked at me. "Oh, we can't have that. Let me see." He brought the bowtie up to my mouth, gently folding it in half so the visible side was safely within the center. "Here, hold this. It will keep your mouth … occupied."

He settled it between my lips, then brought the tie's ends around the back of my head to seal it into place.

He laced his fingers into my hair, then used it to raise my head. "Look into your eyes," he instructed. "But take in the whole scene. Every time you see this dress in the mirror, every time you see that bowtie on me, I want you to remember this."

The front of the dress still hung fully down, demure, elegant, but I could feel when he again uncovered my ass, pulling the back section of fabric to my hips.. His fingers slid around to the sides, and in a moment he had eased my panties down to mid-thigh. I could feel the cool, delicious air on my ass, and the panties' fabric held my legs together, as secure as any bond.

His fingers slid back up to my moist core, tickling along my clit, and I moaned against the silk in my mouth. My body arched, my breasts pressing out on the burgundy fabric, stretching it.

He brought his head by my ear. "Ahhhh, there you go, You are nearly dripping now. And you are glowing, my love. Glowing with beauty and desire."

I could see it in my eyes, the shine, the golden, inner glow which radiated from them. My entire body seemed alive, sparkling, radiating joy.

There was the noise of a zipper, then of foil, and the pressure of his cock against my moist opening. His hand around my waist held me up as my knees wobbled. I held my gaze on my eyes, but I could still see, all around me, the angles of our union. I could see the ripples of his well-defined arm muscle where he held me, the firmness of his legs where I leant against them, and the subtle movements of his fingers under the dress's fabric ...

He slid them, dancing against me, slick. My moan grew more insistent, my body pressing back against his of its own volition.

The barest inch of his head pressed within me, and my breath left me.

I wanted him. I wanted him.

The hand on my hip slid up to caress my breast, the other pressed more insistently against my clit, and his cock retreated, then slid in again, teasing me, tormenting me, with just the barest presence.

I needed him deep within me. I needed him all, filling me …

My voice was a soft groan. "God, Sean, I …"

He brought his lips to my neck, sucking, and I shuddered in delicious agony. I could see his eyes in one mirror, passion-filled, steady. In another mirror I gazed at his thick, dark hair, and I wanted to grab it with both hands, to force him down to the ground, to grind into him until we both lost all control. But all I could do was watch in the mirrors, watch the elegant dress, the controlled presentation, while beneath its layers passions were roiling, fermenting, barely within control.

His voice teased into my ear. "Do you like it when I …"

His fingers squeezed hard on my nipple, his other moved to grab a hold of my hip for leverage, and he sunk himself fully within me, the pressure filling and expanding me. I groaned against his tie, and only his arm around my chest and his steady body behind me kept me upright.

My word was a muffled sigh. "Yesssss …."

His voice grew thick. "And maybe you like it when I …"

He retreated, then slid in again, his hard cock pressing into me, faster this time, and my breath came in stutters. It was all I could do to keep my eyes open.

His voice was a growl. "And when I …"

It was deeper, harder, impaling me to my core, and my nipples stood out hard-edged from within the dress. I could feel my moisture dripping down my leg, shielded from view within the burgundy beading.

His hand slipped within the fabric of my bodice, sliding against my breast, and his mouth found my neck. He sucked hard, the muscles of my sex contracted sharply, and his groan shook me.

"God, Kay, you are … you are …"

His movements sped up, grew harder, and I arched against him, my eyes barely taking in the elegantly attired woman who stood before me. The side views revealed Sean's hard body in its glorious motion, everything I could ever want in a man, and he was mine.

The crescendo grew, cascaded, flowed, and then we were shuddering, joined, soaring into the sky, dancing amongst the stars. The beads glimmered and glistened, sending a thousand candles into the mirrors.

At long last our eyes met in the mirror, shining, connecting in a way I never had with any other person.

His gaze moved to the bowtie in my mouth, down the long, elegant dress in the mirror, then back up to my own.

His lips quirked into a knowing smile.

"Remember."

Chapter 11

I sat on the bed, sliding my feet in the exquisite burgundy high heels to match the gown I wore. The whole experience seemed surreal, as if any moment I would blink awake and be back in my small bedroom in Waterbury, late for school. This was the sort of thing young girls dreamed of. It wasn't something people actually did.

I stood, wiggled my toes, and then carefully walked across the studio to the long mirror alongside the bathroom. The woman who returned my gaze looked nothing like me. Her hair was up in an elegant style, with curls trailing down on each side. The dress shimmered as if it was layered with rubies. Only the Saint Michael's pendant at my breast seemed a glimpse of normal.

Sean pushed open the bathroom door and my breath caught. He was in a formal, black tuxedo, his white cotton shirt freshly pressed, the black buttons gleaming.

I could barely take my eyes from him. I didn't know men existed like this in real life. And here he was, in front of me, and he was all mine.

He grinned at my gaze, then came around behind me, resting his hands on my hips as we looked into the mirror. One of his hands came up to stroke along the edge of his burgundy tie, and my throat went dry.

His voice was a sensual whisper in my ear. "Remember."

My entire body shimmered into heat, and he slid a hand along my hip, turning me …

His phone rang.

He pulled it from his pocket, bringing it to his ear. "Sean here. Sure, Seamus. We'll be right down."

His eyes twinkled when he looked at me. "Guess they're a bit early. They're eager to get the party going." He brought a hand up to stroke along the side of my cheek, and his look became serious. "It'll be good to get this evening behind us."

I turned and picked up my small, elegant purse from the table. It matched, of course, in shimmering burgundy with a thin strap. It held my phone, wallet, and the apartment keys.

He pulled the door open for me, and in a moment we were walking together down the stairwell. We got about half-way down where he took a hold of my hand, drawing me to a stop. He pressed his body against mine, his mouth coming to my ear. His voice was the softest murmur.

"Kay, for tonight, I need you to stay right by me. There'll be the dinner, then the discussion about the Cubans, then the ceremony. After that they're planning on dancing. But once all of that Cuban talk is on record, we'll have what we want. The cavalry will sweep in and gather everyone up."

I knew the plan. The caterers had three large trucks which they'd used to set up for the party. The trucks would soon be parked over in a church parking lot, a few blocks away. Those same trucks would return as the dancing began, seemingly to begin the take-down process. Instead, they would be filled with law enforcement.

He gave my hand a squeeze. "Your only role is to try to help our blonde moppet. If she can get more dirt on Jimmy, that will give our prosecutors even more ammo."

I nodded. "I'll do whatever I can."

He traced his fingers down the side of my face. "I know you will." He pressed a tender kiss against my cheek. "Just stay close. It should be smooth, once they realize they're caught, but you never know."

He slid his fingers to my arm and we continued down the remaining stairs. Once out the door, Seamus's Escalade waited for us in the deepening dusk. Bridgit waved from the passenger seat.

She looked back with a wide smile as Sean and I climbed into the back seat. "Katie, you are a vision! You'll be the belle of the ball tonight."

She reached down to the floor at her feet, and took up a white box, about the size of a double-height laptop. She handed it back to Sean. "A gift for you."

Seamus pulled the Escalade away from the curb as Sean drew the lid open. His brow creased as he looked within. I was confused – it looked like a pile of dark-brown leather straps.

He lifted one of them, and my heart stilled. There was a handgun nestled within.

Seamus's voice was smooth from the front seat. "Taurus PT-99," he commented. "Seventeen-round magazine."

Sean looked up, his eyes serious. "You expecting trouble tonight?"

Seamus shook his head. "No, but I like to be prepared. Our arrangement with Providence and Boston is fairly loose. Their guys will undoubtedly come packing. I like to keep an even playing field."

Sean slipped off his tuxedo jacket, laying it across my legs. He slipped on the shoulder holster as if he'd been wearing it all his life. I flushed. Perhaps this had been standard for him, during his previous assignments. It was still so hard sometimes to remember that he'd been a beat cop once, had worked out of a station and filled out paperwork. It seemed so far from the Sean I knew.

He took the coat up and slipped it back on. I wouldn't have known the gun was under there if I hadn't seen him put it on just a moment ago.

He put his hand over mine, and I looked up into his eyes. They were steeling now, settling into that hardened focus that I knew so well from my childhood, from my father.

Whatever came, Sean would be ready for it.

In a few minutes we rolled up to the warehouse door, and one of Seamus's men ran forward to get the door. We stepped out, and Seamus turned to the soldier. "Remember, all cars go to that church lot. We want the area around us clear. An open line of sight."

The man nodded, then slipped into the driver's seat. In a moment the car was moving off.

Seamus looked around in satisfaction at the empty alley. "We've cleared everything out. Any trouble happens, the attackers will be out in the open. We'll have an easy time of it."

Bridgit tucked her arm into his. "You think of everything. This will be the event of the year."

Sean stepped forward to open the door for them, and my mouth went into an O as I followed them into the warehouse. It had been completely transformed. There had to be at least twelve round tables, each covered with white linen and set for ten with gold-chased china. Large floral arrangements on each table boasted red roses and white baby's breath. Small, twinkling white lights cascaded from a point in the ceiling down to all of the walls.

Bridgit smiled at my surprise. "The team did a good job," she agreed. "Once I got them started in the right direction, they were able to pull it off." She nudged her head toward the stage on the right. "The band will be up there, for the dancing later on." She gave me a pat on the shoulder. "Before that, of course, your Sean has his ceremony."

Jimmy strode up to us, a glass of whiskey in his hand, his face beaming. His normally askew hair had been neatly combed back, and he actually looked half-decent in his tux.

"Everything's all set, Seamus. The caterers are just getting the last of the food in through the warehouse doors, and then we'll send the trucks off. The team is setting up the appetizers as we speak." He waved a hand at the long tables set up against the back wall, laden with a variety of liqueurs. "We'll keep them happy."

Bridgit's eyes lit up, and she strode toward the table, picking up a bottle of Champagne. "Oh, very happy," she grinned.

A glass was poured for me, and Seamus and Jimmy went out back to check on the final preparations.

I took a sip of the bubbly, then looked up again. Sean had worked with Seamus and Jimmy for the past few days, thoroughly sweeping the building, ensuring there were no listening devices anywhere throughout the structure. Then, early this morning, I knew that he added several back in as he strung up those lights twinkling high overhead.

The scene was set.

Soon guests began arriving. Bridgit was the consummate hostess, introducing Sean and me to each arriving group, but the names went in one ear and right out the other. There was an elegant black couple from Boston, a mature, silver-clad, silver-haired Hispanic woman from Providence, a portly man in an ill-fitting tuxedo from Hartford, and they kept on coming. It was an odd mix of a warm family reunion coupled with a high school dance where everyone was sizing the others up. Somehow the group was loudly talkative and carefully distant all at the same time.

Sean barely left my side, staying steadily at my elbow, looking over each new arrival with attentive interest. He seemed to pay special attention to the men, running his eyes along the edges of their jackets, the fall of fabric over the back of their pants.

A waiter strolled by with a plate of mini beef wellingtons. I'd had three of them already, but found it hard to resist the fourth. Sean's eyes sparkled, but he said nothing, his eyes maintaining their smooth sweep of the bustling room.

There was a murmur, and I turned toward the entry. It was Jessica, her blonde curls shining under the twinkling lights, and she was a vision in white. Her dress's lace neckline curled demurely down to a sweetheart shape, and the skirt of the dress fluffed out in sheer cascades. All she needed were angel wings on her back and the image would be complete.

Jimmy was at her side in a moment, his face beaming in satisfaction, and he took her hand. He lowered his head for a courtly kiss, and Jessica erupted in a flurry of delighted giggles. He slid an arm around her waist, and then guided her over to stand with us.

His voice was warm when he spoke. "Jessica, dear, you remember Sean and Katie, right? You saw them in the bar, that time you visited. I want you to stay with them when I'm not around. They'll keep an eye on you." His gaze darkened for a moment as he swept the room. "Too many rough guys around here." His smile returned, and he looked down at her. "I'll keep you safe from them. Trust me."

She looked up at him, her large eyes glowing. "Oh, I do, Jimmy."

Bridgit stepped up, her mouth pressed into a line. "Jimmy, they're ready for the main service."

Jimmy's shoulders tensed, but he sighed, then nodded. He strode up to the stage, then tapped the microphone a few times. "Ahem, hello, everybody. Jimmy here. Please take your seats, and we'll get this meal going."

There was the shuffling of feet, a murmur of conversation, and the group all shifted toward the tables. Sean guided me toward the one immediately by the stage, and I saw that our names were at the place settings on white cards with embossed black script. Sean was on one side of me, Jessica on the other. Then came Jimmy and Bridgit, and Seamus was the last name I recognized.

Sean pointed at the other four seats. "The bosses from the other areas," he explained. "You met them earlier."

I'm sure I had, but in the crowd I could barely keep track of where Jimmy and Seamus were as they moved in and out, never mind strangers. At last, though, everyone found their seats. The tall, black man was sitting next to Sean, with the woman on his other side. The portly man in the tux was alongside the silver-clad woman from Providence.

Ten black-clad waiters bearing plates walked in a line over to our table. Each stood behind one of us, and in unison they laid the plates down before us. It was like watching a performance of precision ballet dancers, but with a culinary flair to it. The plates held a beautiful presentation of five fresh oysters. I tucked my linen napkin on my lap and took up the one closest to me, sucking down the smooth flesh.

Wow, was that amazing.

Sean's eyes glinted. "You eat as many of those as you want," he teased.

I grinned. "Oh, I don't think I need any help from the oysters."

His hand almost reached for my thigh, but he reined it in with visible effort. "Not tonight," he murmured, half to himself.

He took a drink of his water, and I realized that he hadn't been drinking any alcohol all night. He'd somehow deftly turned away offers of drinks or took them to present to someone else.

Jimmy was leaning over to Jessica. "Here, sweetie, you do it like this. Let me." He took up the oyster and tilted it toward her mouth. She obediently opened her lips to him, and his eyes shone with desire as she took in the oyster.

His voice was hoarse. "Oh, yes. Just like that."

She gave a light giggle. "I think I'm liking this Champagne. Can I have some more?"

"Absolutely!" He waved a hand, and in a moment a waiter was at his side, replacing her half-full glass with a fresh one.

There was a murmur from the side of the room, and I turned toward the door in curiosity. My eyes drew to the figure there – and then I stopped in surprise.

Eileen stood there, a black pea coat draped down her body, her mouth open in shock.

Jimmy gave a gargled exclamation. Sean glanced at me in concern, and I knew I had to do something. I rose and half-raced to her, arranging my face to hold a bright look of welcome. "Eileen! It's wonderful to see you! I thought you were going to stay in Ireland through the holidays!"

She continued to sweep her eyes down the cascading, twinkling lights, to the elegant tables with their Riedel glassware, as if she couldn't believe the room was real. "Kate, what is going on?"

I pulled her into a warm hug. "Just a little party for Sean. Nothing important."

Sean had come up to us and I could see the tension glinting behind the friendly smile.

Eileen's eyes brightened with interest, and she drew a long gaze down Sean's well-defined muscles encased in the crisp tuxedo. "And just who is this?"

I chuckled, tucking an arm in on his. "This is Sean, my boyfriend. Sean, meet Eileen."

He put out a hand. "It's a pleasure to meet you, Eileen. Kay has told me so much about you."

Her eyes drank him in. "Well, she hasn't told me anything at *all* about you, so maybe I'll just have to sit with you and hear every last detail." She looked up again, and her gaze grew eager. "But is Jimmy here?"

Her eyes drew to the table where he sat. Her brow furrowed as she took in first Bridgit on one side, then Jessica on the other.

I quickly twined my fingers into hers. "Eileen, maybe I should take you home. Now's not really the best time to have a serious conversation."

She looked over the rest of the table. "The Bostonians are here, and that lecher from Hartford too. Who are they planning on exterminating this time? Last time it was those bastard Lithuanians running drugs out of New Britain. I think there were thirty bodies by the time they finished up. Good riddance."

I blinked in surprise, my mouth hanging open in shock. "What?"

She gave herself a shake. "C'mon, I want to hear what kind of an action they're planning. I think I deserve it, after all I've been through." She waved a hand at a passing waiter. "You, there, set up another seat and place setting between me and these two." She smiled up at Sean. "I want to get to know you a bit better." She shot a heated glance toward Jimmy. "And, Kate, I think you and I have some catching up."

I gave it one last try. "Eileen, wouldn't it be much more fun if you and I went out and –"

She was already sliding into the chair and taking off her coat, draping it back over her seat. Beneath she wore a shimmering gold top over worn jeans. "See, I fit right in," she stated calmly. She looked up as the waiter laid down the plateware before her. "And some of that Champagne, too," she stated. Then her shoulders sagged. "Damn. Never mind, water will be fine for me."

Sean looked across her at me, and I gave a soft shrug. To try to drag her out would be even worse, and it seemed she had no qualms about the discussion that was about to come. Our best bet might be to ride this out with her.

I pulled my chair forward so I blocked her view of Jimmy and Jessica. I leant forward to talk with Eileen in a low voice. "Eileen, I know you've come home into a chaotic situation here. But remember your focus." I glanced down at her abdomen. "Remember what really matters."

She rubbed a hand along her belly, and a crafty smile came to her lips. "You're right, of course. I do hold all the cards, don't I. I'll just enjoy my meal, and then tomorrow when we have our little talk, we'll see what happens." She turned to gaze over to Sean. "In the meantime, why don't you tell me …"

Her flirtatious conversation went on while the salad course was brought. The flavors were delicious, with pine nuts and a fresh raspberry vinaigrette. By the time the filet mignon was presented with its béarnaise sauce, I had half-forgotten the serious undertones of this evening, along with the dangerous combination of Jimmy's flirtations on my right and Eileen's honed readiness on my left. None of it mattered. The cabernet was stunning. The steak was perfectly cooked.

I turned to look past Eileen at Sean. "Maybe we could get in just a little dancing later on?"

His mouth quirked up in a smile, and his gaze drew down my dress. "We'll see," he murmured. "There might be one or two songs before the caterers arrive."

Eileen's gaze brightened, and she leaned against Sean's arm. "You'll have to dance with me, too! I'm Kate's best friend, you know."

On my other side, Jessica was leaning against Jimmy, batting her eyes up to him, and her voice had a slight slur to it. "Ya know, Jimsy, maybe we could do one of those movies, after all. It sounds like fun. All my friends are taking selfies and posting them on the web. I'd show them! Mine would blow theirs out of the water."

Jimmy's eyes gleamed, and he pulled her in against him. "Absolutely, you would beat them by a mile," he vowed. They'd never compare with you. You'd be queen of the school!"

Her gaze went vacant. "Queen of the schhooool …"

The waiters were behind us, taking away our empty plates, and Jimmy scowled as he had to temporarily separate from her. Then the desserts were laid down – a coconut crème brûlée with chocolate shavings on top. A dollop of whipped cream sat in the center.

Jessica's eyes lit up, and she traced her finger through the whipped cream, gathering up a burst of it. She giggled, then wiggled it in the air. She turned her eyes to Jimmy. "What do you think, should I do my selfie naked, only covered in whipped cream?"

Jimmy looked as if he'd fall out of his seat. He nodded eagerly. "That's exactly right," he murmured. "Just you and the whipped cream. Just like that album cover for Herb Albert's band."

Her nose wrinkled. "What's an album?"

Jimmy sighed, shaking his head. "Never mind, sweetie. You'll find out later on, when this party is all over with. I have the back room all set up for you."

I turned to Sean and gave him a nod. While he couldn't hear their conversation, the look in his eyes indicated he had a sense that the tone was exactly what we needed. One of the light garlands streamed immediately over our table, and I had no doubt it was picking up every word. Jimmy's fate was being sealed, one whipped cream dollop at a time.

There was a movement, and I glanced over. Seamus stood up from the table, moving with steady intention over to the stage. He stood before the microphone, and the room quieted down of its own accord. He looked out over the guests.

"I want to thank everyone for coming together. Let's start with a round of applause for our chefs and servers." The room filled with enthusiastic clapping and cheers, and the black-suited men and women bowed from the back of the room.

One of the soldiers escorted all of the waitstaff out of the room, and there was a pause for a moment. At last he came back and gave a thumbs-up signal to Seamus.

Seamus took the microphone up in one hand, and his voice became serious. "Every person in this room is hand-picked. Trusted. You are our core. I wanted to do this face to face, with all of us here, so there'd be no confusion. No issues. We start this as a team, we end it as a team."

There were murmurs of agreement.

He drew his gaze from table to table, his eyes hard. "You've heard what the Cubans did to us. How they disrespected our organization." He waved a hand to me. "Katie, stand up."

I blushed, but I did as I was asked. Eileen looked up at me in confusion, but held quiet.

Seamus's voice added an edge. "This is the woman they kidnapped and abused. She was completely innocent." His eyes darkened. "If we hadn't gotten to her in time, they would have violated her."

The grumbles and growls rolled around the room, echoing off the brick walls. Eileen's mouth opened in shock, and then she banged a clenched fist on the table. "Those bastards! They're going to pay for that!"

Seamus chuckled. "Indeed they shall, Eileen. Glad to have your feisty spirit back with us."

I regained my seat, and Seamus went on. "Those Cubes had spies within this very building. They are trying to negotiate to take half of our earnings. They're looking to castrate us, and then take over completely." His voice dropped. "I say we end this now."

The silver-clad woman across from me nodded in agreement. "They're like cockroaches down in Providence. Think they deserve a piece of all the shipping trade. We've wanted to squash them for years."

The black man by Sean had a tense line in his brow. "They're pretty well entrenched in Boston."

Seamus held his gaze. "So entrenched that, if we pooled our resources, we couldn't carve them out?"

The black man shook his head. "It'll just be messy. We'll probably have to put down fifty, maybe sixty of them to get them fully out."

Seamus nodded. "We have the guns. We have the men." He looked around the room. "Do we have the will to use them?"

A wave of nods moved around the room, and Seamus looked back to the head table. "You four share the final say. Are we in agreement, then?"

The four firmly nodded.

Seamus looked out at the room. "Let me make this clear. Nothing in email or texts. Nothing over the phone. All face to face, like we're doing tonight. We want this done as cleanly as possible."

I glanced at Sean, and my eyes flicked toward the lights.

The corner of his mouth quirked up in a smile.

Seamus waved a hand toward Sean. "Now, for the ceremony."

Sean nodded his head to me. "I'll be right back," he murmured. Then he stood. Jimmy went with him up onto the stage, and escorted Sean around to stand before Seamus.

Bridgit slid over a chair to sit next to Jessica, and she leaned past the girl to speak to me. "You'll remember this night forever," she assured me. "A promotion like this doesn't come around often."

Eileen looked up in interest. "A promotion? He's being made a captain?" She nudged me in the ribs. "You lucky girl! He's quite a catch."

I grinned, a warmth washing through me.

She had no idea.

I looked up at Sean, and he was gazing at me, a smile on his lips. He brought one hand to the edge of his tie, tracing his finger along its edge.

I remembered viscerally how he had held me before the array of mirrors in the dressing room, how I had worn this very dress, how my breasts had pressed out against the fabric. How his fingers had slid down my slick opening …

I held in the moan, crossing my legs, and his eyes gleamed.

Seamus held out his hand. "Sean, kneel."

Sean knelt before him, and Jimmy stood to one side. All eyes in the room were focused on the trio.

Seamus continued to hold his hand before Sean, the gold rings glistening in the light. "Sean Miller, do you solemnly swear to cast aside all other loyalties, and to put –"

There was a commotion from the loading dock area, and I blinked in surprise. This was too soon. They shouldn't be coming in for another half hour, at least. When everyone was relaxed, dancing, and off guard. Not when every man in the room was reaching his hand for his hip, the back of his waist, beneath his jacket …

A stream of men came in from the back doors, their faces set, their eyes aglow. They wore jeans and muscle shirts, and carried a mix of handguns and larger weapons.

The Most Interesting Man in the World came through an opening in the center of his group, smiling in satisfaction, his eyes taking in the scene. Behind him, the weapons were raised and aimed. His voice rang out across the silent hall.

"And now, my friends, I think it's time to say good-bye."

Book 4: Stop One Heart from Breaking

STOP ONE
HEART FROM
BREAKING

OPHELIA SIKES

A WORCESTER NIGHTS NOVELLA

Chapter 1

If I can stop one Heart from breaking
I shall not live in vain
If I can ease one Life the Aching
Or cool one Pain
Or help one fainting Robin
Unto his Nest again
I shall not live in Vain.
-- Emily Dickinson

The Cubans held the room at gunpoint.

My mind detached from the scene, rising above it, and the actors beneath me held still in a quiet tableau. I had been to the reenactments of the Battle of Lexington several times, to the face-off between colonial militia and British soldiers. The line of men, face to face; the tense situation which had – with one shot – launched the American Revolution.

It had always seemed quaint to me. A group of boys playing; a situation from which any sane person could simply have turned and walked away.

I realized now how wildly wrong my thoughts had been.

The men – and a few women – in this room were not just attentive. They were not just engaged. They were viscerally connected to each other in a manner I had never imagined possible. I was somehow aware of every movement, every sound, in a way which seemed supernatural and almost prescient. I knew Sean was torn between an overwhelming urge to leap before me and a desperate realization that staying still might keep the onslaught from beginning. Eileen's hand was curling around the stem of my wine glass, apparently ready to turn it into a weapon edged with shards of glass.

Javier smiled, solidifying his likeness to the Most Interesting Man in the World.

I don't normally trigger Armageddon, but when I do, I make sure my trusty rapist, Raul, is right by my side.

Javier patted Raul on the shoulder, and the arm holding the folding-stock Ruger 10/22 twitched. Javier spread his arms wide, looking up at the stage, to where Seamus, Jimmy, and Sean stood motionless.

"Ah, my friends. So good to see you again. I believe you were just talking about us. I thought it might be useful for us to join into this conversation."

Seamus's jaw was tight. "Seems your gook rat was craftier than I thought. But you know this, you *rafter*. You strike us down, and like the phoenix, we will rise against you. You touch our group, and I fockin' warn you, every Irish soul this side of Little Skellig will flay you alive."

Javier beamed. "Oh, it's Trai you blame for your predicament, is it? Certainly he has been useful at times." His eyes swept across the three men on the stage. "And yet, you might be surprised to hear that Trai had nothing to do with our timely arrival at this little soirée of yours."

My blood ran cold. The streams of white lights overhead crystallized into tiny stars, heralding our doom.

He knew.

Somehow, impossibly, Javier knew that Sean was an undercover cop. And, given that Javier had simply not opened fire, it was likely he was going to use this tidbit of information as a negotiating tool. He could demonstrate that the two gangs had a common enemy. They would merge and form a monstrous beast the likes of which had never been before seen.

With Sean as the sacrificial lamb on the bloody altar of their unholy marriage.

I desperately prayed for the cavalry to come streaming in, for the supporting police and S.W.A.T. and whoever else was involved to surround and take down both groups of soul-sucking criminals.

I silently screamed for Jessica, for Sean, for someone more eloquent to say something – anything – to halt the doom which was descending on us all.

I pleaded –

Javier's voice echoed across the hall, smug, satisfied. "I don't always share advice with my enemies, but –"

I snapped.

I launched to my feet, driving my hand to point at Raul. All eyes – and weapons – swung to me. In an instant I was drenched with cold sweat. A rush of adrenaline coursed through me, steeling me, and I wondered, once it left, if I would collapse onto the floor in a pool of quivering jelly.

I didn't care.

My voice was strong, rich, and echoed off the cool brick walls of the warehouse.

"*I'd* like to share some advice with you, Javier, because even though you were my enemy, you treated me with respect. Let me give you some *advice* about your right-hand man, Raul. Did you know that while the rest of you were asleep, he crept into my room, gagged me, and attempted to rape me?"

The only sound in the room was my heart pressing against my rib cage, thunderously pounding.

Javier blinked, staring at me for a long moment as if attempting to drag my soul out through my eyes. Then his neck muscles steeled as he took in the gazes of the men and women around me, absorbing the fact that they held not shock, but bright fury. He slowly, carefully, turned to look at Raul.

His voice was a rasp of a file drawn across an anvil. "Raul, is what she says true?"

Raul's face flushed beet-red, and he let out a low growl. "She's a fucking *mucker*, Javier! A whore! And you had her –"

Javier's hand flashed. He slapped Raul, hard, full across the face.

Raul howled in fury and spun.

The world stopped. And then three things happened simultaneously.

One. Raul fired, the recoil shuddering him back, shimmering his rage-filled face.

Two. A pair of shots sounded from the stage; a pair of crimson eyes blossomed in Raul's chest, side by side, staring and gaping in wide-eyed vengeance.

Three. A massive fist punched me in the shoulder. I was whipped around, taken clean off my feet, and I plowed face-first into the polished wooden floor.

My breath was gone, and for an eternity I waited for it to return.

The world spun up again into sheer chaos. Tables were overturned to act as wooden shields. Deafening gunfire rang out from all sides. The brick walls echoed with shouts, screams, and the hellfire of purgatory itself.

Eileen crouched before me, her shattered-glass weapon in one hand. With the other she tossed her black pea coat over my body. Her shout echoed with glee. "You fucking showed them, Kate!"

Jessica grabbed several of the linen napkins from the table and pressed them against the wound at my upper arm, staunching the flow of blood which was billowing from my beautiful burgundy dress. Her voice was steady and sure. "Hang in there, Kate. You'll be all right."

Bridgit stepped forward to wrap her arm around my good arm, hauling me half to my feet. "We're getting out of here," she ordered. "Follow me."

I looked back as Bridgit half-carried me toward the far side of the room. Sean, Seamus, and Jimmy had taken cover behind the stack of amplifiers waiting on the side of the stage for the later festivities, now undoubtedly called off. Sean's eyes locked with mine. He leant out of his shelter, looking as if he'd make a run for it, to come like a guardian angel to my side.

A hail of bullets hammered in his direction, and Seamus pulled him back to safety.

Bridgit moved us into the nest of boxes and crates, coming up to one of the boarded-up windows. I looked at it in dismay. If she thought the three of them were going to pry those boards loose before the Cubans finished us all off, she must think we had some sort of Valkyrie power hidden within us.

She stepped forward, undid a latch, and easily slid the entire wooden barrier to the right on a set of small wheels.

My mouth fell open in shock. The full height window was completely open, and before us sat the black Escalade, glistening in the evening moonlight.

Bridgit tossed the keys to Eileen. "Seamus does things his way, but sometimes a woman has to plan for the worst," she snapped. "You drive. We'll get her into the back."

Eileen raced for the driver's side door, hitting the unlock button along the way, and then Jessica was climbing into the back seat, hauling me in after her while Bridgit shoved in my feet.

POW.

A shot whistled past Bridgit's ear, shattering the passenger-side mirror.

Bridgit's head snapped around. "Jesus fucking Christ!" She slammed my door shut and dove into the passenger seat, screaming, "Drive!"

I turned to look out the back window while the g-forces of Eileen's acceleration pushed me into the leather. Four men were standing in the road, guns aimed, their faces bright with hellish delight.

Chapter 2

The Escalade squealed around a corner, I fell against Jessica, and she drew my body into her lap, bracing against the side door. She gathered the napkins more sturdily against my shoulder wound, looking down at me.

Her voice was soothing and steady.

"You'll be all right."

I shook my head. I felt fine. Sure, I could feel the warm, thick liquid trailing down my chest, ruining my gorgeous, beaded gown. Sean was going to photograph me in this. I wondered if he could Photoshop out the blood, the damage done to this work of art. It was nothing, really. A few little swishes with the blur tool, and –

BLAM.

The back window of the car burst inwards, a bullet slammed into the dashboard, and I buried my face into Jessica's torso, a shower of glass cascading down onto me.

Bridgit's voice was calmer than I'd ever heard it. "They're gaining, Eileen. Take the right here. Get up onto 290."

"On it," responded Eileen, her voice a low hum of concentration. The car careened to the left, righted itself, and then there was the steady growl of acceleration as we rose up onto the highway.

There were a pair of pops, but they didn't seem to make contact, or at least nothing valuable seemed to be hit. I saw the Cold Storage Warehouse location stream by, where six firefighters had died in 1999. It struck me how strongly this location could resonate, even though from the highway there was an empty hole. It was like a missing tooth that draws attention with its absence.

My upper arm twinged, and I suddenly wondered just how bad it was going to get.

Pop.

Bridgit glanced back at us, then past us to the car chasing beyond. "Four of them. If they catch us, we'd never take them."

Jessica looked down to me, then up to Bridgit. "We could take a run at an emergency room. They'd let up if –"

Bridgit shook her head. "The bastards would shoot us all dead, then take out the nurses as well. My mother was a nurse. I'd never do that to one of them. They already kill themselves to keep us safe."

Jessica held her gaze. "Maybe a police barracks –"

Bridgit scoffed. "They'll be on donut patrol. By the time anybody came out to look, we'd be a sprawl of corpses, and the Cubes would be long gone."

She shook her head. "No, if we're going to live, we have to take care of ourselves."

She turned to look forward down the road we were screaming along. I pushed up to follow her gaze. Eileen's hands were clenched on the steering wheel, her focus solidly on the road before her, and the needle on the speedometer was quivering at the 120 mph bar. I wondered what the hell the Cubans were chasing us in, that they were able to keep up.

Pop.

Pop.

Bridgit nodded as if in agreement with an unseen voice. "Stay ahead of them, Eileen," she instructed, as if she were laying out the cooking instructions for a nice loaf of soda bread. "They're barely hanging in there. Get us down to Route 16, then go east, to Douglas."

Jessica glanced up at that. "The Douglas state forest?"

Bridgit smiled. "Seamus loves that place. Enough open space in there to remind him of back home. He'll get us back out again." Her gaze hardened. "And those Cube bastards won't last a minute against him."

Eileen found an extra millimeter of juice, and the car edged ahead. The needle quivered to 125. "On it."

I must have faded out. There was throbbing, tense voices, and suddenly there was a whirling and slamming on of brakes. I twisted, groaned, and a flurry of hands was helping me out of the car, tucking beneath me, and carrying me through a darkness fragrant with pine, juniper, and cedar. A moan lurched out of me, and a hand was immediately pressed, albeit gently, to my mouth.

I blacked out again.

Infinity drifted by, gentle, complacent.

Aching pain shuddered through me, and I blinked awake. The full moon's soft, Champagne-colored light filtered through a dense network of trees. I had a black pea-coat over me, and I was pressed up against a sturdy, warm body on either side. My limbs ached, and I stretched.

Bridgit was instantly awake on my left, rising up and turning over. Her face creased into concern. "How are you doing, lass?"

Jessica, at my other side, was slower to rouse, but she blinked her eyes several times. She carefully pried the layer of napkins from my shoulder. "Nothing serious was hit, thank God. But we should still get her to a hospital."

Bridgit's lips pressed into a straight line. "Seamus is coming for us. We wait until he gets here. If we go out on our own, those Cubes will blast us into the next lifetime."

I attempted a smile. "I'm fine. Really. And Sean will be here soon. I know he will be."

Eileen reached over to pat me on my good shoulder. "Absolutely. I saw the way he looked at you, Kate. He'd have to be dead not to get to you."

The blood drained from my face.

Sean could be dead.

I could see it vividly. His body, peppered with bullet holes, sprawled on the stage. Blood seeping out from him, draining away …

Bridgit gathered me up, clucking at me. "Sean is fine," she promised. "He's a soldier, like Seamus. Nothing can hurt them. We just need to tuck in here. Seamus plans. *If he's not fishing, he's mending his nets.* He'll be here, and Sean right by his side."

My anxiety settled, and inexplicably my bladder eased into my awareness. I blushed. "I'm sorry, but I have to … ummm … pee."

Bridgit chuckled. "Of course you do, lass. You've been out for hours. We've all had our turn. There's a stream right over that rise there, by the granite rock."

Jessica looked at me with concern. "You need any help? I'm happy to come along."

I shook my head, putting my hand over the swath of napkins on my shoulder. "I'm sure I can manage. I just have a dress on; that should make it fairly easy."

She nodded. "Well, call if you want help. I'm happy to lend a hand."

I pressed down at the throbbing on my shoulder, and it eased the pain a bit. I climbed up to my feet, and the world swirled around me. Bridgit was there, sturdy, a rock, and I leaned against her for a moment in the shadows until the ground solidified again. Then I carefully hobbled forward, watching for branches and uneven ground. I went from tree to tree, negotiating the shadowed terrain.

Sure enough, just over the low rise was a small trickle of a stream, and the rippling sound of it was nearly enough to make me lose control right there. I carefully hiked up my dress, pulled down my pantyhose and panties, and sighed as the pent-up pressure within me released.

I sighed in relief, and reached for my panties.

Snap.

I froze, feeling completely vulnerable, crouched over the stream, my panties literally around my ankles. My heart thundered against my ribs.

Please, let it be Sean.

A strong arm grabbed me around my chest, just beneath my breasts, holding me in place. Hot breath, stinking of rum, blasted against my cheek, and the accent in the man's voice who held me was definitely of the Cuban variety.

"Got you, you bitch. Took you long enough to get up and away from the others, *puta.*"

My breath wanted to escape from me; it was all I could do to draw it in, let it out. He dragged me back, and I pressed my feet into the rocky ground, snapping both heels like twigs. Clearly they were not meant for outdoor orienteering exercises.

His arm wrapped more tightly, and his hand drew against my breast. His foul breath turned to focus more closely against my face.

"Then again, nobody said anything about you being brought in unharmed."

I twisted hard, trying to break his grip. Agonizing pain shot through my shoulder, and my eyes nearly rolled back in their sockets at the impact of it. A rough gurgling noise coughed out of me, and I fell back, limp.

It couldn't end like this. Not like –

The man holding me groaned, his arms lost their grip, and he fell away.

I collapsed against the ground, dizziness washing over me, and it was a long moment before I could turn. Eileen stood there, her eyes bright with triumph, a shattered-top wine glass in her hand. The daggered edges were dripping with blood.

My gaze trailed down to the man at her feet. His throat had been ripped open, and a waterfall of blood pulsed from him, the stream easing with every passing moment.

Eileen placed her glass-shard weapon onto the ground, then came over to me, helping me re-seat my clothes. She drew me up by my good shoulder, tucking her body beneath me. Then she took up her goblet epee and gave me a squeeze. "One down," she smiled, and then we were walking the short distance back to the others.

Bridgit glanced up as she saw us approach, and took in the smears of blood on Eileen's glass. "What happened?"

"One of them found us," she reported easily. "He won't be reporting us to his friends. We should be safe for now."

Jessica stood, alertly looking around. "You're sure he's alone?"

Eileen nodded. "Sure. Nobody else came to his aid. But we should probably move on, just in case."

Bridgit slid her own arm under me. "We go in deeper," she instructed. "Seamus will find us."

The world weaved in and out, and I had no idea what time it was. I'd have to guess it was the darkest period of the night, but who knew? It certainly wasn't day. We moved slowly, watching for roots and fallen trees, making our way through witch hazel and clumps of club moss. At last we settled into place against a long granite outcropping on a slope, where we had good visibility in all three directions.

Bridgit sat against the wall, pulled me in with her, and sighed as her back met the cold stone. "We just wait here, and Seamus will be here soon."

Eileen stood over her, her voice a frosty snap. "Jimmy, too, you know."

Bridgit muttered, "*You must take the little potato with the big potato.*"

Eileen swung around, throwing her glass-weapon into a mossy patch where it stuck out at an odd angle. The words burst from her in a rush. "You know, Bridgit, Jimmy loved you. He married you for exactly who you were. He adored your spark of life, your bright energy."

Bridgit's jaw tightened. "Don't you talk to me of Jimmy."

Eileen took a step forward. "You know what? I don't think you ever loved Jimmy. I think you only loved Liam. You took Jimmy in, thinking you would mold him into another Liam. And when you couldn't do it, you labeled Jimmy a failure." She crossed her arms in front of her chest. "But he's not. He's just right at being Jimmy."

Bridgit's neck muscles stood out. "Jimmy is my husband!"

Eileen's eyes flashed. "You're God-damned right he is. And you don't even want him. All you want is Liam. But you know what? Liam is *dead*. He's dead, and buried, and he's never coming back."

Bridgit went still, as still as a corpse.

Into that stillness the sound of a foot on a branch echoed as loud as a gunshot. A man stepped into the dark clearing, his face in the shadows, the matte barrel of a gun glinting in the moonlight. His voice was a low rasp.

"Now here is a prize worth taking. It'll be interesting to see who will pay the most for you four – the Cubans, the Irish, or an eager citizen, bolstered by the reward pool ponied up by families of the girls you desecrated."

Chapter 3

The man nudged his handgun toward us, and we huddled together against the face of the cliff. As he came closer into the moonlight I could draw in more details. The pistol looked like a Glock 22 – fairly standard issue for police. It was a .40 caliber, maybe 22 rounds in the magazine. More than enough to take care of us four.

He seemed in his mid-forties, with short-cropped, light brown hair. His face was creased and weathered. Maybe he was a marine, or a hunter of some sort. Certainly he seemed fairly satisfied with the game he'd run down this night.

He looked across us, stopping when he got to my shoulder. "How's the wound?"

My response was terse. "I'll live."

He chuckled. "Good. Because I think, of the four of you, that Bridgit here will bring the most money for me. The rest of you are just collateral bonuses." His grey eyes narrowed. "But don't think of running off. One of you goes, I shoot the rest, and then make your life a living hell. One way or the other, I'll get a meal ticket out of this."

He nudged with his gun. "All right, then, get moving."

We tumbled along in the direction he indicated, Bridgit looping herself under me to help me along.

I glanced around nervously as we moved. There were still two more Cubans out there. They might not have as mercenary a plan as this one here seemed to have.

He noticed my searching eyes. "Don't worry about the others," he scoffed. "We all split up when we left the car.

The other two headed north. They're undoubtedly completely lost by now."

His mouth drew into a smile. "My Dad was Italian. Taught me to shoot, taught me to hunt and track. I never knew it would come in as handy as it did tonight."

We delved down into a valley, then struggled to push our way through a field of pricker bushes. When we finally clawed our way out of the other side, Eileen's voice piped up, tight with fury. "Why do you think it's Bridgit who you should take the most care with?"

I pressed my eyes closed for a moment. I knew Eileen was not always the clearest of thinkers, but surely this wasn't in anybody's best interests.

The man's voice held rich amusement. "Oh, do tell. You think Seamus will care more about the whore who is making a fool of his sister?"

Eileen's voice rose in pitch. "I am not a whore!"

He laughed. "Oh, right, Jimmy wasn't even paying you for those films. You just donated your time and … tits … to the cause. How noble of you."

Eileen gave a strangled cry. "I'll have you know that –"

Bridgit's voice cut across hers. "Jimmy doesn't have any money," she informed Eileen in an emotionless voice. "It's all in my name. If this cock-sucker kidnapper is going to ransom people, and offer up body parts as proof of life, it's only Seamus who would have the money to pay."

Eileen's eyes widened. "Body parts?"

The man nudged with his gun. "Let's hope it doesn't come to that."

Jessica's voice was soft, placating. "If we're going to be together for a few days, while you make the appropriate arrangements, it makes sense for us to get to know each other. I imagine you know who we are. Jessica, Bridgit, Eileen, and Kate. What should we call you?"

He seemed to consider that, and at last he flashed a wide smile in the darkness. "You can call me Ralph."

Jessica nodded calmly. "All right then, Ralph. We want – just like you do – for this to go smoothly. You get your money, we get to go on with our lives. So you just tell us what you need from us, and we'll do our best to comply."

Ralph grinned. "A voice of reason. Keep on moving east. Cell coverage sucks in this neck of the woods, as I imagine you've noticed. Speaking of which, hand over your phones. I wouldn't want yours to blaze into life prematurely."

Eileen, Bridgit, and Jessica all reached into their purses and dutifully handed over their phones. I realized I didn't have my purse with me. It hadn't even occurred to me until then. And the ache in my shoulder was growing louder.

Ralph tucked the phones into a pocket of his heavy jacket, then we were in motion again. We climbed over a thick oak trunk, then skirted around a tight cluster of birch trees, the white bark shining out in the moonlight.

Jessica's voice eased into the darkness, her voice calm, quiet, as if discussing the upcoming shows being featured at the Hanover Theater.

"Well, now, Ralph, I think I've heard of you. Surely that was you who was involved, when that woman from the Rovezzi family was kidnapped?"

His face glowed with pleasure. "Indeed it was. I didn't realize that was known about."

She nodded in encouragement. "Of course it was. You were brilliant. I think you got half a million out of that family before you finally gave her back."

He puffed up. "Sure did. And they were fools, too. I would have taken a hundred. But they were so eager, so willing to do anything, that I milked them for all they were worth."

Jessica's voice was smooth. "I heard the only reason she was retrieved alive was that the cops discovered where you were hiding her. They were able to rescue her before she starved to death."

He shrugged. "Sometimes it is safer that way, you know. No witnesses to identify you later. No loose ends."

Jessica's tone embodied calmness. "But you have to keep them alive until then, in case proof of life is required."

He chuckled. "Some people are picky about that sort of thing. Won't pay the cash until you can prove the blood is still pumping."

"Of course, of course," agreed Jessica. "It's a simple business transaction."

Ralph stuffed his free hand into his jacket pocket. "Absolutely right. Maybe I can finally get out of this frigid tundra and down somewhere south. Maybe Puerto Rico. I hear they have stunning beaches, and a good night life as well. Pour up some rum-and-coke and soak in the sun."

We stumbled and struggled, pulled through briars and sharp-edged branches which lashed our skin. The dull ache in my shoulder had intensified into a searing throb. It felt as if a muscle-bound weightlifter held a screwdriver in his hand and was drilling a screw into my shoulder, turning, turning, turning …

Bridgit drew to a stop, looking down at me in concern. "The lass has to rest. And, before you complain, Seamus will pay well for her. He thinks the world of her."

Ralph made a swirling motion with his gun. "I know he does. But, fortunately for us all, there's not too much further to go. My car is parked just around this bend here. So, carry her if you have to, but once we get there, we can get you all to somewhere warm, and move on with the next stage of our little game."

Bridgit pursed her lips together, drew in a breath, and hefted me back up again. My feet seemed weighted down by heavy dumbbells, and I could barely keep my lids open. It seemed the barest glimmer of light was frosting the trees. Was it finally dawn? Surely an eternity had passed since that long-distant day at the warehouse, with Sean in his tux, standing on stage with that deliciously handsome tie. I could see him in my mind. I could see him ... see him ...

I blinked my eyes open. The group had staggered to a stop in a clearing. A jet black Dodge Charger stood over to the right, its glossy finish shining in the early morning light.

Sean was leaning against the hood, the Taurus PT-99 in the hand hanging loosely at his side. His weary eyes shone with determination.

Chapter 4

It was only Bridgit's arm around me which kept me from collapsing to the frost-dusted ground. The world shimmered. It reflected off the glistening coating of ice on the birch branches. It refracted in the steady gleam in Sean's dark eyes that told me, no matter what, he would save me.

He had come for me.

Ralph's gaze hardened. He waved his gun across the four of us. "All of you. On your knees."

I was exhausted; I easily complied. If anything, it was a challenge not to fall forward onto all fours. In a moment the others were there alongside me, Bridgit with her arm around me, Jessica close on the other side. Eileen crossed her arms across her chest, defiant.

My eyes held on Sean. He still wearing his black tux, although now it was streaked with dark crimson blood layered with charcoal grit and black smears. He looked like James Bond crossed with a gladiator.

Ralph grinned, his grey eyes sharpening. He swept his barrel back and forth across us, like the glistening red eye of a Cylon dispassionately ready to exterminate on a whim. "So, who is it going to be? You shoot me; one of these women dies. Maybe more, if you're not lucky. Care to say which one gets the bullet?"

Sean pressed up away from the car. A sickening tremor ran through me as his left leg shuddered when it took on weight. The realization hit me that he had been through a tumultuous gunfight. How badly had he been injured?

There weren't any wounds that I could see, but surely he would be hiding them, shielding any weakness from his opponent's eyes.

Sean's gaze swept down to me; tense concern drew his brows in. He spoke to Ralph, his voice tight. "She needs to get to a hospital."

Ralph chuckled. "I need to get paid," he countered, shrugging. "She'll last a while, yet. I bet she could even survive with a few more holes put into her." The corner of his mouth quirked up. "Care to test that theory?"

Sean's face steeled. "You touch her, and –"

Ralph stepped forward, pressing the barrel of his gun into the back of my head. It took every ounce of my will not to close my eyes, not to cringe in on myself. I had to be strong. For Sean, for all of us.

Ralph's voice purred from just behind me. "I touch her, and you'll … what? There's just you and me here, boy. The odds are in my favor."

Sean gave a wry smile.

There was movement from the sides of the car. Then, out from the shadows stepped Seamus, Evan, and Jimmy. The three men drew into a line with Sean, separated by enough space to give each room to work.

Thick emotion swelled within me, and I was hard put to assign a single name to it. Comfort. Satisfaction. Serenity. I could almost lay down and take a rest, a rest I craved with every ounce of my being.

Somehow, it was all going to be all right.

I glanced up at my captor. Ralph's brow creased. He swept his gaze slowly, carefully, across the four men, his eyes resting on each one for a long moment.

He hovered, waiting, and then …

He lunged, his arm wrapping around Bridgit's thick middle, hauling her to her feet. He pressed the matte barrel of his pistol against her head, his voice tightening.

"It's always been Bridgit," he instructed the four men. "She's my ticket out of here. You can have the rest. Give me access to my car, and I'll let you get that girl to the hospital. By noon I'll contact you with my demands. A business transaction. Simple. Pay the bill, and we'll be done."

Bridgit stood up straight, her eyes on Seamus. "Take the shot."

Jimmy was gazing at Eileen with concern, but at Bridgit's statement his attention spun. His mouth hung open in surprise. "God, Bridgit, no!"

Bridgit nodded at her brother. "Seamus, you've always been there for me. When our sister, Maeve, died from that botched abortion. When Liam was shot down, murdered in cold blood. You're my foundation. My Carrick-a-Rede bridge over razor-sharp rocks."

Seamus's voice was tight. "I'm here for you, Bridgit."

Bridgit held his gaze. "Shoot. No matter what the outcome, shoot. It's better than what he has planned for me."

Ralph pulled her in against him. "The *figa* doesn't know what she's saying. Let us go, and we'll work this out."

Seamus, like Jimmy and Sean, still wore his tux, and his muscular body flexed beneath the elegant fabric. His brow was creased with exhaustion. I wondered if he, too, had injuries that were not immediately visible. But his eyes shone clear and bright.

"*Nár laga Dia thú.*"

She nodded, her gaze fully on her brother.

I could hear the English version echoing in my mind, even as he drew his gun up, even as the retort of the firing echoed across the clearing.

May God never weaken you.

The blast rocked Ralph's head back, throwing his arms wide, and Bridgit remained still as his body flung back from her, slamming into the frost-coated ground.

For a long moment the tableau held.

Then the world spun up into motion. Sean and Evan raced forward, coming to either side of me. Sean drew me into an embrace, and it was all I could do not to burst into sobs, not to release all of the terror and strain and exhaustion of the past hours. I soaked in his strength, drawing in the stunning feel of his arms around me, his sturdy chest protecting me.

At long last he drew back, his eyes holding mine. One hand shakily traced down my cheek. "God, Kay, are you all right?"

I gave a wry smile, nudging my head toward my shoulder. "I've never been shot before."

Evan growled, and he reached forward, probing at the swath of napkin-bandages there. "You should never have been in that position," he muttered. His jaw eased as he took in the injury. "It's less bad than it looks, though. Who took care of this for you? Jessica?"

I nodded, turning my head to look. Seamus was on one side, wrapping his sister into an embrace, his head nestled into the crook of her neck. Jimmy was on my other side, helping Eileen up, brushing back her red hair. Jessica was kneeling by Ralph's side, her fingers pressed against his carotid artery.

Her voice was low and steady. "He's dead."

Bridgit chuckled. "Of course he is. My Seamus never misses."

Jessica reached into Ralph's pockets, drawing out the cell phones he had taken from the women. Seamus looked at them for a moment, then stood, crossing to her. He took them from her hand, his eyes holding hers for a moment.

He glanced back at Bridgit, then the phones again. "I'll hold onto these for now; put them with Evan's. We can discuss how we proceed once we get to the cottage and get you all warm and fed."

A tremor eased through me, one that had little to do with the ice-cold ground I knelt on or my sheer exhaustion. Seamus and Jimmy were both armed, and both were now fugitives on the run. While Sean had a gun, and I prayed that Evan did as well, I doubted the men wanted to shoot it out in the middle of this deserted clearing.

I looked up to Sean, a wealth of questions ringing in my head which I could not safely put into words.

Sean nodded at me, then looked over to Seamus. "Kay really needs to go to a hospital and get proper medical attention for her shoulder. Let her brother take her there. He's already sworn not to say anything about you. He'll take the Charger and they'll be out of your hair. I'll go with you all in the Escalade, wherever you want, and ensure any remaining Cubans don't cause trouble for you."

I turned and looked at the edge of the clearing. I could see Seamus's car now, its grill barely visible beyond a massive oak. I took in the shattered mirror, the blown out back window, and my heart leapt in my throat.

"I'm going with you."

Evan's voice was a growl. "Kay, I've had quite enough of –"

Seamus stood. "We're all staying together, and we're all going to the cottage. We can talk later about what happens next. But for now, I want you all where I can see you."

Evan's gaze steeled, and tension settled in his arms.

I knew that look. I'd seen it the night we walked through downtown Worcester, during my first year at Holy Cross, and a group of burly young men came toward us on a deserted side street, their eyes sizing us up with interest.

Evan's eyes had hardened, and his lean muscles had compressed, then shimmered.

The men recognized something in him, something primal. They'd crossed to the other side and let us pass in peace.

I put my hand on Evan's arm. "I'm fine, Ev," I soothed him. "Jessica did a good job. And I am hungry. Let's just go to this cottage and rest up."

A chill wind swirled the frost off a patch of leaves, and a red-tailed hawk soared high overhead, his black eyes searching the ground for something – anything – to eat.

At last Evan blew out his breath, nodding. "We stay together," he agreed, his gaze returning to Seamus. "But you'd better have some medical supplies at this cottage of yours."

Bridgit's eyes gleamed with amusement. "Oh, we do," she assured him. "We are prepared."

Sean tucked his arms beneath me and hoisted me up in them. Jimmy slid an arm under Eileen's shoulder, helping her along. The others moved with us as we came to the Escalade.

Seamus glanced back at the corpse. "If we're lucky, the coyotes will drag him off before anybody comes out here. Lord knows they have few enough other things to eat this time of year."

Eileen tucked herself in against Jimmy. "I gave them a snack earlier," she commented with a grin. "This bastard out in the woods last night. Ripped his throat open, when he was trying to rape Kate."

Evan's gaze darkened with anger, and Sean pulled me in tighter against his body. "God, Kay."

"I'm fine," I reassured them. "Eileen got to him before he could do anything."

She grinned. "Damn right I did," she agreed. "Should have castrated him, instead of just killing him quick."

Jessica stepped forward, opening the door. Sean climbed in with me, moving to the back seat, and Evan came in on my other side. Jessica followed to join us in the back row. Jimmy and Eileen took the middle seats, and Bridgit and Seamus were up front, with him driving.

Sean looked at my shoulder again, and his lips pressed together. He turned to face Seamus. "Is it far?"

Seamus pressed on the gas. "West Berkshires. Bridgit has a cottage out there. We'll be safe. We'll take care of Katie, don't you worry. We'll be there in under two hours."

I lay against Sean, breathed in the rich musk and scent which was uniquely his, and his arms came up around me. His lips pressed against my forehead, and the world faded away.

Chapter 5

The world shuddered, searing pain echoed through my shoulder, and Sean's arms drew in around me. His voice was warm against my ear. "Hang in there, Kay. We're here. We'll get that shoulder looked at as soon as we get inside."

My eyes were stuck together, and it took a moment for me to pry them open. It was midday, judging by the sun streaming through the car's windows, and we were parked alongside some sort of a massive log cabin. It was two stories tall, with a railinged front porch which stretched the full length of the building. A large, matching two-car garage stood to the side, and the rest of the world was snow-dusted pines and junipers. A dirt road stretched behind us, twisting into the distance.

Everybody began climbing out of the car, groaning and stretching. Evan took my legs, and between him and Sean they got me out and back into Sean's arms again. Sean carried me up the front porch steps. A pair of Adirondack chairs sat to one side. I leant my head against his chest, thinking of the matching photograph he'd done, hanging in his quiet studio. It all seemed so long ago now.

Seamus unlocked the front door, pressed it in, and we followed behind him.

The place was stunning. High, vaulted ceilings crowned the gleaming wood great room. Beyond it was an elegant kitchen in pine and marble. A massive fieldstone fireplace was surrounded by three large, forest-green sofas. A wide staircase led to the second floor, and an open door to the right presented a view of an elegant master bedroom done in shades of rust. Large windows allowed the beauty of the surrounding forest to shine in from all sides.

Eileen turned in place, her mouth open in an O. "It's like the Log Mahal!"

Bridgit nudged her head at the large oak dining room table. "Put Kate on that. The light above is perfect, and we keep all the bandages and supplies in the cupboard there."

Sean nodded, stepping over with me and carefully laying me down on the table.

Bridgit crouched at the cabinet, coming out with a pile of bottles, bandages, and other wraps. "My mother was a nurse," she muttered, laying it all out on the sideboard. "Saw more than my fair share over the years. Comes in handy."

She turned to Seamus. "Nuke us some hot water, will you?"

"Of course." He headed off into the kitchen.

I felt like a star attraction at some sort of bizarre Quincy episode. The others gathered loosely around me, watching with varying degrees of interest as Bridgit cut away the burgundy fabric from the wound area. I groaned with each slice through the gorgeous material. Surely the dress was already beyond repair, but to have it made so blatantly clear still dug at me.

Sean's fingers twined into mine, and he gave a wry smile.

"I'll get you another one," he murmured.

"I just want to go home," I responded, and my throat went tight. Did I even know where home was any more? Certainly not that tiny one-room apartment in the three decker. Sean's brick studio apartment had been a listening post of Seamus and Bridgit, and we could hardly go back there after this was all over. I was adrift, loose, like floating seaweed tossed on a turning tide.

Bridgit's voice was a mutter. "This will hurt, lass."

She pressed something against my shoulder, and the pain buckled my body, arching me back. Sean's fingers braced more tightly into mine, and Evan drew a wet washcloth across my forehead, soothing me in a rough voice. "Hang in there."

Seamus was back with the hot water, and Bridgit dunked one of her cloths into it. She carefully cleaned away the wound. "You were lucky, lass. There was a lot of blood, but it seems the bullet just tore a chunk out of your deltoid. I've seen this before. It'll heal up, over time, and in a few months you'll be as good as new. In Ireland you wouldn't even be hospitalized for this. Just bandaged up and sent home again."

The creases on Evan's face eased, and he nodded. "One of the guys I know had a similar wound. It hurt like hell, but he was fine."

Bridgit worked quickly, adding in ointments, then bandaging up my arm with fresh swaddling. She added a layer of plastic at the end, taping it carefully to my skin. At last she stepped back, putting her hands on her hips in satisfaction. "All done. You go on up and put on some of my sweats and a shirt, and I'll get a fire going in the fireplace." She turned to Seamus. "And I think we could all use some whiskey."

Jimmy's face glowed. "That's for sure! I'll get the glasses!"

Sean swept me up in his arms. "Let's get you into something warmer."

Bridgit nudged her head. "There are clothes in the guest rooms upstairs. Go ahead and claim any one you want."

Sean brought me up the stairs, turning in to the first door at the top. The room was done in navy blue, with a gorgeous oil painting of a serene autumnal lake hanging on one wall. He laid me on the bed, then turned to rummage through the dresser. He came up with a heavy, black sweatshirt and a matching pair of pants, as well as thick socks.

Evan stepped in through the door, closing it behind him. He put a finger to his lips, then pointed up at the ceiling.

My heart dropped, but I nodded. With the family's penchant for bugging rooms, it could be dangerous to talk anywhere within the house. For all we knew, they used this cabin for meetings with their various bosses, and enjoyed getting a sneak preview of their opponents' stances.

Evan came over to the bed, dropping to one knee beside it. He ran his hand along my face, his brow creased with worry. "You're sure you're all right, Kay?"

I nodded reassuringly. "My arm really does feel much better, now that it's cleaned. Once I get some food into me, I'm sure everything will be all right."

Evan looked up at Sean, and the strength in their gazes sent a flush of heat through me. They would see me through this. No matter what it took, they would keep me safe.

Sean reached his hand into his back pocket and drew out his cell phone. He silently pointed to the icon on the top row of the display. He had a flickering half-bar signal.

Evan nodded, and the corner of his mouth turned up in a smile.

I eased back against the pillow. If Sean had even a ghost of a signal, undoubtedly his contacts were, at this very moment, tracking our destination and planning how to get us out again. We just had to hold tight until the cavalry arrived. Sean and Evan would be ready for it. It would all be over soon.

Evan nodded at Sean, then turned and kissed me tenderly on the forehead. He stood and walked from the room, gently closing the door behind him.

We were alone.

I groaned, gazing into Sean's eyes, and he drew me in, wrapping me hard in his arms. His fingers twined up into my hair as he held me. His voice was low and hoarse. "God, Kay, when I saw that bullet hit you …"

"I'm fine," I soothed him. "Bridgit got me out to safety." I drew back, looking him over. "But are you all right? It must have been like the storming of Normandy after we left."

He gave a wry smile. "Something like that," he murmured. "One of the Cubans jammed his rifle and began using it like a mace. Hit me hard in the thigh before I could take him down. I've got a lump the size of a mango, but it'll heal."

He slid his hand along my hair, and then stopped, his brow creasing in confusion. "Kay, you have shattered glass in your hair."

I nodded. "Probably from when they shot out the back window of the car."

He stilled, and then he brought me in harder against him, holding me close, his breath coming in deep draws. "God, Kay, I am so sorry. I am so sorry I got you involved in this whole mess. If I had lost you …"

I gave him a soft kiss on the neck. "I grew up with four wild brothers," I reminded him. "I won't run from trouble. I would have liked to see you try to keep me away." My eyes drew to his, and his depths pulled me in. My voice went hoarse. "There's no way in hell I could have stayed away from you."

His breath stilled, his lips floated toward mine, and then with effort he turned his head, his fingers sliding down my hair again. "You've just been shot," he murmured tightly, "and we should get you cleaned off. Get all this glass, and blood, and …"

His voice stopped. At last he looked down, gathering me up in his arms.

There was the noise of bright conversation easing up the steps as we crossed to the main bathroom. It was as beautifully done as the rest of the house. Moss green shower curtains, a full sized window overlooking the glistening forest, and an oil painting showed a stag and doe standing side by side in a clearing, him standing at alert as she nuzzled a patch of clover.

I moved to the mirror over the shell-shaped sink to take a look at myself – and winced. There were streaks of blood across my face, in some sort of primitive camouflage pattern. My elegant updo was half undone, curls tumbling in a riot, bits of glass adding random sparkles to the outfit. One shoulder was an elegant mastery of beadwork, while the other was a modern art creation of white bandage beneath plastic.

Sean stepped up behind me, his eyes glistening with pride. "My brave warrior," he murmured. He put his fingers to my neck.

A tremor shone through me, filling me with a golden glow.

A hint of a smile danced at the edge of his mouth. "None of that," he cautioned. "We shouldn't get your heart rate up."

"You might always be the Champagne cork," I countered, twining my fingers into his. "However, I can be the slow, gentle bubbling of a pot of hot cocoa, rising, frothing, until I ease over the edges." The corners of my mouth turned up. "That might not be *too* tough on this shoulder of mine."

His lips pressed gently against my neck. "Your brother would kill me."

My eyes sparkled in the mirror. "Oh, so now you're afraid of my brother?"

His teeth flashed in a smile. "I think I could take him, if you were at stake."

I arched back against him, and he groaned. My voice was a soft purr. "His game is rugby," I warned in a tease. "Just wait until Thanksgiving. You'll see he can play rough."

His hand went to my zipper, and he began slowly, languorously lowering it down my back. His voice whispered in my ear. "Oh, I can handle myself. Just you wait and see."

I could feel every movement of the metal releasing its tight caress of me, inch by inch, along my lower back, then against the curve of my rear. Then his hands were up on my shoulders, sliding the silky fabric down my arms, along my waist, down my thighs, to pool at my ankles.

He looked at me for a long moment, drinking me in, and then he turned for a moment, twisting on the shower. The room filled with the noise of the hot water pounding on the smooth surface of the tub.

His hand went to my bra, he groaned, and stopped. "God, Kay, I want you. I want you more than I've wanted anything in my life."

I grinned at him, sliding my hands under his tuxedo jacket, along the tantalizing smoothness of the white shirt which encased his rippling muscles. "Then let's get you out of these gorgeous clothes."

He let me slide the jacket back over his shoulders, pulling one arm free, then the other. He let the jacket drop to one side. His voice was hoarse. "Kay, I don't know if I can be gentle."

I moved a hand to the burgundy tie, still in place after all we'd been through. "Then we'll have to release that cork of yours in some other way," I teased. "Just for now. In deference to your concern over my scratch on my shoulder."

He groaned as I slid the tie free, trailing it along the side of his neck. "Kay, you've been *shot*."

I began slowly undoing his ebony buttons, one by one, my fingers lingering against his skin as I moved. "And what is that pucker of skin near your hip?"

He wound his hand into my hair, his breathing coming more quickly. "That was different, Kay. I know what I'm getting myself into."

I reached the amazing stretch of body which was his abdomen, and I traced the rippled muscles, soaking in their strength. "And so do I," I murmured, pulling his shirt free from his waistband. "I know exactly what I'm getting myself into." I tugged on the fabric, easing it from his shoulders, and in a moment it joined the jacket on the floor.

He reached into his pocket to retrieve his phone as I worked on the buckle. He set it on a glass shelf suspended from the wall, pushed a button, and the haunting intro guitar notes from The Beatles's *Something* drifted out from it.

I smiled as I eased his pants down along his muscular thighs, past the tight calves. He stepped out of them, then his socks. His briefs were pressed out with his pulsing need for me.

Somewhere in her smile she knows
That I don't need no other lover

I took his hand, gently pulling him through the thickening steam into the shower. "We'll just leave our undergarments on for protection," I teased him. "Keep you safe from actually …" I drew my head close to his as we stepped into the pulsing stream of water. "… from pounding me … hard … repeatedly … against the sturdy tile wall of this tub …"

He groaned, and he half turned me, half pressed against me before reining himself in. His voice was tight with desire. "You have bewitched me, Kay."

I turned to face the front of the shower, facing my forehead into the stream, soaking in the warmth and massage of the spray. I braced my hands against the wall before us. "Then tend to me," I murmured. "Make me shine."

His groan was deeper, and there was a pause before he reached over to the shampoo, took a dollop in his hand, and began slowly, gently caressing my scalp. It was the most amazing sensation I'd ever felt. He moved over every inch, his body firm against mine, his fingers seeking out the glass, untwining the knots, releasing me from the stress and chaos of the past few days. My hair became loose, free, falling in cascades down my back.

He reached past me for a washcloth, then put some liquid soap on it. He slid a hand along my good shoulder, and his fingers tremored. "God, Kay, you are so beautiful."

I arched my rear, still clad in panties, back against him. "You're restraining yourself," I teased.

His groan was a half-cry, and the washcloth followed the path of his fingers, the creamy roughness of the fabric activating my skin like a powerful switch. The soft, sensual feel of his body, the counterpoint of the ridged material, and I was lucky I was holding myself up with my hands. My nipples hardened, pressing out against the wet bra, and I craved that washcloth, that rough fabric, against their tips. One hand left the wall, to go back toward my clasp –

He gave a playful swat to my hand, his voice low in my ear. "Nuh-uh," he warned. "You're injured, remember? I'll just have to please myself on my own."

He pressed his hips forward, sliding the hardness of his shaft along the crease in my ass, and I shuddered with pleasure. Even through two layers of fabric, I could feel the hard knob, feel the slickness as the water and shampoo and soap shimmered between us.

And all I have to do is think of her

His fingers slid up with the soapy washcloth, tracing just along the lower edge of my bra, the index finger slipping within the fabric, and I groaned. His cock pressed more firmly against me, sliding, and his hand wrapped around my waist, giving him more traction against me. His other hand came alongside mine on the wall, and his mouth was at my neck.

His voice was a guttural rasp in my ear. "I think of you, Kay. I think of you every second, you're within me, you're a part of me, and you are … you are … God, Kay …" His body slid hard against me, urgent, fast, and then he was shuddering, gasping, his heart pounding in a way I could viscerally feel. The water streamed, steamed, and it was a long minute before he eased against me, before his breathing returned to a more normal level.

He pressed a long, tender kiss against my neck, running his fingers in a caress along my side. "I would do anything for you, Kay."

I turned in his embrace, looking up into his moss-green eyes. My mouth curved into a smile. "Anything?"

His gaze swirled with passion, and with effort he drew in a breath. "Kay, it's for your own good. That wound might not be life threatening, but it's still a hole in your body. You want to let the scabbing start to take hold."

I reached behind me, undoing the clasp of my bra, giving my shoulders a shake so the good shoulder's strap slid free. The other side was hooked on the bandage, and I had to move my fingers up there to get it loose. "I'm the slow simmer," I pointed out.

His eyes shone with desire. "You weren't a slow simmer that night I took you from behind at the overlook at the Tower Hill Botanical Garden. You were a goddess come to life, filled with passion and desire."

Heat built up between my legs, and my hand slid down his hip of its own accord. "All right, then," I amended. "I have many facets, and for this moment of steam and soap, you'll just have to tease out the simmering version of me."

He drew his eyes down my body, gently caressing my peaked nipples, sliding down to the black lace panties which still shielded my soft curls. "Oh, I think I can do that," he murmured.

He knelt in front of me, and the swirl of desire in my sex deepened, thickened, and the feel of his fingers on either side of my hips sent waves of longing through me. I could feel every inch of movement as they eased my panties down my legs, resting for just a moment against my knees before carrying down to my ankles.

His hands caressed me as he slid his way back up my body to standing, and he brushed his lips against mine, soft, tantalizing. Then he turned me in place, so I stood between him and the stream of water. The gentle pulsing landed on my chest, and I felt the warmth of it course into my heart, spread out through every aspect of me.

He wrapped an arm around my waist, supporting me with his sturdy chest, and rocked back and left.

The stream moved, slid, and then tickled the edge of my right nipple.

I sighed in pleasure, closing my eyes, and the feeling was indescribable. His firm muscles behind me, his steady arm holding me up, and all I had to do was float, breathe, absorb the delicious sensations which coursed through me. He drifted me in slow circles, the stream changing its angle, its target, and my breast glowed with pleasure.

A gentle movement, a shifting, and then the circle of attention slid, drifted, and the left nipple came barely into the stream. My moan was deeper now, and I could feel my juices easing from me, mixing with the water that trailed down my stomach, my back, the length of my legs. Both of my breasts were full to bursting now, fragrant with desire, taut with need. His hand at my waist slid in a caress against my skin, and my whole body pulsed with a sense of anticipation.

Then he lifted me so I was barely on my toes, and he stepped back. The water drifted lower … lower … desire bubbled higher within me, expanding all of my senses, filling all of my thoughts, until there was only the motion of the water, the feeling of his body everywhere, and the steam filling my lungs, filling my ears, filling me …

The water made contact.

I was there. I shuddered, gently, completely, slipping over a line into a world of utter joy and serenity and fulfillment. Sean was here. Sean was all-encompassing. I was his, and I let everything else go.

Chapter 6

All eyes turned as Sean carried me, clothed in soft fabrics, glowing in contentment, down the long flight of stairs. Bridgit nudged Seamus with a grin. "The oldest medicine in the world," she teased. "Does wonders." She waved a hand to the spread of soda bread, herbed butter, a plate of various cheeses, and another with cold cuts. "Sit down and eat up. You must be starving after all that … medicinal activity."

My stomach growled in response, and Sean smiled as he deposited me down on the couch. As I took in the wealth of options, I looked at the meats in confusion. "Are these fresh?"

Bridgit nodded. "We were planning on coming out here for the holidays, and I have a local woman handle the cleaning and shopping for us. The phone's not turned on, and there's barely cell service out here, but we have everything else one could need. The house is fully stocked. So eat up – we have plenty more."

Seamus's brow creased. "Speaking of which …" He held out his hand.

Sean held his gaze for a moment, then nodded, reaching into his back pocket and bringing out his phone. He handed it over.

Seamus flipped through the screens for a moment, then nodded in satisfaction. "Your usage is flat for the past twenty-four hours. No calls, texts, or messages. It's good to know I can trust in you, Sean." He flipped the phone and popped out the battery. "It'll take that parole officer of yours a day or two to sort through the mess and think to follow that signal. By then we'll be long gone. For now, we heal up and grab rest while we can."

His gaze moved up to Sean's eyes. "That Taurus still on you?"

Sean nodded, but his hand didn't move toward the back of his waist, where I could see its outline beneath his t-shirt.

Seamus held his gaze for a long moment, and at last he nodded. "You keep that. There could still be some trouble, and I could use you at my side, until we finally part ways."

His mouth curved into a smile. "But, for now, we drink, we eat, and we celebrate being alive." He turned to me. "Especially you, lass." He leant forward, filling my glass to the brim with Redbreast. "Have some of this. It'll help, in ways other than Bridgit's ointments."

I nodded, taking up the whiskey and swallowing a long draw. A soothing warmth spread within me, and I leant against Sean with a sigh. He took up a slice of the soda bread, slathered it with butter, then put it on a plate and handed it over. He broke off a corner and popped it into his mouth as he did so. His eyes lit up.

"Oh, that's good. Just like mom used to make."

Bridgit nodded. "There's a woman in town who bakes it fresh. Spectacular stuff. She hails from Kerry."

I took a bite, and satisfaction eased through me. It was, indeed delicious. The slice was gone before I knew it, and Sean grinned as he prepared a second for me.

Jimmy nudged Eileen, who sat alongside him. "Drink up, Eileen. You haven't even touched your whiskey! You used to down this stuff like it was water. Could almost keep up with Bridgit here."

Eileen's cheeks tinted. "Actually, I am pretty thirsty," she admitted. "Maybe I could just have some milk?"

Jimmy looked at her as if she'd grown a third eye in the middle of her forehead. "Jesus Christ, you're kidding, right?"

Bridgit stared at Eileen for a long moment, her gaze trailing down her breasts to rest on her abdomen. The corners of her mouth turned down, and she crossed her arms across her chest.

The words came out in a low mutter. "The girl's breeding."

Jimmy froze, his eyes widening, and for a long moment his mouth hung open. Then the warmth of joy suffused his face, and he leant forward, his lips widening into an incredulous grin. "Is it true? Is it really true, Eileen?"

She hesitated, biting her lower lip, then nodded.

He swept her up into a hug, spinning around in a circle with her, laughter bubbling up out of him like water from a spring. "I'm going to be a daddy! I'm going to be a daddy!"

Seamus slowly drew to his feet, a dark frown on his face. "God damnit, Jimmy, don't you think you should –"

Bridgit put a hand on his arm, and he stopped, looking down at her.

She slowly shook her head, her eyes holding acceptance, and I thought I saw a tinge of regret in there. "Let him go, Seamus. He's not Liam. He never will be. He needs to … he needs to just be himself."

Seamus lay his fingers against his sister's cheek. "Are you sure, Bridge?"

She nodded, her shoulders slumping. "I should have known years ago. It'll be better. For all of us."

Jimmy had his fingers laced into Eileen's hair, holding her head to his chest, and he looked over at his wife. His eyes shone with jubilation. "Thank you, Bridgit. Thank you."

She nodded. "Guess you and your knocked-up girl can take one of the other guest rooms, then. Seamus and I will share the master bedroom." She gave Seamus a wry smile. "It'll be like when we were kids, sharing a bed."

He topped off her glass, and raised it to her. "*Cha d'dhùin doras nach d'fhosgail doras.*"

She nodded. "No door ever closed, but another one opened. We'll be fine."

She drank down half her glass, then turned with an amused smile to Evan and Jessica. "Guess that means you two share the last room."

Evan nodded evenly, glancing at Jessica. "We'll be all right." His gaze turned to Seamus. "So you mean for us to spend the night?"

Seamus waved a hand at the darkening world through the large windows. "We're all exhausted, and night's nearly here anyway. You swore you wouldn't do anything to impede us, while we're all together, and I trust your word on that." He gave a wry smile. "However, I'm not stupid enough to test it past your limits."

He gave a long stretch. "Tomorrow I take me, Bridgit, and the two dopes over there out of here. I'll have time by then to set up a fresh car and get my money transferred. We'll leave you here to fend with the turkey and bears."

He glanced at the disassembled phone on the table. "Undoubtedly in a day or two the cops will either have traced that phone's location, or would have figured out that Liam's name on this lease connects to us. They'll stream in like a springtime trout run."

He grinned. "You have plenty of food to last a week, if not more. And, of course, if you're feeling energetic, you can always hike the thirty miles into town and call for assistance yourself. Just watch out for the bears and coyotes."

Evan nodded, his gaze on Seamus. "If you're planning to leave us behind, I am more than happy to behave while we're all holed up here. My priority is to have Kay and Jessica to come through this unhurt. They're innocent in all of this."

Seamus raised his glass. "Kay's been a good girl." He turned to me and Sean. "You know, the offer stands. If you two want to come along with us, you're welcome to. You'd have to start fresh, though. New name, new identity, no contact at all with the past."

Evan's gaze steeled, and Sean shook his head. "I don't think her family would allow that," he stated wryly. "And I wouldn't do that to her. No, I'm afraid that this is where we'll part company."

Seamus took a drink of his whiskey. "The roads diverge, and we have to make our choice. I wish you the best of luck. You're a steady man, Sean."

Bridgit downed the rest of her drink. "Well, Seamus, we have a lot of planning to get done. Let's you and I head into the bedroom and get started on it." She grabbed up the bottle of Redbreast. "With proper fortification, of course."

Seamus stood with her. He turned to the rest of us. "Stars are gorgeous out here at night, but stay on the porch," he advised. "I wasn't kidding about the bears. There are blueberry bushes all along the property, and we have regular visitors. Wouldn't want one of you to get mauled, just as we're about to part ways all peaceful-like."

The two of them turned, and in a moment their door closed behind them.

Jimmy nuzzled at Eileen's neck, and then swept her up again. "Why don't we go explore our room, my darling?"

She giggled with glee. "Oh, Jimmy, you're so romantic!"

He beamed with joy, and then he was carefully negotiating the stairs up. The sound of a solid thud indicated the door was closed, and then there was a high pitched squeal of excitement.

Jessica shook her head. "Why don't we go out and look at those stars for a while?"

Evan looked over at me. "Are you up to it?"

I nodded, drawing to my feet, Sean's arm under my good elbow. "I'll be fine," I agreed. "Delicious food, fine whiskey, and once I get a solid night's sleep in me, I'll be right as rain."

Some ski parkas were hanging on hooks by the door, and we slipped them on, then stepped out onto the front porch.

Seamus hadn't been kidding. With the last golden glow of sunset fading in the west, the sky had sprung to life with a glittering of stars that seemed almost supernatural. Growing up in Waterbury, I'd been lucky to see even a handful of stars against the bright lights of the city. Worcester hadn't been much better. But here, without lights for miles, the night sky had come alive.

Sean brought his hand to the back of his waist for a moment, scanning the woods for motion, then he nodded with his head. We came down off the porch and moved a short distance down the driveway, to the edge of the main clearing. He attentively swept the dark forest, then spoke in a low voice. "We should be all right here."

I looked between him and Evan. I kept my own voice to a whisper. "What the hell happened at the warehouse?"

Evan shook his head. "We had no idea. I was at the command center a block away from the church parking lot, with our brothers on speakerphone, filling them in. One minute everything was going perfectly. We were staging our teams inside the church. We were going to wait until the dancing began before getting them into the trucks. That way there was as short a window of time as possible for them to be spotted and an alarm raised. We had some remote cameras set up watching the area around the warehouse, but everything seemed quiet."

His brow creased. "And then, it was like a tsunami. Waves of cars of Cubans came barreling in, out of nowhere. The men raced in through the loading dock. By the time our guys got on the scene, it was nearly over. Most people were dead or wounded. But certain, key people were missing." His gaze held mine. "Like you."

He glanced at Sean. "When Francesca met with Sean Friday night, she passed to him a key to my car. An emergency backup for him, in case something went wrong. The Mustang has LoJack in it, so we could have traced him if he'd taken it. Besides, he only has that bike of his"

Evan took my hand in his. "As soon as I realized you and Sean were missing, I sprinted back to my car. I found him, Seamus, and Jimmy there."

Sean nodded. "Seamus got us out a back way, and said he knew where Bridgit might have run to, to hole up. When Evan showed up, Seamus almost shot him – but we convinced him that Evan's brotherly feelings trumped any job-related ideals he might have. Seamus took his cell phone and handgun, but he let him come along with us."

I gave Evan's fingers a squeeze. "Thank you."

He held my gaze, his look steady. "You know I'd come for you, no matter what." He glanced at Sean. "No matter what hair-brained situation you manage to get yourself into."

I smiled, leaning against Sean. "Well, but now we just wait until tomorrow, right? Surely the police are planning their action this very minute. They must have followed us, or tracked us, or *something*. In the morning they'll see that the O'Malleys are leaving without us, and just snag them after they pull away. Nobody's at risk, everybody is caught, and we're done."

Sean pressed his lips to my forehead. "That's the hope, anyway."

Jessica yawned. "Well, I think we could all use some sleep, so we're fresh and alert, just in case there is trouble. Is there anything else? If not, I'm heading in."

Evan patted her on the shoulder. "Thank you for watching after my sister. You need anything at all, in the future, you just let me know."

She grinned. "I'll remember that." She nodded and headed back into the house.

I looked after her, a smile playing at my lips. "I think she likes you, Evan."

He flushed and turned to look at me. "Kay, I'm with someone."

My eyebrows raised. "You, the man with a stream of hot dates, is finally settling down? When did this happen?"

His lips curved into a smile. "About a month ago. She's amazing, Kay. I'm sure you'll love her. When all of this is over, I'd like for you to meet her."

I gave him a nudge. "She must be pretty special, to have caught the most eligible bachelor in Boston. All right, then, it's a plan. Maybe you'll bring her down to Thanksgiving?"

He nodded. "I was planning on it." He looked over at Sean. "And maybe, if this all wraps up, you could come as well?"

Sean held his gaze. "You're saying I'd be welcome?"

Evan clapped him on the shoulder. "I'll still say that you could have found a way to keep Kay out of this – but I know how my sister can get. Stubborn as a mule. I don't know where she gets that from."

Evan's eyes sparkled for a moment, then grew serious. "You've risked your life for her, several times. You'd go through fire for her. I'm trusting you. I'm trusting you with her life."

Evan put out his hand.

Sean took it, and the brilliant stars glistened, shimmering against their ebony velvet blanket.

Chapter 7

The barest hint of golden glow edged the room as I blinked my eyes open. I was sprawled across Sean, his rippled chest beneath me, and my hand slid down his side in a languid caress. I reached the firm muscles of his abdomen and grinned.

What was it with guys and morning?

I crept my fingers down through his dense hair, slid them along his shaft, and gave a gentle squeeze.

He groaned, shifted, and his arm drew around me in an automatic motion as his eyes came open. He looked down the length of my body, his mouth widening in a smile.

"Now this is the way to wake up."

I cupped my hand, sliding it more firmly down his length, and his hips rose up off the bed. His breath came out in a sigh.

I reached over to pull myself more fully on top of him, but he shook his head, lifting me and gently rolling me to the side. "Uh, uh," he scolded. "It's barely twenty-four hours since you've been shot, my darling. None of that riding-me-like-a-wild-stallion is going to happen this morning."

I pursed my lips in disappointment. "You're going to let me languish in carnal craving?"

He chuckled at that, then reached over to the drawer beside the bed. He slid it open and put his hand inside. "Look at what I found."

My eyes lit up in anticipation …

He drew out a roll-on fragrance, shaped sort of like a thick magic marker.

My brow creased in confusion. "What are you going to do with that? Tickle my nose?"

He popped off the cap and brought it near my face. "Smell it."

I closed my eyes and gave a soft sniff. It was indeed quite lovely. Some sort of combination of jasmine and ripe peach.

He gave me a gentle pat on the hip. "Roll over onto your stomach."

I dutifully obeyed. The clean sheets felt crisp and nice beneath my body.

He moved near my feet, there was a long pause, and then he placed the roll softly, with the lightest of touches, against my left ankle.

He began tracing a line, slowly, languorously, up the back of my leg, as if he were painting on a pinstripe from one of those pairs of elegant black French pantyhose. I could feel every movement of his hand, and the liquid in the fragrance left a shimmering sensation behind it, cool and alive.

I moaned, and he gave a soft chuckle.

The line traced its way up against the tender skin of my inner knee, and he lingered there for a moment, exerting soft pressure. My body arched in response.

His voice was a murmur. "Slow and gentle," he reminded me. "The colors of dawn revealing a beautiful, rural sunrise. The blossoming of amethyst, tangerine, and deepest crimsons before day begins."

His line moved up, up, along my thigh, and came to rest in the crease just before the swell of my buttocks.

The pen lifted up, and a sigh eased out of me.

A pause, an inhale of jasmine and ripe peach, and the slightest of pressure against my right ankle.

He went slower this time, the seconds stretching, the swirl within my inner knee a sensual slow dance of skin and slickness. Then the line was moving … approaching … delving …

It lifted away.

My legs tingled with energy, with awareness, and I waited …

The barest hint of pressure, right on the lower center of my back. He lingered there a moment, then rose up and around as if tracing the bulbous curve of a heart. He came down, across the curve of my rear, diagonally angling in toward my inner thigh, and I wanted his hand, wanted the line, wanting the wet glistening to …

He came within a finger's breadth of that sweet juncture, and lifted away.

My breath was coming deeper now, the waves of desire washing over me like an incoming tide. The pressure returned again, in the exact same spot at my lower back, but this time the line traced the opposite side of the heart, sweeping around, angling down, down, and I craved …

He slid his other hand along my hip, lifting with gentle pressure, and I rolled onto my back, looking up at him. His gaze was smoky with desire, and his cock throbbed with heat as he looked down me. My nipples stood out hard from my breasts, and I could feel the moisture building further below.

He lay propped up on one arm at my side, and slowly, attentively, he brought the tip of the pen down to rest in my navel. Again he brought it up, out in a curve, then angled down across my hip-bone delving, drawing closer …

The pen lifted away, and a soft moan drifted through my lips.

He chuckled at that. "Seamus took my phone," he murmured, "but let's see if this clock radio can pick up anything." He pushed the button and turned the dial to the right.

There was a bit of static, a slow swell of guitars, and then the lyrics drifted out.

Home, home again
I like to be here when I can.
And when I come home, cold and tired,
It's good to warm my bones beside the fire.

I chuckled. *Pink Floyd* – and I knew well which track came next.

A rich look came into his eyes. "Oh, this'll do quite nicely."

He brought the glistening line in a slow, wending path up my abdomen, through the hollow between my breasts, and carefully, slowly, drew a heart in the center of my chest.

With focused attention he began filling it in.

Another moan escaped me as he swirled the pen near my breast, and his breath was warm against my ear. "Let it out," he softly urged. "Let each breath out sing."

Clare Torre's wordless cry bubbled out from the radio, drawing me in.

Sean leaned in against me and my sigh became a richer groan, my nipples hardening further.

He brushed his lips against mine. "Good girl."

My sex heated, my eyes held his, and then his pen finished with the filling of my heart, and moved to circle, slowly, with absolute focus, around my right breast.

My breaths were now drawn-out moans, almost soft cries of helpless desire, merging in with the song. He circled the pen higher, laying down an ascending spiral which shimmered with energy and jasmine. It climbed higher, higher, and my body lifted with every turn, every inch, and he was nearly …

The pen lifted away, and my cry was tinged with a deep-seated ache.

He brought the pen back to the base of my other breast, and his voice was thick with need. "God, Kay, you are stunning. I want you … I …"

He bit back on what he wanted to say, and renewed his focus on my curved breast, on the rosy peak at its tip. His breath came in deeper draws as he traced its fullness, as the glistening pen slid along my skin, and my groans of pleasure sent a tremor through his hand. When the tip reached the edge of the crimson circle, his finger nearly reached for the tip, nearly followed the desperate urgings of my soul.

He looked down into my eyes, and I knew he was teetering on the edge.

I rolled to my side, slid a hand along his hip, then wrapped my fingers around his firm ass and pulled.

His voice held the tightest edge of restraint. "Kay, you know you're not ready for –"

I pulled again, angling up, and he groaned with understanding. He straddled my chest, I brought my other hand up to cup his other cheek, and then I brought my mouth over his head, already glistening with pre-cum.

I blinked my eyes up to look into his, I groaned with pleasure, and I pulled his length fully into my throat.

He threw his head back, biting down the groan which shuddered throughout his body. The radio echoed his emotion, the singer crying out her need and craving and release.

He balanced on his knees, his hands winding into my hair, and I drew back a bit before sliding down fully again, my chin pressing into his balls, the back of my throat enveloping him. My groan of desire was deeper, richer, and I could see into the very depths of his soul.

He was nearly there, now. I could feel it in the tremor of his fingers against my head, in the flutter in his lashes as he struggled to hold on for just one more stroke.

His voice was hoarse with need. "Spread your legs for me, baby. Spread them wide."

I slid my legs open further, and then tension in them sent sweet agony through them, building with the tracery of glowing lines on my front and back, the lines all pointing to my sweet center, to where I wanted him, needed him, craved him with all that I was and ever would be.

His voice was a groan. "Feel me, my love. Feel me, as I … as I …"

I pulled him in, hard, squeezing down on his cock with my throat, digging my fingers into his ass, taking down every last inch of him. He threw his head back hard, groaning, the music crescendoing. Then the light of morning came blazing through the window, filling me with golden power, as his cum coursed down my throat.

In his abandon he reached a hand back, and with the gentlest of motions, he brushed my clit.

I was released. It was beyond anything I had ever felt before. I was a hot air balloon, and the final rope had been cut, sending me soaring into a cerulean sky. I was a hot geyser, and a dam had eased loose, letting me bubble, lift, release in a way I had never thought possible.

I was expanding, shimmering into a rich, fragrant cloud of jasmine and ripe peach, and I was one with the universe.

I floated, enlarged, gently spun, and then at long, long last I drifted, settled, and eased onto the earth, like a fairy's layer of dew settling onto a field of forget-me-nots.

Time drifted away, slowly reformed, and at long last a fresh energy imbued into my very marrow, revitalized my inner core.

He came down to lie next to me, his eyes shining. He pressed a kiss against my lips. "Ready for coffee?"

I ran a hand through his hair, smiling. "You do know me well," I teased. I stretched then climbed out of bed. I pulled on the sweats and t-shirt, stuffing my feet back into the socks and tucking them into a pair of moccasin slippers. I turned with a grin. "I think I'm going to go breathe in this fresh forest air that I've heard so much about."

Sean leaned back against the headboard, watching me with a sparkle in his eyes. "Watch out for the bears," he teased. "I'll have the coffee ready when you decide to come back in to civilization."

I gave him a wink, then headed down the stairs. The house was silent; apparently everybody else was still soaking in the quiet relaxation that the *Log Mahal* seemed to radiate. The polished wood glistened in the morning sunlight as I crossed the great room and pushed open the door.

I closed my eyes for a moment, breathing in deeply. I'd been kidding with Sean, but there really was something about this place. The juniper and pine glistened in the golden streams of light, and the sky above was a rich, Maxfield Parrish blue. Wisps of clouds drifted by, and it seemed something out of an oil painting. Something far removed from the gritty streets of Worcester or Waterbury or anywhere else I'd ever been before.

I stepped across the porch and down into the grassy clearing which fronted the house. The Escalade was parked to one side, but other than that there was no sign of humanity anywhere before me. The low witch hazel and blueberry bushes presented sprawls in infinite shades of green, and beyond that the forest stretched, seemingly to infinity.

I stretched my arms high above my head, arching my back, feeling, for the first time in weeks, relaxed.

A branch snapped.

I blinked to attention, stepping back a step. I wasn't sure if Seamus was serious about those bears, but I wasn't taking any chances. I was prepared to sprint for the door, to raise the alarm, to –

A movement at the far end of the clearing, a glimpse of pale pink, and then Francesca was standing just within the treeline. She wore a pink silk top with a low neckline, and tight, elegantly shaped jeans. Her high leather boots seemed to blend in with the dark brown trunks.

She made a calling motion with her hand.

My heart pounded against my chest. They were here. I'd wondered how long it would take them to get set up. Surely their GPS triangulation of our position couldn't take too long, once Sean's phone had come to rest. Undoubtedly the remainder of the time had seen them carefully bringing in the troops, laying out a perimeter, and doing all those other things a team did to ensure the safety of all involved.

A grin spread on my face. Soon it would all be over.

I glanced behind me, but the house remained silent. All within slumbered peacefully, completely unaware of what was fermenting just outside their walls. I strode quickly across the clearing, coming up to reach Francesca. She patted me on my good arm, her face aglow with excitement.

"So, you are all right? I heard you'd been shot."

I nudged my head at my left arm, wrapped with the bandage. "That arm just got nicked. It'll be fine, so they say. Sean's leg was bruised, but all in all we're in good shape." I looked behind her. "Is everyone in place?"

She nodded, her eyes sparkling. "Oh, everything is going just perfectly," she agreed. "What's the situation inside?"

"Seamus and Bridgit are in the master bedroom, in the bottom right," I reported. "Sean and I have the first room upstairs. Then are Evan with Jessica, and finally Jimmy with Eileen."

Her brow creased in confusion. "Wait, weren't Jimmy and Bridgit the couple?"

I made a waving motion with my hand. "We can explain it all later. Things have gotten a little complicated in their relationship."

A knowing smile spread on her face. "Oh, Eileen told everyone about the baby, and Bridgit has let him go?"

I blinked, then remembered that Sean had met with Francesca to do his final planning the night before the party. Undoubtedly he had passed along all information he could so that the group could plan well for all contingencies. A flush of guilt went through me at the world knowing Eileen's secret, but I pushed it down. After all, she'd told the people who mattered most. It didn't really make a difference now if the police knew.

I nodded to her. "Yes, that's exactly what happened. The four of them are planning on heading out in a little while, and leaving me, Sean, Evan, and Jessica behind. If you just wait until they drive away, you can capture the four of them without much problem at all. I'm sure Sean and Evan can come up behind to lend a hand, if you need them to. Although Evan doesn't have a gun right now, so only Sean can really be a help."

She tapped an elegant finger to a lip. "Oh, I'm sure they can all help, in their own ways."

She turned to look behind her.

"Did you get all of that, darling?"

There was a movement, and out from the shadows walked Javier, flanked by two husky Cuban soldiers, each carrying a pistol in his hand.

Javier nodded in satisfaction as he looked me over, drawing his gun to aim it at me. "I heard every word."

Chapter 8

A cold sweat shook me, and it was a moment before I could breathe, could take in what was happening. I looked from the pistol in Javier's hand to the bright grin on Francesca's face.

My throat was tight. "Francesca, what are you doing?"

She crossed her arms across her chest, glancing dismissively down the dirt road for a moment. "All those hours I put into my job. The enormous risks I take. And do you know, when I come back from an undercover assignment, that they want me to put all my jewelry into storage at the precinct? The other women I hang out with are draped in diamonds and rubies. They have Coach handbags and Manolo Blahnik heels. I can barely afford sneakers! And I'm supposed to be the good guy!"

She snorted. "Not only that, but you should see how the guys treat me. If I'm dolled up in my undercover clothes, they drool all over me. They fall over themselves lending me a hand." Her face darkened. "But I put the uniform back on, and it's like they don't see me. I'm just one of the guys." Her voice took on a sing-song quality. "Do your own paperwork, Francesca. Stay late to finish those reports, Francesca."

She tossed her head toward Javier. "As soon as I met Javier, I knew he was different. Here was a man who appreciated a woman. He treated me right. He treated me *special*. He rewarded me for who I was – and I returned the favor." Her smile lit, and she held out her hand, showcasing a diamond bracelet on it. "Look what he gave me, just yesterday! This is how I deserve to be treated."

I could barely speak; my lungs compressed with fear. My voice was a whisper. "Francesca, what did you tell him?"

She grinned. "Why, the truth of course. That's what friends do for each other, right? I told him that your darling Sean, apple of Seamus's eye, is his meal ticket to success. He hands over Sean to Seamus, to prove his good intentions, and after Sean is taken care of, the two of them can do business together."

I wove, and it took all my strength to remain upright, to focus on her glistening eyes. "Please, Francesca, no. There's got to be another way."

Her grin grew, and she glanced at Javier for a moment. "See, what did I tell you? The girl has sense."

Javier smiled, nodding his head. "I knew you were an asset to our organization, Francesca, from the first moment I set eyes on you."

Francesca patted me on my arm. "Of course there's another way, my sweet. You just go along with our plan, and get Sean not to cause any trouble. You do that, and we won't say a word about Sean and his questionable background." She shrugged. "It's in your own best interest, after all."

Her eyes narrowed in delight. "And then you also have that innocent girl, Jessica, to think of."

My blood ran cold. She was holding out from Javier after all. Another card, close to the chest. I knew she would use that for leverage if she had to. Yet another way to coerce us into doing what she wanted.

I took in a deep breath. "What is it that you want?"

She rubbed her hands together. "Well, first, we need to get in out of this cold. I saw you guys had a lovely fireplace in there, and all sorts of tasty food. That could do well as a start." She glanced at Javier. "And then, we talk."

I looked between the two of them. "Talk?"

Javier spread his hands wide. "That's all we want, to talk. The police are dismantling both of our operations as we speak. Our men are being rounded up in Hartford, Boston, Providence, and elsewhere. The layers are being peeled off one by one." He shrugged. "We'll both need to set up shop somewhere new and rebuild from the ground up. Why not do it together?"

My brows creased. "Maybe because you just tried to exterminate his entire crew?"

He laughed. "Let's not forget that Seamus was planning to rid himself of us in a less than peaceful manner. These are business negotiations. We let the past be the past, and we look at what the future holds for us. As it stands now, we both have the best chances of success if we work together. Seamus will see the sense of that."

I dug my hands deep into the pockets of the sweats. Fear and the morning's chill were sending tremors through my body. "And what do you want from me?"

Javier waved his gun toward me. "You'll help us get in the door, of course. They'll pay attention if we have a hostage. But after that, I hardly think you'll be important to our talk. When we finish up, I imagine things will go just as Seamus had planned. You and your crew will remain behind in the house. Seamus and I, with our respective groups, will head out together. You won't be able to pursue us, and by the time your help arrives in a day or two we'll be long gone."

He gave a wry smile. "If we were to hurt you, we'd only increase their desire to catch us. By leaving you alive, we're merely the run-of-the-mill criminals heading for the border. We'll make it out before we're caught."

I wasn't sure I agreed with his simplified version of the future, but I bit my tongue. If he was willing to do this the smooth and calm way, I was all for it.

I nodded. "Agreed. I will behave, and I will do my best to see Sean and Evan behave. You can have your talk with Seamus."

A voice called out from the house, and I turned. It was Sean. I could see through the trees that he was standing on the porch, his hands cupped around his mouth. "Kate! Coffee's ready!"

Javier made an elegant, sweeping motion with his hand. "After you."

Chapter 9

Sean's eyes lit up in amused relief as I emerged from the darkness of the woods – and then he stilled. His hand reached slowly, carefully for the back of his hip where the black t-shirt draped over his sweats.

Francesca's voice was light and merry. "Uh, uh, Sean. Turn to the side, and take it out with two fingers only. We see more than two fingers and your girlfriend earns herself a nice exit wound. This one won't be as easy to heal."

Sean's shoulder muscles rippled, but he turned, and the Taurus came up off his hip held only by two fingers.

Francesca motioned with a sweep of her hand. "Put it on one of those silly chairs over there. Then go ahead and open the door for us. Not to worry – we'll be honored guests. I think Seamus will like what we have to say."

Sean stepped to the chair, but he paused there a moment, his gaze steadily on Francesca. "And what might that be?"

She grinned. "Not to worry, dear Sean. If all goes as planned, then Javier and the rest of us will be out of your hair in no time. You, your girlfriend, and the other two will be left behind in the cabin, just as you'd planned."

Sean held her eyes for a long moment, as if judging her, and then at last he carefully placed his gun into the seat of the wooden chair. He stepped back over to the door.

As he pressed it open, he called out, his tone steady but clear. "Evan!"

Evan's feet sounded in quick movement along the hallway, and he was half-way down the stairs before he drew to a sharp halt, his eyes sweeping the group with attention. His hand swept to his hip, hit open air, and he stilled.

Javier nodded in greeting. "Gather up the rest of them. And some coffee, if you have it. It's been a chilly night out there."

The master bedroom door pulled open. Seamus blinked sleepily, then started awake. "What the hell?"

Sean's voice was low. "They just want to talk. Let's see what they have to say."

Javier settled me on the couch nearest the window, with Francesca sitting close at my other side. His other two men arranged themselves behind the couch, their guns out but hanging at their sides. In short order the rest of the household was sitting on the two couches opposite us. Bridgit brought around coffee and muffins for the group, and rousted the fire back into fresh life. For all appearances we were a casual group of friends, planning out a weekend of hiking and fun.

All except Javier's gun, which was resting in his lap, pointed at my abdomen.

Sean and Evan were side by side on the couch across from me, their attention a laser focus. Sean's voice was low and calm. "You have what you want. We're listening. You can put the gun away."

Javier smiled. "Soon enough, Sean. But first, I want to make sure Seamus and I are on the same page."

Seamus's brow creased. "And what page might that be?"

Javier sat back. "We've had a number of misunderstandings in the past. That disconnect was exacerbated by a few … issues … with crew members we could not depend on. For example, Raul was far out of line with how he handled Kate here. I accept he went rogue, and I accept that, when he tried to shoot Kate, you defended her. There are no hard feelings. That's what happens when a member of one's crew becomes untrustworthy."

I looked at my hands, resisting the nearly overwhelming desire to look up at Sean. Javier's words were a clear warning to me, and to Sean. If we did not do everything in our power to help this détente, one word from Javier and the dynamics of this group might change drastically.

Sean was unarmed. Evan was as well. I knew both men were good – very good – with their fists. But if Seamus and Javier decided to shoot them down in cold blood …

Seamus nodded, seeming oblivious to the tense emotions which were twisting tightly on all sides. "I agree – any man in my crew who acts disloyally can expect a brutal end." His mouth quirked into a wry grin. "Which poor Sean here discovered, not so long ago. Luckily, Kate stepped in in time to save him."

Javier's eyes sparkled with amusement. "Lucky for him."

Seamus nodded. "So, what now?"

Javier took a sip of his coffee. "By now I'd assume the cops have rounded up the vast majority of both of our groups. The more they sweep up, the more our men will want to talk, to receive the best deal. We know how this goes. It's the price of doing business. So we'll need to start over."

He looked to Bridgit. "You two have always been admirable planners. I assume by this point you have your finances in order and are ready to move on."

Bridgit's voice was tight. "So what if we are?"

Javier spread his hands wide. "I have done the same, and I have a pathway out of the country. To an ocean-view villa. Warm. Tropical. Glistening white-sand beaches." He gave a stretch. "I can easily take four more with me."

Bridgit's brow creased with suspicion. "Why would you take us with you?"

Javier nodded. "You have access to the distribution network; one that took you years to assemble. Canada, Mexico, Europe, and beyond. Once you create your product, you can move it across the globe with the click of a button. No more need for shipping crates of tapes that can get impounded in customs. You zip up a file and off it goes, and the money pours in." He leant forward. "You have the distribution, but you won't have the girls."

Seamus's gaze narrowed. "And you'll handle that?"

He nodded in satisfaction. "My sister, Aymee, is engaged to a businessman from Cambodia. He has easy access to thousands of girls. Families there live on just two dollars a day, so the parents are eager to sell off their daughters' bodies to make some extra money."

My stomach twisted in horror, and I forced myself to stare at my hands, to breathe in, breathe out. It was imperative I let this transaction go through, to get these criminals out into their car and on their way. Surely the police would be able to track them down, once they were on the road, and bring them all to justice.

Eileen's voice was bright. "See, we are doing them a favor! They get to have some fun sex, and their families can live in luxury! Maybe go out for sushi every once in a while."

I could hear the twinkle of a grin in Javier's tone. "Yes, that's exactly right, Eileen."

He turned to Seamus. "So, what do you say? Our car is parked down the road, and none of your … friends … here in the house have seen it. The eight of us take your car down to mine, trade off, and now we're in a vehicle that's completely unknown to anybody else. I get us to our transportation, we settle in our new home, and we set up shop. Split the proceeds fifty-fifty."

Seamus held his gaze. "How do I know I can trust you?"

Javier shrugged. "I suppose you don't. But since I'm starting fresh somewhere entirely new, I have nothing to gain from causing more trouble before I go. It would only increase enthusiasm in police search efforts. Plus it makes good business sense to leverage your talents and resources."

I twined my fingers into each other, fervently praying for Seamus to take the offer. If he didn't, Javier would move to plan B – to prove his good faith by offering up a sacrificial lamb for flaying alive.

Sean.

My heart pounded against my ribs, and I could barely breathe. Every thought in my head was a mantra, an earnest plea, a desperate cry … *Please … Please … Please …*

At last Seamus nodded and put out his hand. "It's a deal."

Relief coursed through me, and I finally risked raising my gaze to Sean and Evan. I could see the same easing of tension through their shoulders, the infinitesimal relaxing of their bodies back against the couch.

Javier shook Seamus's hand. "I look forward to our relationship."

Sean's voice was low. "So you won't be needing Kate any more?"

Javier's smile grew into a wide grin. "A single-minded focus, I see. You're right, her role in this is complete." He tucked his gun away behind his waistband. "Go on, Kate. You've done well."

My legs were wobbly, but I carefully stood and made my way around the coffee table. Sean and Evan rose as I approached, one on either side, and they moved with me to the back side of the couch. They stepped together to shield me with their bodies.

Bridgit climbed out of her seat. "Our bags are all packed; I'll go get them. She called over her shoulder as she went. "Kate, I hope you don't mind cleaning up after we go. Usually I'd hate to leave a place in this state, but this is a special occasion."

"Of course, Bridgit," I responded, my heart returning to a more normal rhythm. In a moment Bridgit re-emerged with a large suitcase in each hand, her bulk easily moving them with her. She glanced at Jimmy and Eileen. "All right, you two. Into the car."

Eileen laced her fingers into Jimmy's, her eyes bright with excitement. "I can't wait to see where we're going, Jimmy! Do you think they'll have waterfront bars?"

He gave her a kiss on her forehead. "I'm sure they will, sweetheart. And, once we get settled, we'll set up the nursery with everything you could possibly need. This is the new start for us. The life I've always dreamed of."

Seamus's eyes were cold, but he waited for the three of them to be out through the door before following behind them. Javier gave me a smile, then he and his two men left as well.

Francesca sauntered a few steps toward us, drawing her eyes slowly from Jessica, to Evan, to me, and at last to Sean. Her mouth drew into a wide grin. "Sure you don't want to come along, Sean? You're just going to let that crew float away to a tropical paradise, and start their operations up fresh, perhaps larger and more efficient than ever before? Heck, if they have easy access to an eager population of families with young girls, who knows how many films a week they could produce! They could spread out their areas of interest – maybe look into some bestiality … maybe some rough stuff …"

Sean's arm muscles rippled, and I could see the tension in his neck, the effort it took him to stay in place. His voice, when he spoke, was tight. "You go ahead and run with them, Francesca. See how far you get."

Her light laugh tinkled across the room. "Oh, you think your phone was tracked? Quite the contrary, my dear friend. I've convinced the brass that you gave your phone to a group of tourists, because you thought Seamus was using it to keep an eye on you. I gave our contacts the number of a different phone to follow, saying it was your new burner phone. It's in the hands of some college kids on a road trip down to Key West."

She grinned in delight. "Believe me, by the time those dullards get that all sorted out, we'll be long gone."

Sean glanced at Evan, and I could see the building frustration in my brother as well. Neither one wanted to let the criminals out of their sight.

Francesca's eyes gleamed with delight. "Let's see. You two men against the eight of us. You have, what, one gun between you? While we have more than enough." She grinned. "You wouldn't last five seconds." She raised a hand in a wave. "Guess you'll just have to spend the rest of your life knowing you failed. Every time you hear of an innocent girl in an underage video, you'll have to wonder if it's your fault she was traumatized by the horrors she experienced."

Her smile widened. "Meanwhile, I'll be lounging on a beach, getting massaged by the cabana boy, drinking down mai-tais in a fluted glass."

There was a honk from outside, and she turned. "Got to go. My tropical vacation awaits." She strode through the doorway, leaving it wide behind her.

Sean and Evan moved as one to the open doorway. Evan's voice was low and hoarse with frustration. "She's right. We start something up, we'll be hard pressed to finish it and also keep these two safe. Especially with just one gun."

Jessica was already crossing to the master bedroom at a jog. "There's a pump-action shotgun locked to a rack over the bed," she reported. "Saw it when I was helping Bridgit with something earlier. I'll have the lock picked in under a minute."

Sean's eyes went to his handgun, resting on the seat of the Adirondack chair on the porch. "That barely gives us a fighting chance. We might take out one of them – or two – before we're both shot down. And then they'll have free rein on Kay and Jessica."

Jessica's voice called from the other room. "Got it!" In a moment she was back, carrying a shotgun with a beautiful carving of a stag in its bubinga stock.

Sean looked across the three of us, a question in his eyes.

I crossed to Jessica, took the shotgun from her, and racked a round into the chamber. I turned and handed the gun to my brother.

My voice was low but steady. "Go get the bastards."

Sean's eyes shone, and he nodded at Evan. Evan tucked the shotgun bchind his back, and then together the two men stepped out onto the porch. Sean was perhaps a foot away from the chair holding his pistol.

Sean spoke without turning his gaze from the car. "Jessica, Kay, you stay inside. I don't want you coming out here."

Every ounce of me wanted to be by his side, but I understood the situation. If I were anywhere in the line of fire, he would worry about me. That second of distraction could mean the difference between life and death for him – and for Evan as well.

Jessica took my arm and we went over to the window, each of us on one side of it.

The Escalade was packed now. Javier was in the driver's seat, with Seamus alongside him. Bridgit sat behind her brother, alongside Francesca. The remaining four were in the back.

Bridgit turned and gazed at the log cabin. Her look was almost one of regret. Then she nodded and said something to Seamus.

The car pulled smoothly away from the house.

Sean crouched to pick up his gun from the chair, and the two men stepped forward to the stairs. My heart pounded against my ribs. To watch the bastards drive away – to get off scot-free – was near torture. But once the two men started a gun fight, with the uneven odds …

The Escalade pulled across the clearing, and tension ratcheted within me, my breath held, waiting …

There was the sound of tires.

From the far end of the dirt road approached a car I knew intimately. Classic, lean styling. Beautiful dark Caspian Blue coloring. The silvered galloping mustang on its grill.

My brother's car.

Three men were in it, as familiar to me as the freckles on my hands.

The car eased to a stop in front of the Escalade, and for a long moment nothing stirred.

Then my brothers pushed open the doors, climbed out, and crouched behind the sturdy steel, guns drawn.

The cavalry had arrived.

Chapter 10

Seamus nearly kicked his door open, and his face was tense with fury as he climbed out. He spun on Evan. "What the fock is this! You swore you hadn't alerted the cops when we took you along."

Evan swung his arm, bringing the shotgun around to rest across his chest. His voice was calm. "I didn't call anyone," he responded. "You caused this little problem yourself. I imagine the moment they heard how Kay went missing from that party of yours, that my brothers were on the next flight home." He gave a wry smile. "Family can be like that, you know. A bit protective about their own."

He waved his free hand forward. "Sean, I'd like to introduce you to Brandon, up from Miami; Aedan, out from Vegas; and Dylan, the closest. He undoubtedly made the drive from Hartford to Worcester in under an hour. Guys, this here is Sean. You might say he's responsible for Kay being in this mess."

Aedan's eyes flashed, and his coal-black crew cut seemed to bristle. "Maybe you and I will have a couple of rounds in the cage once we're through here."

Evan chuckled. "I might mention that Aedan likes to do some MMA in his spare time. When I was fifteen he broke my thigh, showing me a move. He's improved since then."

Seamus spit on the ground in exasperation. "The girl is fine, as you can see for yourselves," he snapped, waving a hand at the window. "Not a scratch on her."

Brandon's hair was bleached light brown from the Florida sun, and his Miami Dolphin's jacket was zipped up tight against the cold. His eyes held Seamus's. "We heard she managed to get herself shot."

Javier climbed out of the other side of the car, careful to keep the door between him and the three brothers facing off. "One of my men, Raul, made that mistake. Seamus and Sean plugged him in the chest, and he won't be making those kinds of mistakes any more."

Seamus nodded in agreement. "Besides, Bridgit patched her up nicely. As good as gold." His eyes lit up. "But, you know, it's always wise to have these things checked out, just in case. You three should get her to a hospital. The longer we delay here, the more danger she might be in."

Brandon's sea-green eyes flashed to Evan in concern. Evan shook his head in reassurance. "She's fine. We can take our time."

Dylan's voice carried across the clearing, his calm, measured tones the same as he'd used in the many games I'd watched him quarterback through high school and college. "Here's how this is going to go. You guys in the car will come out, one by one, and toss your guns away. You'll lay face down on the ground. Then we'll zip-tie your wrists and call in for support. Nobody gets hurt. Who knows, maybe you'll get a cushy new life in witness protection."

Eileen's howl could be heard across the clearing. "I'm not having my baby in any damn jail! Jimmy, Seamus, take them out! There's only five of them. You outnumber them!"

Francesca hopped out of the far side of the car, drawing a gun from her purse. "I'm as sure as hell not going back," she snapped. "You know how they treat cops in prison?"

Seamus's eyes flashed, and he slid back into the car, slamming the door. Then he had climbed through and all of them were hunkered down on the far side of the car, shielded from the house by its bulk.

Sean and Evan crouched behind the oak railing, taking advantage of the slim protection it provided. They carefully began making their way left toward the back end of the car.

Dylan's tone was calm, reassuring. "Lay down your weapons. We'll tell the D.A. how you cooperated with us. You turn in the people you work with, and I'm sure they'll take that into consideration. Don't start something here that you'll regret."

Javier's voice was that of a kindly grandfather talking to a playful but disobedient child. "You don't belong here. This isn't your fight. Just go on into the house with your sister, and we'll head on by. Nobody needs to get hurt."

Francesca's shout rang out. "They're coming around the back!"

Sean and Evan were at the far end of the railing, their focus on the Escalade's back quarter.

Francesca crouched by the back left tire. "One more step, Sean! I swear I'll drill you right between the eyes!"

Sean looked back to me, and for a long, staggering moment, our eyes held. Everything we'd gone through, every experience we'd shared, streamed through my mind in one long, glorious blur.

He gave me a wry smile.

Evan turned to look to his brothers where they remained crouched behind the Mustang's doors. He nodded at them, then moved immediately behind Sean. He tapped him on the shoulder.

Both men vaulted over the end of the railing.

A hail of bullets exploded from outside the window, and I flung myself onto the ground, throwing my hands over my head. A window shattered somewhere in the master bedroom. Several bullets thunked heavily into the wall of the house.

An agonizing scream echoed across the clearing, and it took all my will not to pop my head up, not to see if it was Sean or one of my brothers. I curled tighter, praying that no bullet made it through those thick log walls.

It seemed like an eternity, but suddenly a silence stretched, and I realized that there had not been a shot in quite a period of time. That could have been five seconds, for all I knew – the world seemed to be moving in odd fits and starts.

Jessica cautiously, slowly, poked her head up over the sill of the window, and my heart thundered in my chest as I did the same.

Javier's two muscle men were sprawled in front of the Escalade, several gaping wounds peppering each man, blood coursing from their bodies. Seamus was leaning face-down against the hood, his hands secured behind his back, and in a moment Evan had hauled Bridgit up off the ground to place her beside her brother.

There was a movement in the open doorway, and then Sean was in front of me, sweeping me up into his arms, drawing me close. "Are you all right? Were you hit?"

"We're both fine," I reassured him, melting against his strength. "How are my brothers?"

"Aedan will have a scar to match yours, I think, but we were lucky. On their side, besides the two soldiers, I think Francesca's got the worst of it. She's got a thigh wound. The blond guy is working on it."

I chuckled against him. "Light brown," I corrected automatically. "That's Brandon. He does lifeguard duty on weekends and has dealt with several shark attacks. He'll handle it."

He ran a hand through my hair. "I'm sure he will. Evan will drive out into cell range and call in for backup. And then I'll get you home."

I nestled into his embrace. *Home.*

I didn't care where it was. As long as he was there with me.

Chapter 11

I groaned as Sean pushed open the door to his apartment and we stumbled inside. The first glimmers of dawn threw the brick walls into a cobblestone-like relief. I looked around at the photographs on the walls, at the neatly made bed, and shook my head. It seemed like an eternity had passed since we were last here. I had been in my beaded dress, Sean in his tux, and an evening of dancing had waited for us.

Now I was wearing someone else's sweats, with only moccasin slippers on my feet, and I was sure my hair looked like a gerbil's love nest.

Sean closed the door behind us, locked it, then turned to look at me. He stilled. "You are amazing."

I chuckled, trying to run my fingers through my hair. "Surely you jest."

He reached out his hands to me, and I folded within his arms. He sighed as our bodies met, and for a long while he simply held me there.

At last he nuzzled against my ear. "I didn't think your brothers were going to let you go."

I smiled. "They can be a mite overprotective at times," I reminded him. "You saw how they leapt on those planes and had the deed records dug out and waiting by the time they landed." I pressed a kiss on his chin. "And you have to agree that these past few days have been a bit ... agitated."

He ran a hand along the tender skin at the back of my neck. "I imagine I'll get more than an earful when we go down on Thursday for Thanksgiving."

My grin reached my ears. "Oh, yes. And I imagine they'll try to draw you into the family football game. And the family cage fight. And the family wrestling match. I have to warn you, they are alpha males, every one of them."

His eyes gleamed. "Oh, I think I can hold my own."

My breath eased out of me as I looked at him. His chiseled muscles, his sturdy resolve, and he was all mine.

"I'd bet on you any day of the week."

He grinned at that, then swept me up in his arms. "You'd better. From that first night I saw you, stepping in the bar's main room, I knew you were going to change my life. I knew I had to let nothing stop me before I had you by my side." He walked the distance over to the bed, laying me down on top of it.

I waited until he lay down next to me, and then I rolled to sprawl on top of him, looking down at him, the whole of my body singing in tune with his. My throat was tight when I spoke.

"That wasn't the first time I saw you," I murmured.

His brow raised. "Oh?"

I traced a finger along his lips. "It was a crash."

His voice was hoarse. "A thunderbolt."

My lips curved into a grin, and I nuzzled along his neck. "A crash of fire-engine red and bumblebee yellow. The drivers came tearing out of their cars, ready to start World War Three." I gazed down into his eyes. "And then you stepped forward."

His breath stilled. "You remember that?"

I nodded. "Chaos was about to erupt with bloody fury, and most people would have run, or pulled back to watch from a safe distance. But you stepped forward to do something about it." My throat went tight. "And I knew you were him. At long last, you were the man I wanted in my life."

He drew his fingers through my hair, his eyes shining. "I am so glad I found you, Kay."

I brushed my lips against his, and my mouth quirked into a smile. "It took you long enough."

He groaned, and his other hand came up against my hip. "It's Tuesday morning. We have two full days and nights before we leave to meet these brothers of yours more properly."

I tilted my hips against his, and my eyes sparkled at the shudder that swept his body.

"Barely enough time for what I have planned for you."

Thank you so much for reading and supporting the cause!

The story of Kate's family continues in the series Bermuda Nights, which features her brother, Evan. Book 1 of this series is *Resonating Souls*.

http://www.amazon.com/Resonating-Souls-Bermuda-Nights-novella-ebook/dp/B00HW24ALE/

You can also get the Bermuda Nights boxed set so you have all four in one complete set!

If you enjoyed Worcester Nights please leave a review!
https://www.amazon.com/review/create-review?ie=UTF8&asin=B00IJPOUGS#

You can also leave a review on Goodreads and any other review site you enjoy. Together we can make a difference!

Be sure to sign up for my newsletter! You'll get updates on free giveaways, great discounts, and the latest releases. I never spam and all names are kept private!

http://www.opheliasikes.com/subscribe.asp

Ophelia Sikes 357

Dedication

To Debi Gardiner of GardinerDesign.com and Bob Evans of ArckArts.com who helped me create the original cover. Bob's Triumph served as the original gorgeous model, and Bob's photography talents are stunning.

To my Dad, who supports me in all my writing projects. My Mom's writing expertise always comes in handy. To Jenn, who provided detailed ideas and suggestions.

To my writing group, especially Ruth, Fred, Dean, and Joan who offered invaluable advice.

To Shala, Remo, Mona, Mary-Anne, and Val, who chimed in with feedback.

To the great folks at Goodreads, especially Heather Jacquemin, Toni, and Tala who delved into specific tweaks.

To Sandra Baublitz, who always does such an awesome job of providing thorough editing and proofing –
https://www.facebook.com/sandrabaublitzediting

To three authors who inspired me immensely when I tackled this project. Glynnis Campbell was the first to show me that amazing storylines and appealing characters could combine with racy language. Eve Carter and Emily Jane Trent then helped me envision these characters and plots in a contemporary environment. Thank you so much Glynnis, Eve, and Emily!

Most importantly – a warm message of appreciation goes out to all my enthusiastic, loyal fans everywhere! Thank you for your support, encouragement, and feedback. It's because of you that I am working so diligently on the sequels!

About the Author

Ophelia Sikes fervently believes that every one of us deserves dedicated, passionate love in our lives – coupled with a soul-deep respect which supports our dreams.

Ophelia adores Worcester, Massachusetts with all its gritty streets, rows of muted-colored three-deckers, and tough-as-nails can-do attitude. She's lived in this area since college, with only a few brief flings in other locations. No matter where else she travels, she's always delighted to return home.

From the row of restaurants on Shrewsbury Street to picnicking at Elm Park, from the summertime boaters on Lake Quinsigamond to the St. Patty's Day Parade, there's just something about Worcester. She hopes she's brought this lively, unique town to life for her readers around the world.

Half of the proceeds of this book's sales benefit battered women's shelters.

Please send along as much feedback and suggestions as you can. The more we can polish these worlds and characters, the more we can help the cause.

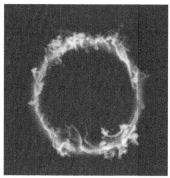

Ophelia Sikes can be found at:

http://OpheliaSikes.com

https://www.facebook.com/OpheliaSikes

https://twitter.com/OpheliaSikes

https://www.goodreads.com/OpheliaSikes

https://plus.google.com/+OpheliaSikes/posts

Newsletter:
http://www.opheliasikes.com/subscribe.asp

Worcester Nights series

Kate's life sucks. She's tending bar at a run-down dive. Her immoral boss fondles every co-ed within reach. The clientele is made up of TV-glazed zombies, drunkards, and ... who is that in the corner?

The Thunderbolt Hits.

She hadn't thought it was real. But when she looks into Sean's eyes, the force of the connection staggers her. Her mind desperately seeks to pull her back - he's an ex-felon. Far too talented with those rippled muscles and toned fists. He's everything she should be staying away from.

She craves him from the depths of her soul.

His touch smolders her skin; his fingers expose her to worlds she never dreamt existed.

But when his secret is ripped free from the dark shadows, their lives teeter on the brink of destruction.

Bermuda Nights series

Amanda desperately needed to get away. Her whole life had been about pleasing others - her straight-laced parents, her rule-bound teachers. When her best friend, Kayla, suggested they hop a cruise from Boston to Bermuda, Amanda leapt at the chance. This was her one chance to light the night on fire.

And then Evan stepped on stage.

Evan was exactly the man her country-club parents would have disapproved of. Ripped abs and soul-deep eyes. Lightning-fast fists. One glance and she knew she has to be his - if just for these seven brief, torturously-exquisite days.

And, oh, Evan could play her. His fingers were connoisseurs of her body, drawing out her deeper notes, sending her soaring to heights she barely knew existed. She lost all sense of self, of rules.

Until the day she saw what she was never meant to see - and her world changed forever.

Italian Nights series

Hannah and her sister, Megan, have been given the trip of a lifetime. They are cruising the Mediterranean Sea. Starting at Rome, they are working their way counter-clockwise through Florence, Monte Carlo, Barcelona, Sardinia, Sicily, and Pompeii. Life is their playground.

And then Hannah meets Brandon.

Brandon is strong, intelligent, loyal, and everything Hannah could possibly dream of in a man. He has also just walked in on his fiancée in bed with his best friend. Hannah is willing to wait as long as it takes for him to work his way through this betrayal.

And then all Hell breaks loose ...

Vegas Nights series

Las Vegas. Sin City. Heidi stepped off that plane ready to re-invent herself. Ready to delve into the glitz, glamour, and fantastical unreality which defines the mantra, "What happens in Vegas, stays in Vegas."

What she wasn't ready for was Aedan.

Billionaire playboy. Supermodels dripping down his well-muscled body. He seemed to have it all. But for some reason he kept appearing where she least expected. And he made her feel a way she swore she never would again.

Like she could trust him.

Until the dark revelation that threatens to destroy her ...

Cozumel Nights series

Sonya thought she was finally free. Her controlling, fault-finding parents had sold the family home in St. Louis and moved down to retire to Florida. Sonya's life could begin anew! But instead, she found herself lonelier than ever, missing her older brother who had escaped to California the moment he'd graduated from high school. So when her parents offered to fly her down to see the new condo and go on a six-day cruise, Sonya hesitantly agreed. After all, how bad could it be being stuck on a boat with her parents for a week?

Oh.

The sole shining light was the bevy of stunningly handsome gay men she tumbled into the care of. They offered laughter, fun, and everything she could ever have dreamed of. And Dylan's arms around her could have been all she desired in life.

If only it could be real.

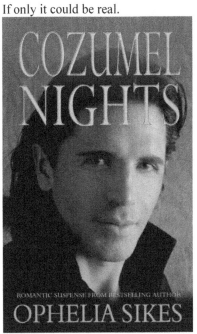

StepShifter Alpha Billionaire Lover
A NYC MMA SEAL BBW BWWM MMF Ménage Paranormal Romance

You've read about the billionaires who like to tie things with ... ties. You've lusted over werewolves and werebears. You've sent your blood pressure through the roof fantasizing about that pair of muscle-bound MMA guys whose sole focus in life is to bring you to the heights of pleasure.

You've perhaps asked yourself, self, why do all of these fantastic lovers have to be in different universes? Why can't there simply be one, all-encompassing, all-possessing man whose endless bank accounts and prodigious sexual talents are mine for the claiming? Or perhaps even two men? And why can't the stories be in short, easy-to-read snippets so I can get through JUST ONE GODDAMNED STORY before the kids start screaming bloody murder or that lazy husband of mine wants another beer from the fridge?

Well, pine no more, for the StepShifter series is here! And what's even better, if you post on Ophelia's page with what you'd like to see the Dynamic Trio do in the upcoming books, your wish is her command. Your fantasies will spring to life in technicolor glory. Well, not really in technicolor, because if she made the book's letters red, green, and blue, then the poor color-blind readers amongst us would miss out on the fun. But while the letters might be elegantly black, like the heroine, the language is absolutely racy. Purple. Red-hot passion. Definitely not for anyone younger than eighteen, or anyone without a serious sense of humor about how consenting adults might choose to pass the night. Or day. Or the time it takes a taxi to get from Grand Central Station to Yankee Stadium.

C'mon. Take a look. You know you want to!

Congratulations! You've found the secret ending page! I'm always curious how many people actually read to the very end of my novels :).

Send me a message via my Ophelia Sikes website:

http://opheliasikes.com/

You've earned a special reward!

Congratulations, and have an awesome day!

Made in the USA
Las Vegas, NV
16 February 2023